**AUTOGRAPH DUTY R**

D0900677

Mike McPhail	Robert E. Waters
James Chambers	Eric V. Hardenbrook
Brenda Cooper	Danielle Ackley-McPhail
David Sherman	Jeff Young
Robert Greenberger	Aaron Rosenberg
Lisanne Norman	Christopher M. Hiles
Bud Sparhawk	

eSpec Books Titles in the Defending The Future Series

Dogs of War - Reissued
The Best of Defending the Future
Man and Machine

Previous Titles in the Defending the Future Series
(out of print - may be available used)

Breach the Hull
So It Begins
By Other Means
No Man's Land
Best Laid Plans
Dogs of War

eSpec Books Titles Related to the Defending the Future Series

A Legacy of Stars by Danielle Ackley-McPhail
From the Archives: The Die is Cast edited by Greg Schauer
Radiation Angels: The Mission Files by James Daniel Ross
Shattered Dreams: The Shardies War by Bud Sparhawk
Devil Dancers by Robert E. Waters
Issue in Doubt by David Sherman
In all Directions by David Sherman
To Hell and Regroup by David Sherman
(forthcoming)

DEFENDING THE FUTURE

IN HARM'S WAY

SERIES EDITOR
MIKE McPHAIL

Books
Pennsville, NJ

PUBLISHED BY
eSpec Books LLC
Danielle McPhail, Publisher
PO Box 242,
Pennsville, New Jersey 08070
www.especbooks.com

ISBN: 978-1-942990-19-2
ISBN (ebook): 978-1-942990-20-8

Series Website:
http://www.especbooks.com/DefendingTheFuture/index.html

Design: Mike and Danielle McPhail
Cover Art: "Recovery" Mike McPhail, McP Digital Graphics
www.milscifi.com

Copyeditors: Greg Schauer
            Danielle McPhail, www.sidhenadaire.com

DEDICATION

To Our Fallen Comrades

PHOEBE WRAY
1935-2016
A teach who inspired women to reach for
their potential; former president of Broad Universe.

S. A. BOLICH
1957-2016
Served her country as a U.S. Army Intelligence
officer in Germany; freelance fantasy writer.

CONTENTS

"It is my duty as a Pararescueman
to save life and aid the injured. I will be
prepared at all times to perform my duties
quickly and efficiently. Placing these duties
before personal desires and comforts.
These things I do, That Others May Live."

– The PJ Creed

A BEACH ON NELLUS
James Chambers

SARAH NUHR FITZROSE SPOTTED THE MISSING PLANET CRUISER, *MERCURY,* submerged beneath clear water at the end of a trail gouged through the jungle to the narrow beach and into the bright, rippling surf. A tongue flick to the sheath of her helmet lit her augmented reality display. Among the illuminated strings of data blinked a red icon, confirming the proximity of the beacon sewn into the abducted girl's clothes.

Sarah scouted the shore for a place to land. The next nearest scrap of earth on Nellus lay 660 miles away across a world covered 98 percent by ocean. She banked the glider and eyed a sandy strip fringed by vine-draped trees and elephantine leaves. Cutting altitude until spray kicked up, she fired her braking thrusters then skimmed her glider's belly across the surface to slow her approach. The glider lurched eastward. Sarah wrestled with it on course, skipping from wave crest to wave crest. She nosed down, plunging the glider beneath the fluid's skin. The sharp drop in speed pitched her forward, knocking her helmet against the cockpit glass. Caught by the undertow, her glider jerked into shallow waters then spun and skidded up the beach, furrowing sand until it stopped hard against a thick wall of entwined tree trunks.

The glider's systems malfunctioned and winked out. The echo of the crash rang in Sarah's ears.

When the shock faded, she punched the cockpit release, lifted the glass, and spilled out onto the soft sand. Wrestling her feet under her, she stood, surveyed her landing, and found the glider's frame crumpled beyond repair.

She activated a sensor in her helmet to initiate a diagnostic app for her vital signs and then confirmed her weapon remained holstered at her waist. Her sleek, black body suit looked undamaged, and seconds later the diagnostic confirmed her stats as normal and verified the com-link to her orbiting ship, the *Sif*. She retrieved her gear bag from the wreck and slung it across one shoulder.

Ahead, an endless ocean confronted her. Behind, the abyssal dark of deep jungle awaited. To either side the pale sand narrowed until it vanished between the two realms. She could swim along the shore or trek through the lush growth to reach the *Mercury*. Either way, she belonged to Nellus now, to its barely charted oceans and its inscrutable jungle untouched since its discovery early in the Myriarchy War.

She referenced her frustratingly limited planetary knowledgebase. Nellus had claimed seven exploratory expeditions before then being ignored because it held no strategic value. The planet's most common fauna, nicknamed *nellies*, resembled, according to their database image, a monstrous mix of lobster and tuna with a long, translucent fin rising from its back. Each had two mouths set vertically parallel and ringed with razor-sharp teeth. They hunted in schools, which could devour their prey completely in seconds, but feeding frenzies often continued with the school consuming its own, reducing its numbers by as much as one third before satiating its hunger. Only Nellus' sea clouds, rare, enormous creatures larger even than Earth's blue whales, preyed on the nellies. The database listed no such predators on land, making the jungle path far more inviting.

She cycled through her full mission plan. Radiant ghosts of terrain maps slid across her view augmented by meager data—water content, soil composition, weather patterns—regarding Nellus' vast oceans dotted by a few scattered land masses. Even the largest of them sometimes vanished beneath its tides. The only thing Sarah knew less about was her objective: the abducted girl.

The Commission's need for secrecy rankled her. With all the resources at its disposal, it had sent her on what should've been a simple recovery run—but the Commission never called on Sarah for anything simple. Her direct lineage back to Earth qualified her as a Registered Agent, eligible for the service's highest ranks and the trust that necessitated. She only pulled missions that required exceptionally hard work or exceptionally difficult choices, the kind that could sway the future of the Commission. Even more unusual, Cultural Relations Commissioner Ariana Dey had issued her orders. The lone Commissioner from Darinthe, the only world to stay independent after choosing the wrong side in the Myriarchy War, Dey stood apart from her ruling colleagues despite talk of her secret romance with Pen Bouchard, the First among the Commissioners. The unspoken bonds and tenuous alliances beneath the Commission's surface seemed as daunting as Nellus' oceans, the rumors of fresh dissent as challenging as its jungles. The lost girl could be anyone and her abduction could mean anything.

Sarah locked the homing signal on her display and entered the jungle. The ground rose in shallow steppes, as if carved by giants, no doubt eroded by varying tides over the course of many centuries. A leafy canopy diminished all but the strongest rays of sunlight, forcing her to rely on the spotlight affixed to the side of her helmet. The homing signal pinned the wreck a mile from her position, maybe half an hour's walk through the tangled vegetation.

Clusters of soft, fleshy vines dangled from the trees. When Sarah pulled on them they snapped and exuded a milky green sap. She gazed above her seeking their origin, but the dusky heights revealed nothing. Dense vine curtains thickened or parted with the subtlety of wind currents tickling water until Sarah realized they moved with a purpose, directing her toward the jungle's core. Whenever she corrected course, the vines closed ranks and guided her in another direction. She walked a few feet, tried again to turn, eliciting the same response. Now the vines grew stronger and coarser. The pathway they shaped offered a tunnel defined by a loose mesh before it tapered into darkness.

Sarah's spotlight penetrated the shadows. At the light's farthest limit, a huge, indistinct mass recoiled from the artificial brightness.

She slid her knife from its sheath on her thigh and slashed at the forbidding vines. Her blade severed the thinnest ones, but only gouged chunks from the largest. Bits of plant matter dropped down and disgorged thick green ooze. Sarah lashed out and pushed onward, moving as swiftly as she could manage.

Behind her something stirred in lumbering pursuit.

The vines rustled, and the ground quivered—then in a moment the vines slithered rapidly together to form a swaying wall behind her, broken only where she had cut them. A menacing bulk trundled along the other side, afraid or unable to pursue Sarah farther. Eager to put distance between her and whatever the vines hid, Sarah resumed her ascent, gripping exposed tree roots and protruding stones until she reached the island's peak. From there she spied an unexpected and unwelcome sight.

Devastation scarred the hillside. A crater roughly thirty feet in diameter. Rocks and soil, spewed upward by the impact, coated the surrounding turf. Trees lay scattered at the edge of the blast area, letting full sunlight pour into the jungle. Sarah's sensors read the crater as cold, hours old. She saw no sign of the object that had created it. One edge had crumbled in on itself. Loose dirt had then been packed down, forming a crude ramp out of the concavity. Wide patches of trammeled soil led up and away like mammoth footprints. Sarah read the signs, and what they said chilled her so much she feared she might already be too late to save the girl.

Chasing the fairy flicker of the homing signal, she raced around the crater, her body suit protecting her against branches and thorns. Pushing faster, she soon reached the shore, sloshing into mud that gave way to shallow water that frothed as she stampeded into it. She struggled against the current as the surf rose to her knees, then to her waist, and she emerged into undiluted daylight. The homing icon flickered. Not far away the *Mercury*'s dim bulk shimmered.

Her sensors showed no activity in the area. She primed her body suit for submersion, switching from filtered air to its internal supply, and then dove beneath the surf. The craft rested twenty-five feet below her. Only a little farther, the shoreline plummeted, the change in depth darkening the water. As Sarah neared the *Mercury* she saw a hole three feet round and scored black at the base of the ship's tail, above the engines, the most likely cause of its crash. She swam to the hatch. Her suit struggled to maintain equilibrium as she dove deeper.

Sarah found the external release along the underside of the rim and activated it. A torrent of air bubbled out from within as water flooded the opening. The hatch flipped back against the hull with a muted clang. On the fringe of her sensor range a mass of small objects appeared. Not waiting for a positive identification, she quickly slipped inside the *Mercury*, sealing the hatch closed behind her.

Automatic systems pumped out the water, allowing Sarah to open the inner door. Four space suits hung along the wall in the next chamber. A door led farther into the craft. The ship's atmosphere remained intact, allowing Sarah to switch back to filters and preserve her internal air supply.

Only auxiliary systems seemed active, leaving Sarah to explore the sleeping machine by the dim glow of emergency lights and harsh brightness of her spotlight. She followed the homing signal to a cabin with an unmade bunk, wall desk, and a chair. A girl's blouse lay draped across the bunk. Squeezing the thermal fabric, Sarah discovered the transmitter sewn within the collar. She tore it loose and swore. The flashing icon vanished from her display. She tucked the useless transmitter into her equipment pack, and then explored the remainder of the ship, except for the rearmost section, sealed tight against water taken on through the pierced hull.

In the cockpit she found the pilot, slumped dead in his seat.

A wound gaped in his side. Pooled blood had grown tacky around him. Maybe the crash had killed the pilot, or he had left the ship and retreated back inside to die, fatally wounded by nellies. Or maybe the abducted girl was tougher than Sarah expected and fought her captors.

Sarah summoned the flight record on the ship's computer. It listed a crew of two and one passenger, all unidentified, offering hope that the girl had survived and fled with the other crew member. Sarah removed her helmet. Despite the ship's clammy air, it felt good to shake loose her short, blonde hair and rub the base of her neck where the helmet clasp chafed her skin. From a small panel in the helmet she uncoiled a thin cable. She popped open the command-deck console with her knife, exposing the innards of the ship's computer, then snapped the plug of her helmet cable into a memory interface and downloaded the ship's records.

The transfer completed, Sarah donned her helmet, then retraced her steps, pausing outside the hatch as her sensors swept her surroundings, finding no signs of life. She swam for the island, making it halfway before the mysterious cluster of small objects reappeared, angling toward her. She kicked faster, pulled harder with each stroke, racing for the shallows. The school gained on her with terrifying speed.

When her sensors showed it within visual range, she glanced back and her stomach sank. Hundreds of nellies approached like a giant whip of teeth lashing the water. She sought a rock or reef for cover, but only barren sand lay between her and the island. A tangle of low jungle growth swayed in the water ahead. She wouldn't reach it in time. Her suit would offer some protection but not for long. She slipped her weapon from its holster and switched off the safety.

As she prepared to fire at her pursuers, her sensors detected a new object—mammoth and rising from below the sea cliff, so big her gear couldn't measure it. Then it appeared, a vast form pouring up from the depths, casting a shadow over her, the Mercury, and the nellies, turning the crystalline-bright sea to twilight. A sea cloud. Unexpected calm blossomed in Sarah's mind as though a force outside herself reached out to reassure her. Then the huge creature twisted—or perhaps merely turned a limb—and the school of nellies scattered. Half disappeared in the sea cloud's grip, or maw, or a fold of flesh. Sarah couldn't tell. The others thrashed, struggling to regroup. Exploiting the moment, Sarah pressed forward to the shallows, resisting the urge to look back at the sea cloud until she pulled herself from the water and into the notch of an ancient tree root.

Away from shore the sea boiled. The partial outline of a behemoth corralled the remaining nellies. Sarah tongue-flicked to snap on her helmet camera then watched the beast roil the ocean, dispersing the school of nellies, consuming those too slow to flee. With grace that contrasted its bulk, the sea cloud slipped back over the cliff, descending to the onyx deeps. After it left, Sarah shut her eyes and rested.

When she had caught her breath, she re-entered the jungle.

She arranged topographical charts on her display, choosing to start at the island's highest point. From there she would survey the terrain and mark the center of her search, hoping the girl had reached shore and survived. She plotted a route to avoid the area of the vines. Compass readings replaced the maps on her visor.

Sarah considered the likely cause of the crater she had spied earlier, a killing machine programmed to camouflage its landing as a meteorite impact, a weapon outlawed after the Myriarchy War, now controlled only by the Commission. Why hadn't Dey warned her of its possible use? Unless Dey knew nothing about it, which lent weight to the rumored rifts among the Commission. Who then had sent a death machine to find a little girl? And where had it gone?

At the peak of the island, Sarah climbed the tallest tree until her weight threatened to snap the limbs. To the east the sun fell lazily to the horizon, its reflection setting the sea afire. Sarah's visor magnified her view, allowing close sight of the ground through gaps in tree cover with enough detail to discern the pattern in their bark. Here and there she recognized the coloring of the vines that had interfered with her earlier. The rustling trees in those places testified to the presence of whatever creature dwelled there. She spied the sea to the west, the water unburdened by reflection, and saw dark shapes sailing below the waves like vast flowing wings. More sea clouds. She scrutinized the island to the last detail, passing over the same stretches of land and leaves until she was certain they held no clues.

Night sped upon her. Sarah puzzled over the girl's absence, fearing her lost in the sea—and then, in the western shallows, harsh light glimmered to life beneath the water. Brightening as it neared the surface, it broke into the air like a miniature sun. Sarah magnified and shaded her view until she confirmed her worst fear. A mechanical demon appeared on shore. Ornamented with heavy weaponry, its brightness blazing stark shadows on the sea, a Cerberus Assassin swiveled and marched onto land. Her scanners detected radiation, indicating damage and a leak in one of its power supplies. Sarah guessed it had submerged to stave off overheating. Finding it unlikely its landing had harmed the machine, she wondered what on Nellus could have done so.

Cerberus Assassins, unstoppable by conventional weapons and capable of operating in the vacuum of space, resembled an articulated tank built in humanoid form for psychological intimidation. They bore an arsenal of powerful sensors. Compartmentalized power sources let any one part of the machine carry on despite damage to the rest. The Assassins had hastened the end of the Myriarchy War. Afterward the Commission—deeming them too dangerous—gathered them together and outlawed them to preserve the tenuous peace.

The machine's glow flickered as it entered the jungle. Sarah marked its progress by the muted light. It gave wide berth to the vine clusters. Sarah extrapolated its route across the terrain. The only unusual feature in the weapon's path was a barren hill of exposed rock, where, almost invisible in the night, a thin column of smoke rose. Switching to thermal sensors revealed a heat source at its base—a fire.

Sarah calculated the distance and found herself closer than the Assassin. She scrambled down the tree, jolted to the ground, then rushed into the jungle, hoping to reach the smoke source first. Heat sensors guided her to the intense infrared blur on her map.

She circled the campsite, her sensors showing only flame, and she heard only the night sounds of the jungle and the surf's constant drumming. She paused on the edge of the firelight and wrapped her hand around the grip of her weapon. To one side of the clearing an opening in a short rock face suggested the entrance to a cave. A second rock wall rose sheer and high beside it. Footprints marred the smooth dirt, those of an adult and a smaller set. Sarah's heart raced. She peered into the crevasse with her spotlight.

The pocket cave stretched back to a nook big enough to hide a person. Propped against the far wall rested a corpse in a uniform identical to that of the dead pilot in the Mercury's control room, his head slumped on his chest, eyes open and glassy, hands clutched over a bloody wound in his torso.

A scraping sounded from the rock above caught Sarah's attention.

She aimed the spotlight beam at the cliff top. A girl stood there, no older than fourteen, clothes torn, face dirt-smeared, brown hair a tangle around her head. She regarded Sarah with a serious, stubborn expression, her quivering arms lofting a pumpkin-sized stone overhead, the stance of a defiant warrior ready to strike.

"Do what I say or I'll drop this on your stupid head," the girl said.

"I'm here to help you, kid," Sarah said.

"Drop your gun and walk over by the fire."

"You're wasting time. Put that rock down and let me help you."

The girl kicked a stone off the cliff. It bounced off Sarah's helmet. "Do what I said!"

"All right, all right." Sarah dimmed the spotlight, lessening the glare in the girl's eyes. She placed her weapon on the sand then walked to the campfire.

The girl followed along the ridge of the rock face. "Now go away."

"Listen, I'm here to rescue you. If I go away, I won't be doing a very good job."

"I don't trust you."

"I'm going to remove my helmet so you can see my face, okay?" Sarah lifted off her helmet, then set it down beside her feet. "See? My name is Sarah. What's yours?"

The girl only stared.

"How much longer you think you can hold that rock over your head?"

A snap of the girl's wrists sent the rock whistling down, thudding a few feet away from Sarah. She flinched but stood her ground. On the crest of the ridge, the girl vanished.

"I'm coming down." The small voice echoed from behind the wall of the narrow cove. "I recognize you from pictures in my father's office." The girl emerged at the base of the cliff and joined Sarah. The orange firelight softened her haggard appearance. "He said he trusts you."

"You can trust me too." Sarah sat crossed-legged and placed her hands on her knees. "I'm not the only one looking for you though."

"You mean the robot," the girl said. "It attacked after we left the ship. We ran away from it into the jungle."

"Did the pilot have a weapon?" Sarah said.

"He lost it in the water when those things bit him."

"The nellies," Sarah said. "Then how'd you escape the robot? How'd it get damaged?"

"The vine monster hurt it. It walked in there to get in front of us, but it never came out. We heard an explosion later. I thought it was dead."

"No, it only laid low to cool off. It'll be here soon. It detected your fire."

"I was cold."

"It's okay. You did the right thing. I'm going to signal my ship to launch a jump pod for us. Then all we have to do is keep away from that thing until it arrives. Okay?"

The girl nodded.

"So, you have a name?"

"Annasol."

"Okay, Annasol, let's move."

Sarah retrieved her weapon. She left the fire burning to misdirect the Assassin.

"They said someone would come but not to take me home. I figured they meant the robot."

"Who said that? The men who took you?"

"Not them." Annasol bit her lip. "The ones in the water."

Sarah snapped around. "Someone's in the water?"

"The gliding things. The ones so big you can't see all of them."

"The sea clouds... *talked* to you?"

"Not regular talking. I just knew what they wanted me to know and knew it came from them."

"What else did they tell you?"

"About the war, how they knew it would happen, and how it would end. How it will happen again."

"Kid, what are you saying?"

"You don't believe me. The pilot didn't either. They frightened him. Until he died, at least. Then I think they helped him feel a little better and he believed. Too late."

Sarah recalled the rush of confidence and security she experienced before the sea cloud laid into the school of nellies headed for her.

"Annasol, who's your father?"

"Commissioner Pen Bouchard. I thought you knew him."

Sarah had accepted many missions from Bouchard, First among the Commissioners, architect of the peace that had ended the Myriarchy War. He faced many enemies, even within the Commission itself—and at least one powerful enough to deploy a Cerberus Assassin and bold enough to target his daughter.

"I do. We're good friends. But you and I have just met, haven't we?"

She led Annasol by the hand into the jungle. Sarah transmitted a coded message to the *Sif* but received no acknowledgment. Atmospheric conditions could obstruct the signal—but more likely the Assassin's jamming equipment blocked it. She scoured her terrain charts for a safe haven and considered hiding in the Mercury, but the Assassin could tear through the hull or simply destroy the entire ship. They had to keep moving to evade it.

Without warning they broke free of the tree line and found themselves on a scant stretch of beach. Water lapped at their feet. Annasol's chest heaved. Nellus' twin moons gazed down at them in cool, unfeeling stillness. Sarah tongue-flicked her sensors and located the Assassin, now past the cave area and clearly tracing their path.

"We're stuck here for now. I can't summon a jump pod from my ship." Sarah crouched to Annasol's eye-level. "Will you do what I ask?"

Annasol hesitated then nodded. "Okay."

"We have to trick the Assassin to where the vines hang and hope whatever's in there can damage it again, maybe stop it."

Terror swept Annasol's face. "No! Then the vines will get us too!"

"We'll be okay if we're careful. I wandered into them when I arrived here, but I got away. The vines themselves can't hurt us. Only what lives inside them. We won't go in that deep. The hardest part is we're going to have to let the Assassin see us."

Sarah's maps indicated that if they walked straight to the vine cluster, they would cross directly in front of the Assassin. She unholstered her weapon and led the way. Soon they heard the clanking, whirring, buzzing of the death machine, so out of place in the jungle. Its lights broke through the foliage. Sarah waited until she discerned its silhouette then took aim and fired three shots. The blasts tore through the leafy curtain, striking the Assassin's metal hide. The explosive rounds merely scarred it. Before the blast echo faded, Sarah and Annasol bolted.

The Assassin pursued.

The night flared into brilliance as the machine fired. A deafening roar erupted.

Shock waves staggered Sarah to one knee, dragging Annasol down. She lifted the girl and plunged ahead again. A second blast flared, closer, shoving Sarah and Annasol into the air. They sprawled on the ground. Sarah whirled to confront the third blast she knew would follow. Instead she faced only silence and the jungle gloom. Obscured by smoke and shadow, the Assassin froze, and Sarah realized she and Annasol had entered the vines' territory.

Dangling lines already gathered and shifted to form a path that would seem inviting to whatever swam into it when water submerged the island. To succeed, Sarah needed to embark down the dark tunnel, but the Assassin seemed unwilling to follow. She debated firing another round at it but feared nothing short of letting the machine glimpse Annasol again would bait it. She didn't think they were fast enough to risk exposing themselves at this range, though. Then the grinding of gears resumed, and the Assassin's arm probed the sheath of vines.

Her hope refreshed, Sarah lifted Annasol and jogged along the path. Vines flexed to guide their passage. The Assassin stalked them, its steps slamming the ground. Sarah pushed herself to run harder, faster, until she reached a clearing, across which awaited a massive shape obscured by vines. The Assassin closed. A cannon emerged from its shoulder and swiveled to aim. Sarah waited another breath and then— clutching Annasol to her body—leaped to one side of the path as the cannon barrel flamed.

The shell blazed into the clearing then burst into an electric ball that spewed a cascade of sparks through the trees. One-handed, Sarah shoved Annasol behind her, steadying her weapon on the Assassin with her other hand. From the clearing edge, the machine re-aimed. Sarah blasted at the thing, her shots only scorching its plating. The telltale whine of a building energy charge turned Sarah's blood cold. She couldn't protect Annasol from another attack. Then a bulging shape appeared behind the killing machine, looming over the Assassin like a miniature mountain. Fleshy blackness swirled like a gelatinous storm cloud and grasped the mechanical nightmare.

The robot glowed and crackled with energy at the vine monster's touch then appeared to malfunction. Thick vines, flush with internal fluid, entwined the Assassin like steel cable, broke off its extruded cannon, and crushed its shell. The vines swelled to the width of a tree trunk. The Assassin's energy weapon reported, but the blast ended in a muted flash. Its upper torso vanished into the vine monster. Small thunders sounded as it unleashed what weaponry it still commanded. Sarah shuddered at the power of the thing. She and Annasol had been too small to rouse it fully, unlike the machine—or the sea clouds, upon which Sarah figured it preyed when the island sank. As the Assassin's legs slid deeper into the shadows, Sarah lifted Annasol and fled.

Outside the vines' territory, the girl clung to Sarah, who brushed her hand through her hair, whispering, "You're okay. We're safe now."

Sarah took them to her ruined glider, where she tucked Annasol into the soft flight couch. Then she removed the outer layer of her upper body suit and wrapped Annasol's shoulders with it to quell her shivering. Tired and hollowed out, Sarah leaned against the hull of the glider. When the tightness in her chest eased, she reached for her transmitter.

"Don't."

Annasol reached and stopped her. Sarah frowned at her.

"What's wrong?"

"They want to talk to you."

"Who? The ones in the water?"

Annasol nodded.

"The sea clouds can really talk?"

"Sort of. You'll see. It won't be long."

Sarah met Annasol's gaze for a moment then faced the sea where a shape rose to fill the emptiness. A heartbeat later, it vanished in a myriad flourish of sharp, glowing whitecaps...

... and Sarah *knew*.

The knowledge came in an instant. One moment she was alone in her mind, and the next everything they wanted her to know crowded out her own thoughts. She jolted from the shock, staggered several steps, and then, lightheaded, propped herself against the glider.

Annasol clambered from the cockpit. "Did you hear them?"

Sarah nodded. Tears welled in her eyes.

"What did they tell you?"

Screams and fire, people dying in mobs, clawing across each other for a last gasp of life. Pen Bouchard's decapitated body on the floor of the Commission chambers, his head lanced on a pole. A blinding circle of pure light enveloping Earth before it vanished. True darkness falling as suns died. Nellus's oceans evaporating in steaming, radiation-steeped plumes, leaving the sea clouds to shrivel in the sun like beached jellyfish. The beasts in the vines withering and blowing away. Her own death in the vacuum of space, drifting amidst the wreckage of the Sif.

Sarah now knew what Nellus knew, secrets hidden during the Myriarchy War, secrets the sea clouds had destroyed past expeditions to hide. Time and distance meant nothing to them. All events happened simultaneously, the entire universe laid bare before their consciousness, a jealously guarded truth.

"They told me who sent the Assassin," Sarah said. "It was... it was your father."

"No, it wasn't. You're lying!" Annasol said.

"They told me what happens if you make it back, and I... I believe them."

Annasol leapt from the glider cockpit and splashed into the surf. She faced the dark sea. It should've made Sarah's choice easier, but her gun filled her hand with venomous, dead weight. The trigger pricked her finger like a fang.

"I can't bring you home, Annasol," she said. "Somehow your father understood that."

"Why not—?" Annasol spun around. The sight of Sarah's gun aimed at her locked her in place.

"They didn't tell you...?" Sarah said.

Annasol trembled, unable to answer. Tears ran down her cheeks.

"If you return, the war starts over. I don't know exactly how, but you're the catalyst. Your father knows it. So do others. Somehow someone deduced it from what little data was gathered about Nellus—or the lost expeditions here sent back more data than what was reported. Anyone who finds you finds all Nellus represents. That's something people will kill to possess."

"Who? If who finds me?" Annasol said.

The gun wavered in Sarah's hand. "I don't... I'm not sure. They didn't say...."

Sarah shifted her gaze toward the sea beyond Annasol. The open water, its ever-rolling waves and unseen currents, its strange ecology, and unknown depths. Ever-changing, yet ever-present. A vast mystery, like those lingering in her mind as to who'd abducted Annasol and what they had hoped to accomplish. To hide the girl? To protect her? And why had Arianna Dey sent her after the girl. Had she known about the Assassin? Dey, Bouchard, secrets, and hard choices. A meager seed of hope took root in her mind.

Trembling, Sarah holstered her weapon. The moment she removed her fingers from it the sense of calm the sea clouds had imparted to her when they saved her from the nellies returned, gently nudging aside her anger, fear, and horror. They had wanted *her* to take the first step, to make the hard choice. She knew that without knowing fully what it meant.

"You'll stay here. The sea clouds will watch over you."

"Don't leave me alone!"

Sarah paused as a new thought unfurled in her mind. "They'll make it so we can always talk to each other. You won't be alone. I don't understand it all. They can't show us everything at once like they see it. That we can see any of it is because they're helping our minds adapt."

"Sarah, I won't really be alone if I stay?"

"Wherever I am, I'll never be farther than a thought from you. And I promise I'll come back for you as soon as it's safe."

Sarah hugged Annasol and then stayed until she fell asleep in the glider cockpit. Then she hiked half a mile along the shore and beckoned a jump pod from the *Sif*. Without the Assassin's interference, the signal patched straight through to the ship's automated system.

Half an hour later, she left Nellus.

Four hours later she convinced Bouchard and Dey the girl she'd gone to rescue had died on Nellus, her body lost to the sea. She provided the homing transmitter and the *Mercury*'s data as proof and reported the Cerberus Assassin, struggling to hide her rage at Bouchard for sending it after his own daughter. If Bouchard felt any remorse or grief, he betrayed none of it.

Six hours later, Sarah talked with Annasol.

She learned the girl's favorite color, blue, that Nellus offered lots of good things to eat if you knew what to look for, and that the sea clouds watched over Annasol when she swam in the ocean. Sarah recalled the visions of war that had played in her mind, fading now and less certain with her increasing distance from Nellus.

Her entire life seemed less certain now.

She had betrayed the trust of her position, traded it for the trust of a lost girl and a difficult promise, for prospects for a better future. An endless ocean to one side, an abyssal jungle to the other, and in between a patch of warm, shifting sand upon which she hoped to find firm footing.

CHILDREN OF THE LAST BATTLE
Brenda Cooper

C HIARO LEANED AGAINST THE WALL OF HIDDEN CAVE, TRYING VAINLY TO LISTEN FOR footsteps and keep track of seven children at the same time. Three-year-old Liam grunted with happiness as four-year-old Bryan trounced him in an impromptu wrestling match. The genetic changes designed to make Bryan a strong already manifested in a broader build and more height. Bryan barreled Liam to the ground, the two boys a tangle of chubby limbs on the smooth floor of the cave. Liam's lower lip quivered, but just as Chiaro pressed away from the wall to limp toward them, Bryan pulled himself free, helped Liam up, and hugged the smaller boy. Liam quieted.

That was when Chiaro heard the scrape of feet on the ledge above the cave mouth. She and the children stilled until David's voice floated down from above them. "It's okay."

Chiaro stepped to the side and held herself ready to assist the returning warriors. David dropped to the cave floor first, followed by his wife, Marissa. The oldest of the children, Chelo, and her younger brother Joseph raced to them. As their parents scooped them up, Marissa whispered, "Not there...there's blood there..." and Chelo looked at her with wide eyes and shifted the position of her small arm on her mom's bony shoulder. Marissa's sleeve was stained dark with old blood and caked to the wound.

Kayleen's mother, Ryu, hissed, "I need help." Marissa turned to help Chiaro make sure that Ryu managed the jump without falling. Ryu's right ankle was so swollen that Chiaro wondered how she managed to get back at all. The small, dark woman sank down to the cave floor, and tiny Kayleen sat beside her, not touching her, but mumbling soft words that Chiaro couldn't quite make out. Kayleen was the one talker among all the kids, the one who spoke a sentence or a paragraph or even a book for every thought that settled in her head.

A slide of gravel announced Justin before he hopped down all by himself. A soft grunt acknowledged the sting in his feet as he landed. He stepped quickly across the cave and scooped his daughter up, burying his face in the unruly fall of Alicia's dark hair. Her lavender eyes stared at the low corner of the cave's mouth where the adults entered.

Bryan also watched, his usual perpetual motion stopped, his attention on Alicia. Elinia, the other child with the most strength genes, had turned her face to the wall. She would still see – this one had an extra eye in the back of her neck – but she apparently thought no one could see her. The kids each had coping mechanisms. Hiding her face was Elinia's, but it hurt to see. Bryan scooted closer to Elinia, offering her his presence and knowing enough, even at four, not to touch her in this state. He always seemed so old for his age, so much more like a little adult than a child.

Chiaro listened for more footsteps.

Branches rustled in a soft wind just below them. Far off, ordnance burst loudly enough to silence the busy seed-stealer birds, although they started to croak again just a moment afterward.

Chiaro spoke Alicia's mother's name. "Dawn?"

David shook his head. "They appear to have sent everyone who can walk after us, in some glorified idea of a final battle." He looked drawn, his misty-blue eyes full of worry and jaw tight. "We have to go back. Now." He hesitated a moment. "We could lose. Get the children in the skimmer."

Chiaro blinked as fear raced through her nerves. "We're leaving the cave?"

David looked at her as if the question made no sense. "We might not be able to get back to you. If we win, we'll bring the skimmer and get you last. But if not, I don't want you stuck here. You could starve." David glanced toward Justin, who held Alicia tight as she wriggled against him, her small hands fisted. David frowned. "We're dropping you at the top of the High Road where we camped last summer. Ryu will stay with you, help you with the kids. She can't fight anymore anyway."

Chiaro struggled to take it all in. Dawn dead. Alicia motherless. Leaving the last safe place they had. "Why so close to town?"

His voice was full of pain. "We *can't* leave you here. The kids couldn't walk out. This is the best bad choice. You might get caught, but there's a cliff you can back up against if the demon dogs come and a good clearing that should keep you safe from paw-cats. And if we don't get back..."

He didn't need to finish that sentence. If they didn't get back, Chiaro and Ryu could surrender. That might kill them, too, but it would be easier than dying in the wilds of Fremont. Chiaro hobbled over to Elinia and scooped her up before turning around and asking, "What happened?"

"The locals ambushed two of our teams on the way into Artistos. They killed all of the other team and Dawn. We killed seven of them."

Seven, when they had only lost one. She glanced at Marissa, who had started cleaning her own wound. Almost two. The colonists vastly out-numbered the new arrivals from Silver's Home. When Chiaro helped to choose Fremont for their new home, no one realized there was already an established colony. Even though the unexpected residents stubbornly rejected the genetic mods Chiaro and her people used for trade goods, they were strong and resilient, and they worked together. Chiaro had known for months that peace was the only way to keep a foothold on Fremont. That, or give up on the one rich continent and take the other, which was so actively volcanic it wouldn't do. At this rate, they'd have nothing. She'd met some of the opposition leaders before the arguments turned physical, and felt sure they could have been debated into peace. Once. Not anymore. But it hadn't been her place to make decisions. She didn't have the special genetic traits needed to lead or to fight. She was smart and fast, but a thinker more than a doer, and a bit of an empath. Not a leader. Besides, her left foot had been bitten by a snake and hadn't fully healed. So she had stayed behind running logistics, and eventually childcare. She had counted the dead. She'd lost count now, but it was close to two hundred out of three hundred. Chiaro swallowed, looked at David's tired, angry eyes and nodded.

Two hours later, she and Ryu stood at either end of the skimmer's back door, helping the kids climb out one by one and setting each of them down carefully on bare dirt. The children shuffled to the edge of the small clearing, silent in the way children of war understood. Late afternoon sunbeams illuminated Alicia's dark hair and Kayleen's out-sized feet and left Elinia and Bryan's faces in darkness. Chelo was the last child out, her round face grave with worry as she counted the other children.

Marissa handed Chiaro a bundle. "There are two stunners in here, and backup charges for them. Two pairs of Night Eyes. A small perimeter mesh. Blankets." She glanced up at the sky. "It might get cold."

Chiaro tucked the bundle under her arm. "I'll keep them as warm and safe as I can."

Tears glistened in Marissa's eye, but none fell. She hugged Chelo and Joseph, her face a mask of not-quite-hidden pain. Then Marissa reached for Bryan and Elinia, who no longer had parents, folding them into her last hug before she turned back to climb into the skimmer.

Marissa was the best of them. Chiaro whispered "stay safe" at her retreating back.

When David stopped to hug Chiaro, he touched his ear. "We'll try to keep in touch."

Even though neither Chiaro nor Ryu could walk well, they were almost as fast as the children. They moved away from the skimmer, away from the wide road that led down to Artistos, and toward the sheltering bulk of the cliff. Dry leaves crackled underfoot. Chiaro used a stick to probe ahead of them, trying to scare away any snakes and uncover poisonous plants as they went. The whole damned planet felt poisonous. It smelled that way, too, sharp and acidic with cloyingly sweet florals.

Periodically the distant whine of the skimmer or the higher report of a hand-rocket penetrated the trees, slightly muffled and only a little frightening.

The light began to turn the gold of early evening as they settled the children on rocks or cleared patches of dirt and fed them nuts for dinner. Bryan and Chelo chose spots on either end of the line of children, playing protector and looking out into the forest while they chewed on their rations of dried redberries and djuri jerky.

A crackle in her ear alerted Chiaro. Justin's voice. "We left the skimmer in the woods. In case you need it. I'll send you the coordinates. We had to ditch it; there are rockets falling around us. We didn't think they had any left. We'll go back to it and try to come get you around daylight. Hug Alicia for me. Tell her Daddy loves her."

Chiaro inched closer to Ryu. "You heard that?"

Ryu nodded.

Wordlessly, the two women dug the small perimeter alert system out of the bundle and started stringing it up in nearby trees. It was simple. A series of small cameras set to alert them to movement, with different tones and colors sent to Chiaro and Ryu's wrist monitors when anything larger than a butterfly crossed. The best locations they could find left them a safe area inside the perimeter twenty meters in front of them, twelve to their right, and fourteen to their left. Behind them, the rocky cliff formed a barrier, although snakes or lizards could swarm down it. They finished putting the remaining food away in time to watch the sunset turn the twisted twintree in front of them into a sinuous silhouette and a tent-tree near the cliff into a black lump the size of a small building.

There were enough blankets to wrap the children in, two to a blanket, leaving Elinia with her own. Chiaro and Ryu had one between them to share. Chiaro handed it to Ryu. "I'll take first watch."

"Wake me when you need to."

Chiaro propped her swollen ankle up on a nearby rock and set her stunner next to her. The strap of the Night Eyes dug into her scalp, but she didn't pull them down. They could help spot movement and life in front of her but at the cost of her peripheral vision. She had never liked them. Elinia had the genetic version of a Night Eye, and so did Justin, although Justin had told her more than once he wished he could turn it off. Neither she nor Ryu had it, but she wasn't going to wear the damned goggles until she had to.

As the stars winked into being, Chiaro began to hum softly, hoping to send the children to sleep. She sipped sparingly from her canteen between songs, falling silent only when everyone else seemed to have drifted off.

From time to time the boundary lit pale blue lights on her wrist, which she kept squeezed between her knees to hide the glow of the light. Two moons rose. Wishstone, then Destiny. She looked for a third since the original colonists had a superstition that three moons meant good luck, but there was no sign of Hope or any other of the seven moons. At least the double moonlight made pretty shadows on the dark forest floor.

Chiaro tried to picture the others safe, but there had been so much death she kept seeing the dead in her imagination instead of the living. They didn't look broken. They looked like she had last seen them, each of them resolute and grim as they had headed out of the cave for battle.

There were other groups of survivors, but she had been in the cave for a year and everyone except the children and their parents seemed like mist. She'd give her good ankle to be back on Silver's Home where the skies were never this dark and still and she didn't need to worry about any kind of predator—not animals or people.

Kayleen whimpered in her sleep.

Far off, a pack of demon dogs howled after prey, probably a herd of djuri or one of the other, fatter, grazing animals.

Ryu turned over, groaning.

A meteor streaked a wide white scar across the dark sky; light enough to dull Chiaro's night vision. Chiaro shivered, once again thinking of home, where they had defenses against such things, where the ground didn't shake once a month or more, where many of the birds had been designed to sing beautifully.

Little Elinia woke, untangling from her blanket carefully and saying, "I need to potty."

Ryu stretched. "I'll take her. I can't sleep anyway."

Of all the children, Elinia was the most body-conscious.

She watched carefully as Ryu and Elinia walked hand in hand toward one of the few trees inside the perimeter.

Bryan sat up. "Stay here," Chiaro whispered.

He pointed toward the tree, his eyes wide, and quietly pushed to a stand.

Chiaro looked where he was looking. Everything except the limping woman and the small, wide girl was still. Nothing seemed to move except them.

Chiaro tugged her Night Eyes down over her face just in time to see a red streak of cat fall expertly from the tree onto Ryu's back.

Ryu staggered.

Chiaro aimed her stunner, but the cat was fast and sinuous, and she could just as easily stun Ryu. She hesitated. The two beings danced together in her glasses, both hot with red light, almost impossible to tell apart.

Ryu cried out. One of her arms fluttered at the cat. Like a butterfly assaulting a stone.

Bryan leapt toward the attack.

It didn't matter if she stunned them both. Chiaro fired at the same time that she hissed, "Bryan, come back!"

Her shot went wide.

Bryan kept going, only now he blocked a second shot.

Chiaro glanced at the other children, awake now except for Kayleen, who seemed able to sleep through gunshots. Chiaro leapt from her rock, scampering east to try for a clear shot that didn't compromise Bryan.

Bryan reached toward Elinia.

A heavy *thunk* sounded at the same time that the cat twitched. A long dark line told Chiaro it was an arrow.

She turned, staring into the forest. Three human-shaped heat signatures made a rough half-circle just outside of their perimeter. Chiaro shot at the closest one, then ducked and changed direction, heading away from the children.

If only she could see what the cat was doing. It hadn't fallen.

Her foot slowed her down. She twisted and got off another shot. Missed.

Something slammed fire into her right arm.

She screamed and fell, watching the slender, hot shape of the man who'd shot her. She wanted to rip the glasses off so she could really see his face, but her arm wouldn't move.

He fell, his body making an audible thud as he landed. Stunned.

She turned, found Bryan just a few feet away, holding Ryu's stunner.

An arrow sped toward him, missed, but found Elinia's belly.

"No!" Chiaro screamed.

Bryan shot the third man before he turned toward Elinia.

None of her enemies moved. Nevertheless, Chiaro shot them all with a stunner a second time for good measure and then raced toward Bryan and Elinia. Bryan held Elinia's still form against his chest as he sobbed quietly. The cat had disappeared somewhere. Ryu lay with her good leg crumpled under her, her throat and side both bleeding. Ryu's face and part of her torso were bloodied and raw and she didn't so much as twitch at Chiaro's approach. Nevertheless, Chiaro extended her shaking hand to Ryu's neck, hoping for a pulse.

Nothing. Chiaro turned toward the children, fighting back tears. She plucked Elinia's body from Bryan's arms, careful of the arrow which had pierced the child's chest. She picked him up. "You saved us."

He buried his face in her shoulder, fighting back sobs as she carried him back toward the other children. She had no idea where the cat had gone. Hopefully off to die quietly. Others could come. Cats or people or demon dogs or snakes. The three enemies they'd stunned would eventually wake. They had to leave.

But this was where Justin and David would come looking for them.

Indecision and shock made her dizzy.

She counted the children. The Night Eyes made it easy to count to six, although it took a few moments to sort out who was who with her arm on fire and her head swimming with worry. Chelo sat quietly beside Liam, who had silent tears staining his cheeks and shirt. Joseph was on her other side, silently observing. Alicia – the one most likely to take stupid risks – was up and walking around the inside of the perimeter. Kayleen had started to stir.

A thought struck Chiaro so hard it nearly drove her breath from her chest. It wouldn't do for Kayleen to see her mother's body. She reached into her pack and took out some medical spray, aiming the can at her left arm, closing her eyes as she pressed the release trigger. A cloud of thick droplets covered the wound, stinging like hell for a moment before bringing a blessed near-total numbness. She tested. The arm still obeyed her. It felt clumsy, but she could use it. She picked Kayleen up and settled her sleepy form on her left hip. She kept the stunner in her right hand. She asked Chelo, "Will you lead us down the hill?"

Chelo nodded.

"Stay right behind me. Hold hands. Keep Bryan next to you. Then Joseph and Alicia. Liam can take the back." Normally, she would have put Bryan in the lead. She snorted a hard, painful breath. The child had saved them all. But even though Bryan was the bravest, he had the most tender emotions. Surely he was in as much shock as she was right now. Maybe more.

They might have to go into Artistos. If she could even get that far with her limp. If she did, they would kill her. Almost certainly.

It didn't matter. The children mattered. They needed to get far enough away that Kayleen wouldn't see Ryu. Then Chiaro could stop and think harder.

They followed the main path. It was the only safe thing to do with one crippled adult and six war-shocked children. The woods rustled around them. Night birds called back and forth to each other.

She had left Elinia's body behind. But what else could she have done?

Chiaro hadn't brought a way to brush away snakes. She could only hope not to step on another one. Her leg throbbed at the memory that brought up. Damn Fremont anyway.

After twenty painstakingly slow minutes, she stopped to rest in a fat part of the path with rocks conveniently placed along the sides. She set Kayleen down.

Kayleen immediately asked the impossible question. "Where's Mom?"

It couldn't be hidden. "You mom and Elinia are both gone. I'm sorry."

"Gone?" Kayleen's face crumpled and she repeated the word. "Gone. They're gone. Mom and Elinia. Gone. Gone."

Chelo sat beside her and took her hand.

Such tiny children to be taking care of each other.

Chiaro took a step back and touched her ear, signaling to Justin, Marissa, or David. Anyone that would hear her.

Battle discipline meant waiting for an acknowledgment.

None came.

She sat next to Bryan to rest her foot and think. He scooted next to her, not touching but close. Just the way he had treated Elinia.

She glanced toward the children. They were all quiet, eyes wide and exhausted. None of them had slept more than twenty minutes since the night before.

All of their parents could be dead.

She hadn't heard anything that sounded like battle for a few hours, but it was the very middle of the night. Perhaps all of Fremont except her and the children slept.

They needed a place to wait safely for daylight.

She dug into their packs and handed each child some jerky. Bryan put his in his pocket, but the others ate. She passed around a canteen. After everyone drank, she spoke softly. "We're going to walk a little bit more. We're looking for someplace safe to sleep. We'll walk in the same order, except Kayleen will be behind Chelo."

Bryan looked at her. "I'll be last." He held up his hand, which still had the stunner. "I can use the stunner."

She stared at the gun, surprised he still had it. But he had saved them once. "Be careful with it."

She kept them on the main path.

About fifteen minutes into the slow walk, a bird with wings as wide as Chiaro was tall swooped down in front of her, pulling up just inches from her face. The wind of its passage ruffled her hair. To their credit, the children didn't scream. Chiaro started trying to watch above them as well as in front.

After an hour, she couldn't keep moving. The knee of her bad leg trembled. All of the kids were slowing.

The next fifteen minutes felt like forever.

A clearing opened at the edge of the path, the lights of Fremont's only town, Artistos, sparkling below them. Pillows of rough grass made as good a place to stop as any she had seen. She ran her fingers through the grass, looking for anything stinging or dangerous. The sharp blades drew blood from two fingers but wouldn't hurt someone moving slowly through it. "Be careful," she told the children. They sat in a close circle, huddled together for warmth. There were no blankets left, and Chiaro shivered.

Although she couldn't make them out in the depth of the night, the rockets they had come here in, the *New Making* and the *Journey*, rested on pads in the middle of the grass plains that swept from below the town to the sea. If the night had gone well, she and the children might already be on their way to the ships.

She tucked Kayleen into her lap and stroked her head, keeping her quiet.

From time to time, Chiaro touched her ear. Nothing. No response.

Had everyone died but her? Was she alone with the babies? How could she possibly protect them? Since there was no one else to take a watch, she stayed awake.

The colors of the grass plains had just started to show mottled greens, silvers, and blues when she heard the skimmer above them. Someone had come for them!

She touched her ear again. Nothing. She spoke into the mic, heard her own voice reverb through an apparently empty channel.

Had they simply lost communications? She had to get back up the path. But she still couldn't afford to move fast. Dawn and dusk were both full of predators on Fremont.

Hurriedly, she woke the children. They all needed to take care of business. She made them do it right there, under her watchful eyes, hurrying them as much as she could. Just as Kayleen was finishing, the whine of a medium-range rocket split the air, followed by a deep *whump* and then a crash of trees as it landed.

Chiaro stiffened.

The children raced to her, swarming her legs, almost tripping her.

Light spilled faster across the plains, turning the grasses golden and pale green now.

The skimmer whined away, light flashing on its silver wings.

A dark cold settled into Chiaro's heart. They would have seen the bodies. After the rocket landed, they couldn't have stayed. Not really. They were lucky it hadn't destroyed the skimmer. It was the last one they had left of the three they'd brought, the only way for anyone to move quickly here.

They might not know she lived, that their kids lived! She tapped her ear again and again, desperate. "Hello?"

Nothing.

Whoever fired that rocket was probably close.

No point in going up. Not now. Now that there was light, she put the children in front of her, Bryan leading, Chelo in the back, closest to Chiaro. She started them down, humming softly.

Her foot hurt. Her arm hurt. Her head felt like mush with exhaustion and anxiety warring inside of it.

A deep rumble came from the direction of the sea. Bryan stopped so abruptly that Liam stumbled into him. Bryan pointed.

Once again, she followed his finger.

The noise intensified. Steam. And out of the steam, out of the noise, the *Journey* rose straight up from the grass plains, slowly at first and then faster.

Chiaro drew a deep breath in, searing her lungs with it on purpose. She blew it back out. Again. Again. They were alone. They were alone on a planet full of people who hated them for no reason other than what they were. The people who lived here didn't know the kids, but they already hated them. It was fear, really. She knew that. Marissa knew it. Some of the others knew it. But knowing it was fear instead of hatred hadn't stopped the fighting. One emotion killed as easily as the other.

Back at the beginning, when the conflict between the two groups was still talking and astonishment, Chiaro had met many of the colonists. They were like her, except slower and weaker, and less quick of mind. Mostly. But they had hearts and they loved their families and they raised animals and got sick and died. They were human. Her ancestors had been like them.

The children had been born after the war started and grown up mostly hidden in the cave. Sometimes on nice days, they'd been taken for skimmer rides to far away safe places where they'd swum in pools of cool water or just walked on beaches that the colonists had never been able to get to.

She had no idea how to fly the skimmer. Or the *New Making*. She was no pilot.

Fear chittered along her nerves and throbbed in the cut on her arm in spite of the medical spray.

Voices came from behind her.

She turned, unable to see anyone yet, but they were talking about the ship.

Chiaro hissed at the children. "Run. Run like the wind."

Bryan grabbed Liam's hand and headed toward a rock. Chelo and Joseph raced down the hill in the middle of the path, Chelo glancing back from time to time.

Kayleen and Alicia stayed put, Kayleen's arms wrapped around Chiaro's right leg.

A man and a woman rounded the corner, still watching the plains and the place where the *Journey* had been.

Alicia raced *toward* the strangers, her dark hair bouncing up and down as she ran, her shoulder bent as if she could actually knock these people down. She was fast – all of the children were faster than the normals here.

The woman immediately flipped her gun up.

Chiaro screamed, "They're children!"

Alicia stopped. The man's gun pointed at her, Chiaro.

"I can't do it," the woman said. She was watching him, while he watched Chiaro.

Alicia slammed into his legs with little effect.

He stared at Chiaro, his eyes a little wide. "Even your children fight?"

"When they're frightened." She remembered Bryan and his stunner. Hers hung loosely in her fingers, while two guns were pointed at her. She couldn't tell if they would stun her or kill her, but if Bryan shot one of these two, the other might shoot him.

The woman kept her gun trained on Chiaro while the man picked Alicia up and trapped her against his hip with one arm, telling her, "Stay put."

Miraculously, Alicia behaved. Probably biding her time until she could find a soft place on the man's arm to sink her teeth into.

"I'm Therese," the woman said. "And this is Stephen. We run Artistos now. I'm sorry about your friend and the other child."

So they had seen. Therese sounded as exhausted as Chiaro felt.

Chiaro dropped her gun, hoping Bryan would do the same. She looked behind her. Chelo and Joseph had stopped a good distance away, but she couldn't see Bryan or Liam. Maybe they could get away. And what? Be eaten by a paw-cat or a pack of demon dogs? Her people were gone. Chiaro looked at Therese. "Elinia. Her name was Elinia. She didn't deserve to be shot."

Stephen's face had been set hard, his brows drawn together in thought. He softened a little. "Good to know. You should come to town with us."

She hesitated. "What will happen to us?"

Stephen dropped his gun arm a little, aiming at the ground, his other arm still clutching Alicia tight to him as she tried to squirm free. "We decide important things by Town Council. So even we can't tell you that now. But I can tell you I am sick of death. We may not be able to keep you safe. People are angry and lost and bitter. All of us. But I don't think they will execute children."

She swallowed. "I would die for them."

"Maybe you won't have to."

He didn't sound certain. But she would die here anyway now, at these people's hands or by the sharp teeth of a predator. She couldn't even walk fast, let alone run. She took three sharp breaths, trying to find her way forward. "Bryan?" When he didn't answer she repeated, "Bryan? Good boy. Come to me."

Bryan peeked out from the side of the rock, the stunner in his hand.

"Drop it. Like I dropped mine."

He hesitated.

She held her breath.

Stephen said, "Bring it to me. Carefully."

Bryan looked at Chiaro, who nodded. He slowly edged himself away from the rock, bringing Liam with him.

Stephen bent down and let Alicia go. She rushed to Chiaro's side and started to untangle Kayleen from Chiaro's legs.

Bryan walked so solemnly Chiaro wondered for a moment if he understood what he was doing, and what it meant. He couldn't, of course. He was only four. But when he handed Stephen the stunner, the man said, "Thank you."

Therese picked up the gun Chiaro had dropped, and then sat down in the middle of the path, sobbing. Chiaro stared at her for a moment, not quite comprehending, even though Therese's sobs made her want to cry. Maybe it was just stress and exhaustion. Maybe it was surrender. Maybe it was the loss of her way home, her friends. She didn't even know who was alive anymore. No one had answered her. She slipped the silent, betraying earset into her pocket and started down the path to retrieve Chelo and Joseph.

CONTAINED VACUUM
David Sherman

ACCORDING TO *JANES COMMERCIAL STARFLEETS OF THE CONFEDERATION OF Human Worlds*, the unidentified starship off the *Dayzee Mae*'s port bow was the SS Runstable, which had vanished two years previous, along with her crew and cargo.

Sergeant Tim Kerr, of the Confederation Marine Corps, stood on the bridge of the *Dayzee Mae*, watching the derelict ship on the display. The ship's acting captain, Lieutenant Junior Grade McPherson, had just finished briefing him. The *Runstable*'s cargo had been destined for twenty different worlds, none of which were near enough to this jump point to explain why the ship might be where it was. And all of the containers she was carrying when last heard from were missing; the superstructure made a narrow tower over the empty container deck. It was emitting a distress signal but carried no friend or foe identification.

"She must have been taken by pirates," McPherson said, "then abandoned here. This location is far enough from normal trade routes that she wouldn't be found quickly. We don't have a surveillance tech aboard," he added apologetically, "and we lack the necessary equipment to detect life forms on her. So you'll be going in blind."

Kerr nodded silently, his gaze intent on the latest display, which showed the starship in fuzzy detail. Her near-space running lights were on, but her passenger hatch and a bridge hatch were open. No lights showed through the open hatches.

The *Dayzee Mae* was a civilian starship, confiscated by the Confederation navy when they caught her supporting an illegal alien slavery operation on the twin worlds Opal and Ishtar. McPherson and his crew were ferrying her to the navy base on Thorsfinni's World where another crew would transport her to wherever the Court of Inquiry determined she should go. So, naturally, she didn't have military-grade sensors. She did, however, have one piece of military equipment never before found on a civilian freighter. The THB, Tweed Hull Breacher, was used by Confederation Marines to cut their way into hostile or potentially hostile starships. The THB carried by the *Dayzee Mae* had been used by the Marines when they boarded and took her.

Finally, Kerr said, "It could be an ambush. I want to use the THB and force an entryway. We'll enter through the rear of the bridge."

"You've got it, Sergeant." McPherson gave a wry grin. "You are our expert on hostile boardings."

Kerr grunted. He hoped the boarding wouldn't be against a hostile force; he and his men had seen enough action on this latest deployment, and were on their way home. Second squad, third platoon, Company L of 34th Fleet Initial Strike Team's infantry battalion had been given the assignment of providing security on the *Dayzee Mae* during her transit to Thorsfinni's World because the squad had suffered badly in the action on Ishtar. Two of the fire team leaders and one other Marine were still nominally on light duty, and two new men weren't completely integrated into the squad yet. Chain of command thought this duty would give them a chance to rest and recuperate.

"We're Marines," Sergeant Kerr said a short time later, when some of his men groaned at being told about the boarding mission. "Everyone in Human Space expects us to do anything necessary, at any time, in any place, regardless how difficult."

"We're Marines," Corporal Rachman Claypoole—one of the injured fire team leaders—muttered. "We do the difficult immediately. The impossible might take a little longer."

"That's right, Rock," Kerr said. "Now go to the arms locker to check out your weapons and armored vacuum suits."

"With chameleon overalls?" Corporal Chan asked.

"Yes," he said. There was no telling who or what they might find aboard the derelict. The invisibility provided by chameleons could prove to be vital.

"*Armored* suits, sir? Are we expecting trouble, Corporal Claypoole?" asked PFC Berry, one of the two new men in the squad.

There were vacuum suits, and there were *armored* vacuum suits. One protected the wearer from the vacuum of space, and the micrometeorites that swarmed through it. *Armored* vacuum suits protected the wearer from the flechettes that could shred an unarmored suit, and almost every other known projectile, including plasma weapons, such as the Marines' own blasters.

Claypoole snorted. "We're Marines boarding an unknown starship in interstellar space. We don't have an invitation. No shit, we're expecting trouble."

It took more than two hours for the Hull Breacher to travel the 200 klicks between the *Dayzee Mae* and the derelict. Three fire teams of Marines stood waiting quietly, sweating into their armored suits, doing their best to ignore itches, thinking—or trying not to think—about what might meet them on board the SS *Runstable*.

It's odd, Kerr thought, *that she's here. And nobody noticed her when the* Grandar Bay *came through here on our way to Ishtar.* He struggled to quell the knot that tightened in his stomach at the wrongness of the situation.

The pilot, EM3 Mark Resort, brought the THB into contact with rear of the *Runstable*'s tower as smoothly as any first class could have, touching the starship's hull with barely a bump. He grappled the THB to the hull with its magnets, and fired up the cutters. Everything went smoothly, and in mere moments he had an opening cut through the rear of the outer hull of the *Runstable*'s bridge deck. It only took a few more seconds for him to cut through the inner hull.

"First fire team, go!" Kerr snapped. He briefly touched helmets with Resort before leaving the THB. "Good landing, squid. You can drive me anytime."

Corporal Chan showed no lingering effects of his wound when he darted onto the bridge and led his men toward the port side. Corporal Claypoole and his men ran to the starboard as soon as Chan and his fire team cleared the breach. The six Marines spread out, covering all directions with their plasma blasters.

Kerr entered the bridge more slowly, walking without using his boots' magnets to hold him to the deck—the *Runstable*'s artificial gravity was still on—and stood between the first two fire teams. Using his helmet's light gatherer screen, he looked around; it showed him everything in stark black and white, with a few shades of gray, and negatively affected his depth perception. The bridge was about ten meters deep and thirty wide. Centered on the side the Marines had entered was the captain's chair, flanked by the navigator and helmsman's stations. They faced large displays on the opposite bulkhead. The displays were blank. Consoles were lined up below the displays—probably crew stations. What looked like airlock hatches were at either end of the bridge compartment.

Kerr couldn't discern any damage in the odd view through his light gatherer. The knot in his stomach tightened further. Something was very wrong here; this wasn't a simple derelict starship. He looked to his rear. Corporal Doyle and his men stood stolidly just inside the bridge. But Kerr knew that was an illusion; they had to be shifting their weight, even jittering, inside their armored vacuum suits. His motion detector didn't pick up anything other than his Marines.

Kerr advanced to the captain's station. Keypads on the armrests of the chair were clearly labeled, and he opened the airlocks at each end of the bridge. "Heads up," he said. He quickly found the *Runstable*'s log. He scanned though it, beginning with the most recent entry, while copying its contents to his comp.

"Find anything interesting, Honcho?" Claypoole asked.

Kerr shook his head, not caring that the gesture wasn't visible. "Everything looks normal, right up to the last entry, dated about two years ago. The last entry is interrupted mid-word." His comp beeped, signaling that the download was finished. Done with the log, he checked the starship's systems. As near as he could tell, none of them were damaged, just offline—including nearly all life support—with one exception.

"The ship's gravity seems to be on throughout the ship," he announced over his comm's squad circuit. Then, "Check out the compartments beyond the airlocks. First fire team, left, second to the right."

"Aye-aye," Chan and Claypoole answered.

They were back in moments. Each had the same report: The compartments were smaller than the bridge and had storage lockers that all seemed to be empty, with with airlocks at the far end that were open to space. Claypoole added that there was a ladder heading below in the compartment to the bridge's starboard end.

Kerr thought for a moment, then said, "Listen up, second squad. We're going to check this girl out, top to bottom. Rock, is Wolfman up to running point?" Kerr looked at the reddish blur that was Lance Corporal MacIlargie. It had to be his imagination, but he could have sworn that MacIlargie's armored vacuum suit gave an eager twitch at the question.

Third fire team joined the squad at the head of the ladder, a shaft with a handrail on each side that descended into the bowels of the tower.

Kerr gave the route order. "Second fire team, me, third, first. Go."

"Aye-aye," Claypoole said. He pointed at MacIlargie and said, "You heard the man. Go."

"Right." MacIlargie gripped one of the handrails, pointed the muzzle of his blaster between his feet, and stepped into the shaft. The rail drew him down.

Claypoole let MacIlargie's helmet clear the level of the deck, then followed. Another deck appeared seven meters down.

"Into it, Wolfman," Claypoole said.

All of the spaces on this level were open to the corridor.

The level was surprisingly smaller than the bridge level. By examining the *Runstable*'s schematics stored on their comps, the Marines saw that the difference was conduit space behind the bulkheads, allowing the power, life support, and other commands to flow between the bridge and all other areas of the starship. When they located the well-concealed access panels, everything looked to be in order behind them; there wasn't enough room inside to hide a body, alive or dead.

It was at the third level below the bridge that they finally ran into a closed compartment.

Kerr signaled Claypoole, who banged his armored fist on the hatch. His armor augmented his strength so that he hit the hatch almost hard enough to dent the plasteel. He pressed the "announce" button, hoping there were lights inside that would flash to alert any occupants who might not be able to hear someone banging at the hatch.

When there was no response, Kerr motioned Claypoole aside and stepped to the hatch himself—if a frightened civilian might die because of what he was about to do, he wanted the death to be on him, not on one of his men. He slapped the "open" plate, and the hatch slid aside.

MacIlargie leaped through the hatch before it was fully open and spun to one side. Claypoole was on his heels, and spun to the other.

"Dammit!" Kerr swore. He didn't wait for Berry to complete the fire team's maneuver before he darted through and joined Claypoole and MacIlargie. "I told you to wait for me."

"Sorry, Honcho," MacIlargie said. "I didn't get the word."

They found a corpse huddled in a storage closet of the otherwise empty room. The lack of atmosphere had kept any bacteria or mold from living and taking root anywhere in the starship, so the corpse hadn't rotted. Instead, its own intestinal flora had grown and burst the abdomen from the inside, splattering gore around the interior of the closet.

Berry gagged—a strictly reflexive action, as the remains gave off no stench in the absence of atmosphere in the compartment.

"You upchuck in that helmet, you'll be in trouble, Marine," Claypoole snarled, choking down his own gorge.

"Right. Trouble," Berry gasped, turning away from the sight.

Kerr's stomach was stronger, or he was better prepared for the sight when he looked into the closet.

"How do you think he died?" Claypoole asked.

Kerr's shrug went unseen inside his chameleoned armor. "Starved. Maybe dehydrated. Do you see any signs of violence?"

"No," Claypoole said softly. "He doesn't look like sudden decompression killed him, either."

Kerr noted the corpse's location on his comp, then ordered, "Move out."

They found three more desiccated corpses before they reached the lowest deck of the tower. One, they assumed, was the ship's surgeon, as the otherwise unidentifiable corpse was in the infirmary.

"Where are the rest of them?" Claypoole wondered out loud.

"In the subdeck?" Kerr said. "Maybe ejected into space? Maybe sold as slaves somewhere? Maybe set free on some out-world?" Disgust came into his voice as he added, "Maybe nobody will ever know." He shook his head, unseen inside his chameleoned armor.

"A-Are we checking the subdeck?" Corporal Doyle asked nervously.

"We're checking the whole damn ship," Kerr said flat-voiced. "Doyle, you asked, you lead the way."

Doyle audibly swallowed. "Aye-aye, Sergeant Kerr. Summers, me, Johnson," he said, giving his fire team's order of movement. In infra, Kerr saw Doyle's armored suit turn as he looked side to side along the passageway for access to the subdeck that ran below the container deck.

"It's to the right," Kerr said, glancing at his schematic of the *Runstable*.

"To the right, Summers," Doyle repeated. He followed in Summers's wake.

The subdeck was one continuous cavern, interrupted at regular intervals by evenly spaced pillars that kept the decking and overhead from flexing away from—or into—each other. Despite the breadth and length of the hold, it felt claustrophobic; the overhead was less than five meters above the deck. The machines that kept the *Runstable* and all its systems operating were arranged on this deck. Cargo-moving cranes and lighters were drawn below deck and battened down. Ship's stores were stowed and marked as such near access shafts from above.

Kerr turned his helmet's ears all the way up and listened. He didn't expect to hear any sounds, not in vacuum, but he thought that vibrations through the deck might register through his boots as subsonics, and straining his ears might help him "hear" the vibrations. All he felt was the faint thrumming of the gravity generators.

"Fire team leaders," Kerr ordered, "use your motion detectors. Have one man use his light gatherer, the other his infra. Leaders, use both. I want to know immediately if anybody detects anything. Do it now." Kerr himself used his light gatherer and infrared screens in conjunction. He compared what he could see with the schematic on his comp and found that six aisles cut between the machinery and stacks of other containers that ran the length of the subdeck. He climbed to the top of the nearest machine housing and looked as far as he could, which wasn't much more than fifty meters—there wasn't enough light for the light gatherer to see any farther, and what he could see was dim. Still, he saw what looked like cross-passages between groups of machine housings and other equipment.

"Listen up. We're going the length of this hold. First fire team, take the starboard-most aisle. One Marine in the aisle, one on top of the machinery on each flank of the aisle. Second, the next, third, the next. Same top-bottom-top spacing. When we reach the far end, everybody move over three aisles. That'll put third fire team on the outer side. If you see anything that looks like it's been opened, let me know and check it out. Questions?"

"Is 'do we gotta' an appropriate question?" MacIlargie asked.

"Stand by for a head smack when we get back to the *Dayzee Mae*," Claypoole snapped before Kerr could respond.

"Dumb question, huh?" MacIlargie said.

"Dumb as they come," Claypoole confirmed.

"That's enough," Kerr barked. "Get into your positions and move out."

Kerr kept an eye on his men and saw that they didn't rush, but looked into everything that might have been opened, and checked behind everything that could be checked behind, just as he told them to. It took more than an hour to cover the three hundred meters to the bow, but the only thing they discovered that seemed out of the ordinary was almost none of the machinery was operating—just what was needed to provide gravity and to power the near-space running lights.

Kerr checked his men visually to make sure they were all present, and verified that with the display on his comp.

"All right," he said, "shift over three aisles." The fire teams were in their new positions within two minutes. Kerr made one more visual check, and ordered, "Move out."

Fifty meters on, Fisher's icon on Kerr's display suddenly began blinking red.

"Chan, report!" Kerr snapped.

"Fisher's down," Chan came back. "I don't know what happened."

"Hold your position, I'll be right there." Kerr was in the central of the three aisles along which the Marines were moving. He clambered to the top of the machinery between him and his first fire team and began crossing it toward their position as fast as he could.

He was halfway there when something too fast to make out flashed past his vision, barely above foot-level. His head jerked in the direction the blur seemed to have come from, and thought he saw a faint blip of red, but it was gone from his sight before he could be sure.

"We aren't alone down here!" he shouted. He snapped off three rapid-fire plasma bolts from his blaster. The first two bolts of star-stuff slagged a hole through the thin metal casing of a container that projected higher than the rest of the machinery. The third bolt went all the way through and ended in a brilliant flash of light from behind it. He dashed to the edge of the machinery he was standing on and leapt down from it to join Chan. Along the way he wondered, *Are there Skinks here?* He didn't know anything else that would flash like that after being hit by a blaster bolt.

To Chan on the fire-team circuit, "What's Fisher's status?"

"Something blew right through him!" Chan said. "Through and through. His body suit sealed his wound and sedated him. I slapped patches on his armor, so he's not losing air." His voice grew haunted. "But what the hell hit him?"

Kerr remembered the blur that was too fast to see, and shuddered. The only thing he could think of that went that fast and could punch a hole right through an armored vacuum suit was a railgun. But railguns were only used by Skinks, and were crew-served weapons. This seemed to have been a personal weapon. He remembered the flash of light that met his third shot; the Skinks vaporized in a flash of light when they were hit by a plasma bolt—nobody knew why—but that was in the atmosphere of a planet, and how could they be flaring in the vacuum of the abandoned freighter? These Skinks—if that's what they were—were also somehow able to detect where a chameleoned Marine was, and get close enough to shoot him. *What is happening here?*

"Railgun, I think," Kerr said, answering Chan's question. *Now I know why the gravity is turned on,* he thought. *The Skinks, or whoever, need it for themselves.*

"Does anybody have anything?" Kerr shouted into his comm. "Motion detector, infra, anything?"

"No," "Negative," "Nothing," the answers came back.

"All right," he said, knowing that nothing was actually all right. "I got one. Probably the one that shot Fisher. But it doesn't matter if that's the one—you know there are more."

"D-Do you think this was a trap?" Doyle asked.

"That's damn likely. Maybe more than just inside the ship." Kerr not only thought there were more Skinks in the Runstable's subdeck, he was afraid they also had a warship near enough to jump here and destroy the Dayzee *Mae.*

He toggled to the long-range comm. If the comm could get through the bulkhead of the subdeck and make it to the distant starship, he could give them a warning. He climbed to the top of the machinery he was taking cover behind and found something to hunker down behind while he used his comm.

"*Dayzee Mae, Dayzee Mae,* this is Hellhound. Over." Nobody had expected the Marines to have to contact the *Dayzee Mae* except over the THB's ship-to-ship comm, so they hadn't assigned comm call signs. But he was certain that Petty Officer Craven would realize who was calling— who but a Marine would call himself Hellhound?—and that the call meant trouble.

"...llhou...ae. How do...ou read m..." came the reply.

Kerr swore before toggling his comm to transmit. "You're badly broken, *Dayzee Mae.* How you me? Over."

It took a moment for a reply to come. It was as broken as the first.

"...ellhoun...Mae. Yo...br...en. Say...gin...las...Ove...."

Damn, Kerr muttered. He could make out enough to know that the *Dayzee Mae* couldn't hear him any more clearly than he could hear them. *Well, you do what you can with what you've got.* "*Dayzee Mae*, we've got Skinks. I say again, we've got Skinks. Over."

"*He...nd, Dayz...* Inks. I do...un...and. Ov..." It sounded like McPherson's voice.

"Skinks. I say again, Skinks are on the *Runstable*. Over." Kerr heard the CRACK-*sizzle* of blaster fire behind him, and hoped his comm picked it up—that would let McPherson know that the Marines were in a firefight, even if he didn't realize they were fighting Skinks.

Then: "...inks! Ski...!...ere are Sk...ks...*Rus...ble*?"

"That's affirmative, *Dayzee Mae*. We've got Skinks. Over."

"I...stan...Skin...affir...?...ver."

"You got it, *Dayzee Mae*. We've got Skinks big time. You best watch for a Skink starship coming in. I gotta get back to the fight. Hellhound Out." He turned off his comm, sure that the Dayzee Mae had gotten the basic message, and looked around the side of his cover in time to see a dim spot of red. He snapped off a bolt of plasma at it, and was rewarded by the sight of a flash of light that could only be a dying Skink.

The Skink he had shot earlier was to his right, perhaps seventy-five meters distant. As was this one. He groaned. That put the first Skink, and probably more, in front of third fire team, Doyle's.

"Doyle, are you topside or below?" he asked. His comp told him, but he needed to make sure his weakest fire team leader knew where he was.

"T-Topside. Closest t-to the hull," Doyle answered nervously. "Summers is below. J-Johnson is topside inbound."

All right. Doyle knew where he and both of his men were. "Everybody," Kerr ordered into the squad circuit, "look, and use your infras."

"But Skinks don't show up well in the infrared," Claypoole objected.

"As cold as it is in vacuum, any warmth will show up," Kerr said. "Do it!" And wondered why the two Marines in three already using their infra hadn't spotted the Skink that shot Fisher.

Three rapid plasma bolts burned a line from Kerr's left almost to his direct front. He thought he saw a flash of light.

"I got one!" The shout came from Lance Corporal Little.

"Your fire gave away your position. Move!" Kerr shouted back.

"Already did, Honcho."

Kerr shifted to look around the edge of his hiding place—just in time. He'd barely moved over before something punched through the plasteel housing right where he'd been. *Damn, that was close—too close!* He scooted backward until his feet reached a drop-off. The whole time his eyes jerked side to side, scanning the area around the machine he'd been behind, seeking any sign of the telltale slight reddish tint.

"Who's still below?" he asked into the squad circuit. "Chan, I know you are, but stick with Fisher."

"I am, Summers."

"So am I."

"Who's that, Berry?"

"Ah, yeah, I'm Berry."

Kerr dropped over the edge his feet had found and studied the schematic of the subdeck. He knew it showed the location of the permanent items, those affixed to the deck. It was the other items, the crates of ship's stores, that he couldn't count on showing up.

"Berry, have you seen anything?"

"No, Sergeant. I don't think they can see me. I think they're all on top."

"I think so, too. Rock, Wolfman, can either of you get down to where Berry is without exposing yourselves to the Skinks?"

"Probably, but one of them fired a projectile of some kind close to me," MacIlargie said.

"Then stay where you are. Claypoole?"

"I'm already joining Berry."

"Summers, try to get to Berry without going topside. Claypoole, Berry, I'm on my way to you. Chan, if anything happens to me, you're in command. If that happens, I want you to get everybody out of here. Go back the same way we came in if you have to. Got it?"

Chan's voice was leaden when he said, "I get everybody out if anything happens to you."

"Everybody else, let me know if you see anything. If a Skink shoots and you can tell where the shot came from, return fire, then change your position before they fire back."

Kerr was moving while he gave the orders. He reached Claypoole and Berry right after Chan acknowledged his orders. Summers joined them a moment later. Kerr waved at the three to touch helmets with him. He'd give them their orders via conduction rather than comm, on the off chance that the Skinks were able to pick up his transmissions and understand his words.

"Both shots that we made were at targets fifty, seventy-five meters ahead. We're going a hundred meters forward, then go topside and see what we can spot from there. Questions?"

"What if they're set up in depth?" Claypoole asked. "We could come up in the middle of them."

"We won't all go topside and stand where they can see us. I'll go first and look over the edge. Anything else?"

"Does anybody have a periscope?" Summers asked.

"Nobody," Kerr answered. "But that's a good idea. Everybody, keep an eye out for anything I can use as a mirror to look over the top. Now let's go. Summers, me, Claypoole, Berry. Go as fast as you can and still keep a sharp eye out. Go."

The four Marines moved out at a brisk walk.

Thirty meters on, Summers dropped to the deck and fired his blaster straight ahead. Kerr had fired an instant earlier; he fired before he dropped. The two had seen faint red glows emerging from between two bulks another twenty-five meters beyond. One of the two faint red spots terminated in a brilliant flash.

"Spread out and line up so you don't have any of us in your line of fire!" Kerr shouted. He waited for a few seconds, aiming his blaster where he'd seen the enemy emerge. No more came.

"All right, stay down and move back. We'll get into the nearest side passage to our rear."

Before they got there, half a dozen or more incredibly fast slugs slammed down where they'd just been—even though they couldn't hear, or even see the paths of the projectiles, they could see the holes the slugs punched into the deck.

The four Marines awkwardly skittered backward, propelling themselves with knees and elbows.

"Two on the right, two on the left," Kerr ordered.

It took longer than he was comfortable with, but they reached the cover of the side passage without being shot at again. Kerr and Berry went to the right, Claypoole and Summers to the left.

Which wasn't the case with the Marines left on top. Kerr didn't see a flash, but he did hear MacIlargie's excited shout:

"Ooo-eee! Did ya see that? I must have got a whole squad with that shot!"

"I-It wasn't only you," Doyle said. "J-Johnson fired too. So did I."

"Somebody give me a realistic assessment," Kerr snapped.

After a few moments of silence, a voice said, "Sergeant Kerr, I saw three plasma bolts going down range. Before I could locate a target in the area where they converged, there were three or four flashes. I didn't see anything in infra after that."

"Little?"

"That's me."

"Identify yourself when you give a report."

"Will do, Sergeant."

"You did a good job with that report."

Little grunted at the compliment.

I wonder when he learned to give a report that way, Kerr thought. *Maybe he's due for a promotion.*

"You left something out, all of you. How far away was your target—your targets?"

"Not much more than twenty-five meters," MacIlargie said.

Kerr swore, and rolled onto his back; twenty-five meters put the Skinks right on top of him and the Marines with him!

"Claypoole, one of you watch the top. It sounds like we're right in the middle of them."

Claypoole swore something unintelligible, then said, "I'm on it."

So now what, Sergeant? Kerr asked himself. He shook himself. *I'm a Marine sergeant. When in doubt, act decisively.*

"Claypoole, you and Summers head left. Let me know when you're halfway to the next aisle. Go."

"On the way," Claypoole answered.

Kerr looked at his motion detector. He saw Claypoole and Summers withdrawing, but didn't detect any movement topside.

While he was looking up, he saw another plasma bolt burn through his vision. "Report!" he ordered.

"Johnson, Sergeant. I thought I saw something."

"But you didn't hit anything?"

"I don't think so," Johnson said. "Sorry, Sergeant."

"Don't apologize. I'd rather have you shoot at nothing than not shoot at something and get one of us killed because of it. And always move after you fire; your bolt gives away your position."

"Corporal Doyle already told me to move."

Doyle. He always comes across as timid and not a very good combat Marine. But he knows his stuff, and trains his men well.

"We're there, Honcho," Claypoole's voice suddenly said.

"Cover us," Kerr answered.

"If anything red shows, we're ready to flame it," Claypoole said back.

"Berry," Kerr looked to where his infra showed his greenest man was. "Go. I'm right behind you." Kerr started moving, but had to pull up short because Berry didn't move.

"Berry, go!"

"Did you see what those slugs did to the deck?" Berry said, almost in a wail.

"Yes. And that's what the next slugs will do to us if we're still here when they come." He grabbed Berry's shoulder and shoved.

The young Marine stumbled, but quickly gained his balance and ran until Claypoole reached out and grabbed his arm to keep him from running off by himself.

"Doyle," Kerr radioed to the senior Marine above, "what's happening topside?"

"N-Nothing. We haven't s-seen anything since before Johnson's last shot."

"Well, everybody be careful of what you shoot at, because the next thing your infras pick up might be the back of my head."

"Roger, Sergeant Kerr," Doyle said. "Did everybody hear that?"

Kerr decided that Doyle had the situation under control topside, and took a last glance at the top of the machine housing he and Berry had just been behind, on the other side of the aisle where the Skinks had almost caught them. There was nothing there. He began climbing up the stack to his front.

He was almost to the top when Doyle's voice shouted over the comm, *"They're coming! Fire!"* Then to Kerr, "Honcho, I see a mass of them coming at us across the top. Including where you are."

"Are there any on the deck?" Kerr asked.

"I don't know, I can't see the deck from my position." Kerr could almost hear the CRACK-sizzle of Doyle's blaster as the corporal fired time and again.

"There are some coming toward me and Fisher," Chan reported. "I'm getting him into one of the side passages."

Holding onto his position with his feet and one hand, Kerr activated his heads-up display and switched it to show his men's positions. Chan and Little were in the same aisle where he and the Marines with him had been shot at. As he looked, he saw the two turn a corner, out of the aisle. He checked his motion detector. That showed a large number of

CONTAINED VACUUM - David Sherman

forms moving rapidly along the tops of the machine housings and along two aisles.

"Claypoole, Summers, go left and open fire forward, Skinks are coming that way. Berry, go right and fire back the way we started out. I'm going topside to take them out here. *Move!*" He didn't wait for acknowledgements before lunging high enough to get his head and arms over the top and began firing.

The nearest faint reddish glows were only ten meters away.

Kerr didn't take the time to aim, he just pointed and shot. The many hours he'd put in training in snap shooting over the years came to the fore—at this range the only way he could miss was if he did it deliberately. In his mind, he could hear the blood-curdling screaming the Skinks made when they had charged the Marines on Kingdom and on Haulover—every place where the Marines had fought them—except now the Skink charge was silent. As in those other fights, a brilliant flash met each of his plasma bolts. He was killing the Skinks as fast as he could point and press his blaster's trigger-lever.

In seconds, the Skinks were close enough for Kerr's light gatherer to make out details, and he could tell that their vacuum suits weren't armored. At least they had no protection from the Marines' plasma blasters; the bolts burned straight into the suits, and the Skinks flamed in the suit's atmosphere just the same as they did planetside. The heat of their immolations was so intense that they reduced the suits to cinders.

Even though they were smaller than men, there were too many Skinks, and they were too close. One flared up just as it was diving at Kerr, blinding him with the intensity of its flash. Something slapped against his helmet and he fell backward, to the deck below. Momentarily dazed, he didn't hear Claypoole's, "Got that one for you, Honcho!"

But before he could see again something slammed into his helmet and knocked him backward, sending him crashing to the deck below. Shaking his head to blink the dazzling stars and circles out of his eyes, he realized that the wind he felt on his cheek was air rushing out of the side of his helmet.

Don't panic! he shouted at himself. He'd dropped his blaster in his fall, so both hands were free. He groped with one to find the break in his helmet, while reaching for his patching kit with the other. In seconds, he had a patch slapped on the gash in the side of his helmet—he hoped it would hold long enough for someone else to make a better patch. He looked for his blaster. But before he found it, another Skink jumped onto him, knocking him onto his back. He rolled to the side and pushed at the body that lay across his chest. The Skink was light enough that, even still half-stunned and struggling for breath, by using his armor to augment his strength, Kerr was able to shove the Skink off of him.

The creature scooted farther away before it scrabbled to its feet. It pulled a wicked-looking knife from somewhere and lunged at Kerr. Even though the Marine couldn't sidestep fast enough to avoid the blade, his armor easily deflected it. Kerr slammed his armored fist into the Skink's faceplate, shattering it. Red flecked mist geysered from the enemy's helmet. Kerr clearly saw his foe's face before it collapsed—sharply convex, with pointed teeth, the final bit of proof he needed to know that he and his squad were fighting Skinks. The Skink's hands slapped at its face as it fell, as though trying to force air back into its broken helmet.

Kerr looked around for his blaster. Before he could find it, another Skink dropped onto him from above, staggering him. He instantly recovered and threw himself backward, hoping that his superior size and the hardness of his vacuum suit's armor would crush the Skink.

But the Skink didn't die; it shoved at Kerr's back with enough force to lift him and fling him away, and then another Skink landed on the Marine's chest, slamming him back down. This time, Kerr felt something crack under his back, and the Skink he was on top of stopped pushing at him.

Kerr lunged upward, forcing the Skink on his chest to lift off. Palms up, he slammed the sides of his hands into the Skink's neck, just below its helmet. The Skink dropped the knife it had just drawn, and clutched at its throat. Kerr folded the fingers of his right hand and shot the armored knuckles into the Skink's throat. It collapsed backward.

Kerr spun about and saw the Skink that had earlier jumped onto his back was stirring, groping for a knife, and trying to rise. He raised a foot and stomped on it until it stopped moving.

He looked up; no more Skinks were jumping or falling over the edge to fight with him. Neither did he see a plasma bolt burn through the vacuum. If he hadn't just been in violent action, he might have thought all was as serene as the subdeck of an empty container ship ever gets. He looked to his sides. The Marines he'd stationed to cover the aisles weren't firing. He could barely make out their shapes with his infra screen, but they seemed to be looking at him.

"Second squad, report!" he ordered into his comm.

No one replied.

"I said, second squad, report," he repeated. "So speak up. Chan first."
Still no reply.

Kerr looked to his left and saw Claypoole and Summers stand and come toward him.

"Claypoole, talk to me, Marine!"

Claypoole gestured, but didn't say anything. Then he was there, touching helmets with his squad leader.

"Can you hear me, Honcho?"

"Of course I can hear you. What do you...Don't tell me."

"I don't care, I'm going to tell you anyway. Your comm's busted. Chan and Doyle both report all present and accounted for. The bad guys are gone. No casualties."

"Except for my comm."

"Seems that way. Now hold still while I fix that patch on your helmet. I think that's what knocked out your comm."

"All right." Kerr waited patiently for the moment it took Claypoole to layer on a second, better patch. He stared at the dead Skinks at his feet while he waited.

"Good as new, Honcho," Claypoole said, touching helmets again.

Kerr looked at the bodies on the deck around his feet. "We've finally got Skink bodies for the science people," he said. "Get the rest of the squad here to collect them for transfer back to the *Dayzee Mae*."

"Aye-aye." Claypoole broke contact to radio to the rest of the squad.

Before anybody else arrived, the three Skinks Kerr had killed in hand-to-hand combat flared into brilliant, brief flame, hot enough to scorch the chameleon coverings over the armored vacuum suits worn by Kerr, Claypoole, and Summers.

Back on the *Dayzee Mae*, Kerr gave a succinct after action report, leaving out nothing despite its brevity. "I estimate there was an entire platoon of Skinks on the *Runstable*," he said near the end. "We killed all of them. Or at least we killed every one of them who fought us." He shrugged. "It's possible that some hid from us as we left the *Runstable*."

McPherson shook his head in amazement that one squad of Marines could be ambushed by such a superior force, and totally defeat them at the cost of only one Marine wounded.

"Any word on Fisher's condition?" Kerr asked, as though he knew what the starship's acting captain was thinking.

"Only that he's in a stasis bag," McPherson answered. "We won't know anything more until we get back to Thorsfinni's World."

Kerr nodded and looked at a display on which the SS *Runstable* was visible. "What are we going to do about her?"

"I don't have any crew to spare to take her to port," McPherson said. "All we can do is report her position and hope she's still here when a salvage ship comes for her."

"And that the Skinks haven't manned her again in time to ambush the salvage team," Kerr said.

"And there weren't any Skink bodies to recover?" McPherson said.

"No, sir. All the bodies flared up as soon as the fight was over."

"How do you think it happened?" McPherson asked.

Kerr shook his head. "Dead man's switch, maybe. Maybe there was another Skink hiding someplace where he could set off incendiary charges placed in their suits. Maybe they spontaneously flare after they die." He shook his head again. "Maybe we'll never know."

An earlier edition previously published in *Armored,*
ed. John Joseph Adams, Baen Books, 2012.

THE OATH
Robert Greenberger

THE DECK PLATING RATTLED, ADDING TO THE CACOPHONY THAT MADE IT DIFFICULT TO concentrate. There were concussive sounds coming from all directions although it appeared there were few direct hits on Biânjîng itself, but Jasmine Yue found it difficult to discern anything with assurance. All she knew was that the red alert klaxon woke her far too soon after her twelve-hour shift ended, then she was back in her scrubs and out the door of her cabin in under five minutes. As she hustled into the Emergency Room, adjacent to the colony's clinic, it was clear casualties, other than nerves, were light—for now.

CMO Dhruv Naccarato, tall, dark-complected, and with impossibly straight black hair, nodded at her arrival, her hands attending to a leg wound. Yue immediately donned surgical gloves and awaited instructions.

As the pair silently worked on the victim, a man Yue did not recognize, she was given the highlights: a score of small alien spacecraft had arrived, somehow avoiding Quatrième's planetary defenses, and opened fire on the Biânjîng colony. They had been firing back and forth for the last half hour.

There had been archaeological remains found on two of the other colony worlds, but they dated back centuries or millennia, confirming humans were far from alone in the universe. Yue settled on Biânjîng, the fourth human establishment on an alien world, helping establish the Quatrième colony. She arrived just as the last of the dome was completing, allowing oxygen to flow and humans to breathe. The scope of the years-long project astonished her along with the promises of new discoveries, never anticipating she would be part of the first contact with a living alien species after just four years. This was not how anyone had hoped for a living first contact to go, although it did confirm the worst fears of some factions still on Earth.

"Focus," Naccarato snapped, forcing Yue to blink twice and study her colleague's hands. They were carefully repairing vein damage to the man's left leg and Yue needed to keep the area sponged clean. Noise around them increased as more injured arrived, more than the small medical staff could reasonably handle.

"I need more hands," Naccarato snapped, her voice betraying a trace of her Indian heritage. "Tell Rocky to send whoever he can spare."

Another nurse confirmed the order and hurried off to signal the deputy commander while Yue began arranging the dermaplast that would be packed around the wound to protect it from infection and help new skin grow.

As the pair began to close the torn skin, the loudest *whoomph* yet reverberated through the casing. Heads snapped up, brows knit in concern, and everyone hushed leaving the various machines to hum by themselves, waiting for someone from CentComm to let them know what just happened. Seconds later, the speakers flared to life and the red alert signal was cut off.

"Remain in place," the stern voice ordered, one Yue didn't recognize. "Alien vessel down half a klick from Biânjìng. Other ships are either de-stroyed or fled. Remain on highest alert."

After the message repeated, silence fell over the Emergency Room but that lasted only seconds as doctors and nurses resumed work, giving orders, receiving confirmations although everyone's voices were now subdued. Volunteers, anyone with EMT or even basic First Aid training, were beginning to arrive. Naccarato, to her credit, afforded them a quick acknowledging look and then directed them without pausing with her patient; freeing the more experienced medical staff to tend to the direst of injuries. The colony had three operating rooms, all of which were in service, which was why she and Yue were working in the ER. The energy level rose but there was efficiency, not panic.

Still, Yue worried what would happen to the colony and to the in-habitants of the alien starcraft that lay just a short walk away.

It was less than an hour later when Naccarato, finally done with the man's leg, was summoned to an emergency department heads meeting, leaving Yue and the others to clean up the work space and begin invento-rying supplies to determine future needs. After all, this could have been an exploratory attack, a first wave attack, a case of mistaken identity or any number of reasons to provoke an assault. It would take time to fabricate some of the supplies and they would have to be prioritized with whatever repair materials were required elsewhere in the colony. One reason Quatrième was selected for colonization was its mineral composition, assuring a sustainable human colony could grow and thrive over the years.

Scuttlebutt ran faster than sound and certainly faster than Commander Bracken normally informed the crew. Everyone was buzzing, swapping rumor and innuendo, searching for fact.

"I bet they're bipeds," Derek Chamberlain said as he handed Yue a cup of something hot. It was sweet tea, something the flirty doctor knew she liked.

"Will we get a chance to examine them?"

"God, I hope so, Jas," he said. Chamberlain was classically handsome, down to the cleft in the center of his square-jaw. His auburn hair peeked out from beneath his surgical cap and there were bloodstains on his scrubs but she was noting, instead, how the top strained against his chest. He'd been working out.

"That'll be something for the medical journals," he continued. "Of course, you've got the surest hands on staff, so no doubt you'll be able to assist on the autopsy. We'll get to weigh and measure, feel in our hands, something not of this world."

"Aren't you being a bit..." her words were cut off by a fresh set of loud noises coming toward the clinic. It wasn't a new attack; the sounds were wrong for that. But Yue finally identified the motorized hum of multiple gurneys and heavy boots moving quickly. She anticipated more injured colonists, maybe someone found in the wreckage One wing of the Biânjīng complex had been nearly obliterated. The loss of life was still being tallied and the clinic had already readied stasis tubes for the dead. A proper morgue was in the phase five plans, but that was years away from becoming a reality.

A blue light suddenly bathed the clinic and Emergency Room, signaling that quarantine protocols were being put into place. She heard the extra set of heavy metal doors snap shut, creating a chamber that would protect any who entered their space. The Sufacide Helios Triple Emitter UV-C disinfection system pulsed, bathing everyone and everything in sterilizing radiation. Anyone entering the chamber would be similarly disinfected. But Yue couldn't fathom why it was needed.

The pneumatic hiss of the double-doors caught her attention and then the patient atop the first gurney. Whatever the patient was, could not be human; the proportions were wrong. Instead, it was something covered in a spacesuit, initially making the number of limbs difficult to determine. The suit itself was torn in spots, a thick-looking white, gray, and black outfit with tubing and pouches spaced irregularly. The helmet was not hard, like the Terran ones, but seemed soft and pliable. Proportionally, the body seemed taller and wider than human norms but who knew how much was a result of their flight suit?

As the first gurney was settled into position, a second rolled right on by, headed for an OR. She caught a glimpse of the second alien, and saw the suit was punctured in places, definitely looking deflated in comparison. Following the second gurney was Naccarato, who paused long enough to address her and Chamberlain. There was a mix of emotions on her face making it hard to read her.

"You two are up," she said, her head nodded toward the first gurney. "The other is dead. I'll begin supervising the autopsy to see what we're dealing with."

Yue couldn't take her eyes from the alien on the gurney, her stomach doing a little flip at the momentous event. Was she really being asked to touch it? Where to begin?

"Up for what?"

"That one is still alive but we gather it's hurt so you get to fix it," she said and to Yue it appeared the woman wished it was her performing the history-making duty.

Chamberlain blinked at his superior. "Did they bring a medical manual? We haven't the first clue how to treat an alien! What if they can't breathe our air or need their equivalent of a blood transfusion?"

"Derek, we're all in uncharted territory so we're all going to be making it up as we go along," Naccarato said. The sound of voices behind her made her let out a heavy sigh.

Entering their quarantined space was CentComm's second officer, Mark Rockwitz, short, balding, whippet-thin and always looking like he'd rather fight than talk. As he was bathed in the UV rays, Rockwitz grimaced but headed right for the trio, eyebrows rising, asking, "Why haven't you gotten started?"

"I thought I'd actually give my staff some direction. You can accompany me to the autopsy," Naccarato said, clearly wishing Rockwitz were anywhere else.

"CentComm is busy enough but I'm now stuck here to oversee what you find. I don't want this to last any longer than it has to," he barked.

"You're in my world now," Naccarato shot back. "It will take as long as it takes because we're in virgin territory. Watch all you want, but do *not* rush me or get in my way."

Rockwitz's face expressed his displeasure, especially since he couldn't argue with the CMO. This *was* her world and this *was* an unprecedented moment for mankind. Yue found herself wishing she could assist her boss despite having an alien of her own to tend to.

Chamberlain and Yue cautiously stepped over to the gurney, keenly aware that armed security men stood at every entrance beyond the quarantine doors with one, rifle in hand, hovering nearby. Yue looked more closely at the figure, not seeing any evidence of recognizable respiration. There was no outward sign the alien was alive at all and part of her wanted to peel away the suit and see what it looked like while another part wanted to go into hiding. She'd read way too much fiction and seen way too many videos where the alien's blood was toxic or it went crazy in an oxygen atmosphere or immediately impregnated warm, breathing life forms or skin contact allowed mental manipulation or they resembled us and it was love at first sight. None, not even that last option, appealed to her.

The doctor snapped on a series of scanners and devices surrounding the gurney, including the bright light which revealed how reflective the spacesuit was, causing everyone around the gurney to squint. No doubt the engineering and sciences teams would love to reverse engineer every nonorganic portion of the patient. Of course, Naccarato and Chamberlain were also just as eager to explore alien tissue and organs. All Yue wanted to do right now was see the face of the unknown and not vomit in the process.

"Chamberlain, this thing on?"

"Yeah, Dhruv, you're live. What do you see?"

"We're taking measurements. Do the same, please." The gurney already registered the body in its suit as weighing 161.479 kilograms, making it the heaviest living being in Biânjìng. Yue retrieved a digital measuring device and was not surprised to see the alien topping out at 2.24 meters.

"He's big one all right," Chamberlain said.

"He?"

"Gotta call it something, Jas," he said with a grin. "Want to name it?"

"How about prisoner number one," the nearby guard suggested.

"Got dibs on that," Rockwitz called over the communications system. "He can be number two."

"'He' is fine for now," Yue replied, ignoring the back and forth. She wasn't feeling jocular at the moment, too tense to be anything but serious and procedural. She promised herself there would be time to process her emotions later.

Long seconds passed as the sound of scissors and a scalpel worked at peeling away layers of the dead alien's suit. One of the station's biologists, laden with devices of her own, had hurried past Chamberlain and Yue to join the autopsy next door. Someone else carefully gathered the suit scraps, putting them in an orange medical waste bag.

"It's going to get crowded in here pretty quickly," Chamberlain said, noting the gawkers and those slowing down as they hurried by. He began tentatively touching portions of the spacesuit, getting a sense of its flexibility. Cautious, she noted, he did not go near the various pouches in case they carried weapons, booby-traps, or pets.

"Did any of the pouches rupture?" he asked the microphone directly above him.

"Yes," Naccarato replied. "Three and they're identical. We think they may be some sort of breathing apparatus."

"Okay, I'll bite: breathing what?"

"Stand by," she told him. Chamberlain shrugged at Yue as they both tentatively explored the suit. She tested the suit, poking at it with her index finger, reaching deeper than she imagined to strike something solid. It had to be the alien itself.

A deep, muffled rumble emerged from the helmet.

"It's alive," Yue exclaimed. The guard by her elbow immediately trained his weapon on the alien.

"Say again?" Rockwitz demanded from the other room.

"The alien is alive," Yue said, forcing herself to be calm. "I was examining the suit and it emitted what I can only take to be a groan."

"I have it in my sights," the gun-toting man said.

Yue forced herself to read his badge, learning his name was Dorbyn.

"It's in pain," Chamberlain said. "Stand down, soldier, that thing is not going anywhere."

"You would be too, if you'd just crashed on the surface. His partner is most definitely dead or doing a damn good job of playing possum while we strip off his suit," Naccarato told him. "Can you save it?"

"Are you shitting me? I don't know how it works! How am I supposed to treat it?"

"We need you to save it," she commanded.

"Only if you're certain it will not harm anyone aboard," Rockwitz ordered.

"And how do you either of you propose I accomplish your goals?" the doctor asked, studying the body, which had yet to move on its own.

"We'll work as quickly as we can in here to figure that out," Naccarato assured them although her voice didn't convince Yue. "So far, we think they also breathe an oxygen-nitrogen mix. Mitterand is doing a crash experiment to confirm that."

"We're coming in for a look-see," Chamberlain said and beckoned for his nurse to follow him. She began to follow then noticed Dorbyn was inching closer to the alien.

"No shooting my patient," she warned him.

"He moves, my orders are to fire," he told her without taking his eyes off the prone figure.

"Not in the clinic," Chamberlain yelled as he headed into the other room. As they entered, it was dim with powerful lights focused on the torn and presumably bloody form of the alien. Enough of the spacesuit had been peeled away or cut off to reveal a roughly humanoid figure of indeterminate gender.

Naccarato didn't even bother to look up as they entered, fixated on the form and speaking aloud, mostly for the recording being made. Rockwitz, also looking at the alien, uselessly paced around the table while Mitterand stood at an adjacent table, running tissues through an analyzer.

"The alien is bipedal with two arms, each ending with hands that have two opposable thumbs, one at each end, making for a total of six fingers. It has no discernible fingerprints or fingernails, each finger rough to the touch. No hair on the epidermis."

Chamberlain gaped at the exposed epidermis, congealing blood or fluid at various wounds, its, well, beige skin bruising chocolate brown in spots. Yue followed him, uncertain how they could begin to treat the creature since anything down to a simple sterile gauze wrap could prove fatal.

"Is it a threat?"

"I'm sorry?" Chamberlain said to Rockwitz.

"If you fix it, will it post a threat to us?"

"You shot their ship down and dragged him someplace where he is seriously outnumbered. Even if I knew *how* fix him, I suspect he's dealing with trauma and wouldn't be up to anything more than a few attempts at a fight."

"Not good enough. What if it has something...extra?"

"What? You mean like heat vision? Atomic breath? Some alien venom? There's no knowing but I aim to find out."

That stopped Rockwitz in his tracks. "That is a clear danger to everyone here. Better we dissect them both, find out what makes them tick, so we're prepared whenever they come back."

"I'm not about to kill my patient," Chamberlain began to protest.

"Rocky, if we save one," Naccarato interrupted, "we might be able to communicate. That's more valuable."

"And that is a risk I am not ready to take."

"Not your call," the CMO said. "Derek and I took an Oath. Our obligation is to save lives, human or not."

"That is an enemy combatant that has threatened every life in the colony. Your oath is to your fellow humans, first and foremost. That should be very, very clear right now," he said, his tone defiant.

"I'm a doctor and my first oath is to heal," Naccarato said, with Chamberlain and Yue also nodding in agreement.

"The Hippocratic Oath was never intended to cover hostile aliens," Rockwitz shot back. "Hell, if you follow that, aren't you pledging yourselves to Apollo? I think we debunked his authority thousands of years ago."

Chamberlain made a dismissive noise, earning him a glare from the military commander.

"What?"

"We've moved way beyond that original oath. It was something that's evolved over the centuries but we still place a priority on preserving life."

"Where does it say alien life?"

"Funny you should ask, since it's been discussed ever since the remains were first found on Einstein. We just haven't settled on the final language. But the intent is that life is life. So, once I figure out how it—he—works, I can figure out how to heal it."

"And it's funny you should bring up oaths, because I took one, too. It was to defend and protect everyone living on this colony. Part of it includes protecting you and me 'against all enemies, foreign and domestic'." Rockwitz gestured at the dead body. "That's as foreign as it gets. And remember, doctor, they fired first."

Chamberlain seemed to ignore the bluster as he circled the body, joining Naccarato toward the head. She was using a magnifier and tweezers to examine something around the mouth.

"Did you hear me? That other alien is an enemy combatant."

"Patient first," Chamberlain called over his shoulder then, to his superior, "what do you think they do?"

"Maybe filter the air, act like krill?"

"They're big, so what do they eat to maintain mass?"

"Did you hear me?" Rockwitz repeated.

Chamberlain spun about perhaps more forcefully than intended. "Which do you think is more important? Having a living, breathing alien we can learn from or two dead bodies that can tell us only so much?"

"We're safer with two dead bodies," Rockwitz shot back. "They fired on us and arrived in force. Doesn't that tell you anything?"

"Honestly, it raises more questions than anything," Chamberlain said, now tracing the line of fine hairs down the cheek to the very thick neck. "I would think we want answers."

"'And I do bind myself to conform, in all instances, to such rules and regulations, as are, or shall be, established by the government'," Rockwitz recited. "I represent the government in this case, which is something you should not forget. You know why we haven't rewritten the Oath in centuries?"

"Laziness? Now hush," Naccarato said. She was plucking something from between the fine hairs and the slit in the mouth. "Could be his lunch."

"No, because there is a chain of command to ensure order. And that order also means the protection of the civilians living here. We can't have it walking around, infecting or killing everyone."

"You have your chain of command, and I have my own. Here's one for you to consider: 'A physician shall respect the law and also recognize a responsibility to seek changes in those requirements which are contrary to the best interests of the patient.' So, you wanting him dead is contrary to his interests," Chamberlain said.

'You don't know it is a he!" Rockwitz said, his voice rising.

"I'm all for changing those requirements if it means we can save a life," Naccarato said. "After all, maybe Derek is playing the part of Androcles."

Rockwitz blinked at that, opening and shutting his mouth a few times.

Yue took pity on him and recounted the fable about Androcles and the Lion, thankful it was a favorite story from her youth. She agreed, if they saved this alien, it might be the first step in understanding one another, saving lives.

"Do you agree with them?" he challenged.

"As it happens, nurses take their own oaths, tracing all the way back to our guiding light, Florence Nightingale. Part of the current pledge involves following the instructions of the physician in charge of the patient. Then there's 'I will not do anything evil or malicious and I will not knowingly give any harmful drug or assist in malpractice.' I think letting anyone living die is malpractice. So, I guess I side with Doctor Chamberlain."

"Feeling ganged up on yet?" Chamberlain asked.

"Mock me all you want," Rockwitz said, iron in his voice. "This thing is a threat. We may never be able to talk to it. It may see us as being in the wrong and feel it has every right to kill us all. It is a chance I am not willing to take. You can quote all the oaths you want, but even if you do manage to do the impossible and save its life, it then becomes a prisoner of war. Make no mistake, Doctors, that I consider the attack on our home as an act of war. Doesn't matter at all why they attacked, they were the aggressors. A proportionate response was to defend ourselves and frankly, I'm just as happy most of them skittered out of here rather than letting us blow them all up. They can go home and tell them we're something to fear and maybe they'll stay away."

"Or they could come back with more friends," Chamberlain challenged. "That's why I have to go back and try and save him."

"*It*. We got lucky just one ship crashed near us and maybe you think we're lucky because we have a live specimen, but to me, it is a continuing threat to the safety of all who live here."

Naccarato and Chamberlain continued to probe the body as Rockwitz finished talking. Neither rebutted him or even acknowledged their superior officer. The rising tension in the room was making Yue feel increasingly uncomfortable and she was able see both sides. The alien was a tangible example of the dangers of living away from Earth but it was also a living being with rights she considered to be, well, inalienable.

"Don't you think there can be a middle ground....sir?"

Rockwitz stared at her as if she were the alien then he exhaled and indicated she should proceed.

"We can try and save the alien, which is the right thing to do. I strongly believe God put us all in the universe and would approve of this. But, since we don't know the motivation behind the attack, the living alien would pose a possible threat. We have storage units just beyond our colony. Couldn't we just keep it there until we figure out how to talk to it?"

There was a long silence as Rockwitz stared at her and the doctors continued to work and explore. Mitterand, for her part, had been listening and silently nodded in approval.

Chamberlain cocked his head and Yue followed him back their still-living patient.

"You're wasted as a nurse. You should be a diplomat," Rockwitz finally said, following them. "But I would still outrank you. We can't take any chance of reprisal, especially if we get it wrong and save it but make it a wounded animal. Box it up and we could all be in for a world of hurt.

"Here's the thing you all forget. Your oaths are lovely, but are directed at you and your patient. That's one. Me, my oath is to protect everyone. Do you know our current population? I bet not, so let me tell you. We are standing at six thousand four hundred and twelve. Probably a few less with the deaths its people caused today. My decisions mean life or death on a far greater scale. Also, we're isolated from Earth and the other colonies. We send an SOS, it'd be wasted because no one could get here quickly enough. That makes every decision I make here all the more important."

The doctors remained quiet, letting Rockwitz effectively talk to himself. Instead, they were deeply focused on examining various portions of the alien's body, taking temperatures, and tissue samples, placing various fluids in vials for study. Mitterand arrived to collect and label each item, beginning the various devices required to study and attempt to understand their patient.

Yue watched, fascinated and frightened at the same time. None of the exposed organs looked at all familiar and no doubt it was all guesswork how the alien breathed or functioned. Every now and then, she watched the agitated second-in-command wander the room, seeking some acknowledgement, or better yet, validation of his position. She sympathized and understood the responsibility he bore. The colony's premier, Stanislaus Mueller, would arbitrate should this reach her but she was no doubt overseeing rescue-and-repair operations. No doubt she'd want a peek at the first alien life form encountered by mankind, but it could wait until the populace was considered safe. To Rockwitz, that would happen only after both were dead and no longer a threat. Yue never would want the crushing responsibility either role carried. Instead, she was perfectly content helping heal and ensuring the population could grow nice and healthy. There were always new things to learn as humans adapted to the differing gravity and solar radiation on Quatrième, comparing those readings with the ones from the first three colony worlds.

There was a sharp yell and she realized she had forgotten all about the guard.

She looked down. The alien now writhed as it made muffled noises, none of which sounded good. Of course, she was projecting and had no real clue. None of them did.

Chamberlain took a quick look at the body then gave the guard a sharp look. "Lower the weapon and let us work," he commanded.

The guard looked beyond him to Rockwitz.

"Let him die," the commander instructed. The guard only slightly lowered the weapon at the instruction but the words infuriated Yue. She was uncertain what to do, but was determined to follow Chamberlain's lead. She glanced in his direction, only to note his attention was fixed on their patient. She was surprised how quickly she had accepted that designation for the body before her, but also it felt right to her.

"I think he's running out of air," she said.

"I'm taking the helmet off," Chamberlain said, reaching for the head.

"You could kill him instantly. We don't know if the air here will be good for him," Naccarato said over the speaker at the same time Rockwitz snapped, "You will not!"

Once more, the guard raised the weapon, vaguely aiming it higher, more toward the doctor, which alarmed Yue.

"You told me to heal him, so it's my call. Jess, let's go. Scissors."

She deftly handed him the tool, completely focused on the action, tuning out everything else around her, which was probably for the best. She could already hear the buzz of voices in the background. Once committed, she doubted Rockwitz would interfere with Chamberlain.

"We can't work effectively with you aiming that at us!" she yelled at the soldier.

"I have my orders," he replied.

"Your superior said let him die, not shoot him. But you're making *me* nervous. He's not a danger, but *in* danger."

The soldier looked up, expecting a reply from Rockwitz. There was nothing but silence.

Chamberlain and Yue carefully but decisively cut away the seals around the helmet and removed it carefully, making sure the head was supported with a pillow. Like the fatality, it had an egg-shaped skull, pale beige skin, and a thick covering of the hair over what were presumed to be nostrils and mouth. If it had ears, she hadn't noticed them. What she did notice was that it noisily inhaled the station's air and didn't adversely react. It might have been too far gone, it might have been just sleeping. That suddenly changed when it gurgled, fluid seeping through the facial hair. As it emerged, it turned from blue to a reddish-orange.

"Capture a sample," Chamberlain directed.

Deftly, she brought a petri dish to the alien's face and let the presumed blood drip into it, then covered it. But, before she could put it down, there was the unmistakable sound of choking.

"Suction," he ordered, a hint of tension in his tone.

She grabbed the hose, thumbing it to life, and gently worked around hair and orifice. The liquid was thicker than blood and did not suction easily but she was patient and worked to get it all, as the breathing steadied.

Once done, the alien stopped choking and they continued to peel away the spacesuit, revealing more of its form. He seemed to lack a rib cage and there were protrusions that might be natural or the results of the crash. Repeatedly, she was told where to angle the various cameras being used to record every second of the procedure.

"Is it awake?" Rockwitz asked over the loudspeaker.

"Maybe, probably not,' Chamberlain replied. "Want to come look for yourself?"

"I didn't think so," Chamberlain said. "Chief, we need to uncover the corpse and do a body comparison. I need to know what I'm working with."

"Let the dead stay dead," Rockwitz ordered.

"In here, your authority has its limits," Naccarato said as she hurried back into the other room.

Over the next twenty minutes, Chamberlain and Yue removed every vestige of artificial covering then sponged the skin clean to get as un-obstructed a view of the body. The scale now registered the naked body at 129.59 kilograms The patient behaved, not choking after that first bout, and had the courtesy to remain alive and unconscious as it was measured, scanned, and subjected to a complete Synchrotron X-Ray study. As each aspect was completed, computers began an analysis, until finally Naccarato needed authority to reallocate computer-processing time, something Rockwitz grudgingly allowed.

Naccarato and her own nurse, a petite, dark-haired woman named Diane McFadden, had already completed their own work. They had worked steadily, but quickly. Everyone was eager to begin comparing notes, try to learn some lessons from their alien visitors, but there remained work to be done. In the meantime, Chamberlain and Yue staunched bleeding and wrapped the wounds, of which there were many obvious ones. With great care, they tested disinfectants on the blood samples before applying them to the alien. Several seemed to react badly until they found an aloe-based gel that seemed to work. Through her gloved fingers, she sensed the alien's skin to be thicker than a human's, but also spongier. Underneath, though, there was a similar arrangement of veins and arteries, tendons, muscles, and what appeared to be multi-faceted bones. She had to keep reminding herself not to gawk and to be alert for instructions. Thankfully, the guard had lowered his weapon, but remained poised, just in case.

Naccarato came in with the preliminary results from the computer analysis and held up the tablet for him to read while he continued to work.

"The blood oxygen is out of whack, something is wrong with our patient," he said, urgency filling his voice. He took command of the digital displays and after shuffling through several screens, spun about and left the room. Yue followed; certain something was very wrong.

"He..."

"...or she..."

"It, whatever, is about to lose an organ. It's no longer drawing blood from what I can tell."

"What does it do?"

"I don't know."

"What can we do?"

"Give it the other guy's. He doesn't need it."

"What?" Rockwitz thundered, as he neared the pair.

"If we don't try to transplant that organ into this body, this one may well die, depriving us of a chance to communicate."

"I can't let you do that, doctor," Rockwitz said.

"The hell you can't."

"If we operate and kill it, and the aliens find out, they may accuse us of conducting illegal experimentation or torture..."

"And how the hell will they find out?"

"For all you know they're telepathic. In the name of security, I forbid the procedure. It recovers and lives or it dies on its own."

"Remember that oath I took? It takes greater precedence over your paranoia," Chamberlain said. He began rattling off a list of tools and supplies to Yue, who obediently began collecting items, focused on the process, letting the men yell at one another.

"'The health of my patient will be my first consideration'," Chamberlain said, almost like a mantra.

"This is insubordination," Rockwitz yelled.

"Another debate for another time," Chamberlain said. "You can put on surgical gloves and actually get your hands dirty, or you can get the hell out of the room."

"You understand you're putting us all at risk, which I doubt goes with any of the oaths you've taken," Rockwitz said as he took a step back.

By then, Chamberlain had tuned him out and began giving instructions to Yue, who obediently followed his every command. The laser cut through the epidermis and a tube sucked away the blood, capturing it to reinfuse into the patient. Within minutes, the doctor and nurse had fallen into a rhythm. She had no idea how long they'd be working or if it would do any good. But there was a patient in need and she would honor that Practical Nurse Pledge, hundreds of years old and now being practiced among the stars.

HOPE'S CHILDREN
Lisanne Norman

"THE SHUTTLE WENT DOWN ON THE OUTSKIRTS OF HIDDEN VALLEY, NEAR CENTERTOWN."

"Damn! We can't send men in there. It's Vess territory. There's scanners all over the area!" Then, regret mixed with resignation: *"It has to be the kids."*

The voices faded in and out then, the blackness engulfed Cassie again. When she finally came to and opened her eyes, she found she was curled in a ball at the heart of a dense bush.

With patience born of experience, she listened carefully for the sounds of woodland critters—bird calls, the rasping of crickets—but all was well, there was no one nearby. Pulling herself to her knees, she pushed her way through the thorn-free center and into the spiky outer branches using her pack to keep the sharp thorns at bay. Cursing under her breath, she rubbed her scratched hands.

No time for that, she thought as she grabbed up her pack and got to her feet. *Time to get to the village.*

A faint breeze sent puffs of dust up into the air as she walked. Ahead, the outskirts of the village rose through the already gathering heat haze.

Autumn on Hope was always hot. She trudged along, sweat forming on her brow, plastering her hair uncomfortably to the back of her neck. As she got nearer, she saw a watch tower with one of the Vess looking out toward her. The Vessian sensor panels ringing the village were between her and the entrance. Would they still let her pass, or would they zap her as too mature?

Her heart in her mouth, she strode between them. A faint tingle buzzed through her and then she was out of range and heading toward the entrance. One obstacle down, one more to go.

A group of four Vess were now standing at the village gate, along with the obligatory human translator.

"Halt. What brings you to our village?" the human asked, stepping forward.

"Cassie Stringer, returning to join her group," she said, faking more tiredness than she actually felt. "What's the problem?"

"They want to know what your business is here."

"I live here. I'm coming home. What's it to you?"

The man glanced sideways at the group, talking to them in their guttural language then waiting for a reply.

Cassie stared at the nearest Vess, making the other blink its large eyes and look away. Tall as the average human, their skin was pallid, the nose two mere slots in the face above a small mouth. If she looked hard, she would see a faint pattern of scales on the skin. She didn't bother today, she just wanted this confrontation to be over.

"They wish to know why you left," the human said.

"I went to visit friends in Barford. There's nothing wrong with that, is there?"

"You should remain in the village of your birth. The Vess don't encourage travel, you know that."

"We're the only ones who *can* travel," she snapped back at him. "I'm home now. You gonna let me in or what?" she asked, putting a petulant belligerence into her tone. "I swear you make more of a fuss than they do."

"Let me see the bag." The interpreter held out his hand for her pack. "Gotta check it for contraband."

She handed it over and he rifled through the contents before handing it back to her.

"Someone was generous with food," he said.

She shrugged. "They had extra."

Since the two species had different dietary needs, the villages and work camps survived on food air-dropped by the humans at war with the Vess, but every now and then the military would include a batch of MREs for the villages. The kids, working as couriers like Cassie and her small group, knew to save the meals to use on their missions. It meant a few days of poor rations until the other food drops took up the slack, but they could handle that.

"Arms up for a pat down. Can't let you bring in any weapons."

This was her main worry. Spread about the many pockets and the lining of her old padded coat were the supplies she'd need for her mission—contraband in the eyes of the Vess, and the human collaborators, but necessary to her.

She stood with her arms held out, and as the interpreter began to frisk her, the nearest Vess grasped him by the shoulder and pulled him back, barking an order at him.

The interpreter scowled and began to argue. The guard backhanded him, making him stagger and spit blood.

He straightened up and wiped his mouth with the back of his hand. "He says don't go out again or you may not be allowed back in. They're beginning to crack down on who gets out and you look near the age limit."

"Bite me," she muttered under her breath, annoyed by the interchange, even though she had expected it. She knew what the Vess had said, and it wasn't that.

A sudden blinding pain behind her eyes caused her to stagger slightly. A hand reached out to steady her but she pulled away from the interpreter even as she heard the voice in her head. *"She has to understand the Vess. We haven't the time for compassion."* Then it was gone and she was righting herself and setting off down the main road.

"You all right, kid?" The voice of the interpreter followed her.

"Yeah, fine," she said, rubbing a hand across her eyes. Dammit! The sleep memories weren't integrating properly! How much longer would it take until they did?

The village was a collection of buildings, most broken in some way, be it gaping windows or doors, or roofs that would no longer keep out the winter rains. As she paced between the ruins, she sensed young faces peering at her through broken panes of glass, or the few dirty intact ones, following her movements with suspicion. Of the few adults she knew still living here, there was no sign: they knew better than to show their faces when the Vess were about.

She left the dusty road and stepped up onto the boardwalk, heading for one of the larger and better preserved buildings. It looked as dilapidated as it had when she'd left a couple of months ago, the blue paint faded, and the white now the color of the ever-present gray dust. It looked deserted.

"Where are you?" she muttered, eyes darting around as she stopped at the door. Were they still there?

The door suddenly opened and there stood Gemmy, her fine features wreathed into a smile.

"I knew you'd be back," she said happily, darting forward to hug her. Behind Gemmy in the dim light of the main room, the others stood awkwardly, waiting for her to enter.

She laughed, tucking the scruffy fly-away ends of Gemmy's hair behind her ears. "Yes, I'm back," she said, linking her arm through the younger girl's and stepping into the house.

"Why was you gone?" Matt demanded as she shut the door behind her.

"Had to go outside," she said, "but I'm back now." She glanced round the main room: nothing had changed except it looked even shabbier than before.

"We got a job," Les said. It wasn't a question.

Cassie waited a minute before answering him, looking at the kids one by one, gauging their mood, searching for the slightest sign that something was not as it should be.

"Yeah," she said, moving further into the room. "Some Ranker's been shot down five miles or so from here. Need's us to go save his sorry ass. They want him back. Seems he's got information can help the war effort."

"This ain't a war," Les said, gathering up the throwing knives he'd been sharpening. "It's a rout. We got nothin' to fight back with."

"Intel is what'll help us win. This Ranker has more of it," she said, throwing her pack onto a sagging easy chair.

"Intel didn't stop him gettin' shot down," Les muttered, going over to the rough table and pulling out a dining chair to sit on.

"There's food in my pack," she said. "Who's on kitchen duty?"

"Me and Gemmy," Matt said, walking over to her. "What you got?" He picked up the pack and hefted it. "It's heavy."

"Take it and see," she said, sparing a moment for a quick grin, no matter that it was forced. "Bread and tins of beans, some chicken and tuna, and half a dozen packs of those potatoes you add hot water to. Some MREs too."

"We'll eat well tonight," Gemmy said as Matt picked up the pack and headed for the kitchen door.

"Where'd you go?" asked Pete.

"I needed to go for special training," she said, taking off her coat and sitting down in the empty easy chair.

"Why d'you need special training?" Gemmy asked, perching on the arm of the chair.

"Dunno," she said. "They said do it, so I did."

"Was it sleep training?" Pete asked, who'd had a session or two of that himself.

"Sleep training's the easiest," Matt said, coming back in from the kitchen with a roll of cookies from her bag. "You get all plugged up, then you go to sleep and suddenly it's morning. Then they get you to practice what you just learned."

Most of the kids had been outside the village with her at some time to get specialized resistance training. On this world, only they could move freely and were above suspicion because of the Vess' belief in the sanctity and innocence of childhood.

"Some was. More of their language this time, and some other stuff," she finished vaguely, trying to remember. Scenes flashed before her eyes, too fast to see or make any sense, but she remembered the pain. She reached up to rub her upper arm — she could almost still feel the ache there. With it came the memories of being shoved into a cell with two of the Vess, being left there for days, fed when they were fed, and manhandled by one of them. Not for that Vess, the attitude that kids were out of bounds to them. The least of what he did was to grab her and drag her aside at feeding time until he and his partner had eaten. Then she was allowed to approach her food.

Pushing herself up out of the chair, she forced herself to smile broadly at Gemmy. "Let's start getting dinner ready. Do you still get food regularly from Prinny? Has she had that baby yet?"

"Not yet, but she reckons it'll be any day now. She always sees us right 'cos we don't cause any trouble for her, unlike the kids on the other side of the village."

"Good to know she's looking out for you." She let the door bang behind her as they headed down the dim hallway to the kitchen.

A small fire burned in the grate, heating the few feet of the room around the sofa and chair they were sprawled on. Except for Les, who sat on the floor by the fire, once again sharpening his knives on his ancient oilstone.

"That was so good," Matt said. "Wish we could eat like that every day."

Cassie looked over at him. "One day we will."

"One day," Les said, checking the edge on one of his knives before putting it down to pick up the next. "It's always one day. Won't come before we're all grown and rounded up by the Vess for the work camps."

"You never know," John said. "Maybe this time the Ranker really has important Intel. When do we leave?" he asked Cassie.

"At midnight," she said. "There's no moon right now so it'll be full dark and easier for us to sneak out of the village. We'll have to avoid Vess search parties and patrols."

"Who you taking?" Gemmy asked, yawning hugely.

"I'm leaving you, Matt and Sean behind, Gemmy. We only have two days to get to the Ranker and get him out of here before the Vess find him. Now go get some sleep, we leave at midnight."

The kids had dragged their sleeping rolls into the main room as near to the fire as they could. Only Cassie was still awake, worrying about her mission and about those she'd be leaving behind. This was her last op, because even with the meds she had to take, she was over the age of puberty by several years. Any time now the sensors might detect her as an adult and deliver a killing jolt of energy rather than the faint buzz they all felt as kids.

"You're taking a risk with the sensors," Les said quietly as he sat up. "Thought for sure they called you back because of that. Never expected to see you again."

She hesitated, then decided to be honest with him. "You wouldn't, except for this mission," she said quietly, pushing herself up on one elbow to look over at him. "It's really important we get the intel this Ranker is carrying."

"And us? What happens with me an' Steph an' Pete?"

"You come with me. You're too close to adulthood yourselves to risk out here any longer."

Les nodded, slipping his knives into their sheaths on his bandolier. "Good. Didn't fancy staying here till they came to cull us for the work camps."

"The others will be okay, they're still young. With any luck, I was told, this will all be over before they reach puberty."

"So it's personal; we gotta get this Ranker and his intel out of Vess territory if we want to survive."

"That's the gist of it," she agreed. "I'll brief you once we've left." She checked her watch. "Time we got up."

They'd already packed the things they'd need for two days in the open, so with quiet efficiency the four of them were able to grab their bedrolls and packs and make their way quietly to the rear of the house, opening the door and slipping out into the darkness.

Silently in the moonless night, they made their way past the sensors, making for the lightly wooded land at the rear of the village. Keeping low, they ran toward the tree line, not stopping until they were a good fifty feet into the more densely packed forest. Starlight filtered down through the occasional breaks in the tree canopy, helping them navigate their way.

Cassie took advantage of a brief stop to take off her pack, then her coat, and begin to pull items from the inside of the padded areas. First came the parts for a gun and bullets made of Kevlar, then several magazines for it. She pieced it together quickly and stuck it into the waistband of her jeans. A map and compass followed, and finally a small device the size of a pack of cards. This she switched on, angling it to all the compass points. Getting no response she turned it off and stowed it in her pocket.

"What's that?" Pete asked. "Something we should know about?"

"It's a tracker," she said. "The Ranker has a tracer in him, and the tracker will tell us when he's nearby."

"You don't know where he is?" John asked in disbelief, shoving his fair hair back out of his eyes. "We gotta *find* this guy, too?"

"I know roughly where he is," she said, opening the map and checking their bearing with the compass. "The tracker fine tunes his location, that's all. He'll be hiding, waiting for us."

She fumbled inside her coat some more, pulling out a thin case. Some of the padding was stuck to her fingers and she shook them to dislodge it before standing up and pulling her coat back on. The case she stowed in an inner coat pocket.

"What's the mission?" Les asked. "Get the Intel and get out to the pick-up point?"

"Get the Intel," she said, setting off into the woods. "And get him back if we can."

"And how do we get him past any sensors?" Pete asked, trotting after her. "They'll kill him for sure."

"I got a drug to give him once we're past the sensors," she said. "It'll bring him back again, so they said at HQ."

"So they say. Has it been tested?" Les demanded.

"Not in field conditions," she admitted. "They think the sensors give a person a huge electrical shock that stops their heart, but they haven't been able to get hold of a sensor yet to test it. So we're kind of field-testing this for them."

"So what do you do?" Pete asked.

"It's in that case," Les said.

"Yeah," she said. "It's a shot of epinephrine. I have to stick it in his heart to start it up again. So long as we have the intel, that's what matters most, though. The shot is to test if it works or not."

"Does this guy know he's kinda disposable?" John asked, catching hold of a narrow tree bole as he slipped on damp leaves.

"He's bound to, unless he's also some kind of dumb," Les said, ducking under a branch. "Most he'll know is we have a way to revive him," Cassie said. "Best not see problems before we need to. Now let's stop talking in case there're any patrols out and about."

Cassie pushed them hard, stopping only a couple of times to rest, drink, and to check the map. This time they hunkered down among a rocky outcrop ringed by bushes.

"Break out your rations," she said, taking off her backpack.

"Mission rations," Les said, pulling his MRE out and tearing it open. "No heaters."

"Makes sense," John said. "What d'you know about this Ranker?" he asked, alternating bites of his chicken pastry with some beef jerky.

"Keep your voice down," she said, stripping off her wrapper and beginning to munch on her food. "There will be patrols out here and we don't want to draw their attention. His name is Lieutenant Ryan, and he was on an infiltration mission at one of the work camps. He escaped and was picked up by our side, but the Vess managed to track him and shot his ride down. He's on the run now, trying to stay free 'til we can meet up with him."

"Where are we exiting with him?" Les asked.

"To the east side," she said. "You know the place, by the river. You've been there before."

He nodded, taking a slug from his water bottle. "I know it. If the coast is clear, should be easy to get him across—if the sensors don't get him. All we need is the intel, right?" Les's brown eyes regarded her unblinkingly.

"Right," she said.

"Just checkin'," he said, breaking eye contact. "Need to know what our priorities are. If we're followed, or there's a patrol, getting us and the intel out is more important than the Ranker. Jus' want everyone to agree 'cos once we're out there, no time to argue about it."

"You're right. No time to argue," she agreed. "Any trouble, we leave him and run for it."

"It's only for two days," the voice said. *"They won't touch you, they treat their own young with kid gloves, and are good to all of you in the villages. Just listen to their language, work out what they're saying. With the sleep tapes you had, you should pick that up in no time."*

"Can't I do it by watching from here?" she'd asked. *"I can see them right enough, but they don't know I'm here with that two-way mirror. Besides, you got interpreters. They know their language!"*

"No, you need to be in with them," the stern-voiced general said, cutting through what the female officer, Lieutenant Pierce, had been about to say. *"The interpreters work for the Vess not us. We need our own language experts. You're getting too old for this. Next time you pass through their sensors could be your last. We have to make as much use of you as we can."*

"General, I protest! She's still a child, not one of your soldiers! You know her father wouldn't have approved of this!"

"Her father's dead, Pierce. She goes in the cell with them now, that's all there is to say about it!"

Someone was shaking her, their hand firmly over her mouth as she thrashed her arms trying to dislodge the grip.

"It's me, Les," he hissed in her ear. "Quiet! There's a patrol only a few yards from here!"

She blinked her eyes, finally focusing on his face and nodded slowly, letting her hands fall to her sides. She shivered as the memory began to fade, cursing herself for nodding off.

He removed his hand from her mouth and sat back on his heels as she gasped for air.

Sitting up slowly, she listened for the slightest sound. She heard the snap of dead twigs and branches as the Vess moved slowly through the underbrush about thirty feet away from them. Their voices carried on the still air, quiet, but understandable to her.

"Take a look," she mouthed at Les as the sounds gradually grew more distant.

He nodded, getting silently to his feet, slowly climbing the overhanging rock until he could just see through the cover of a bush. He remained there until they could no longer hear the voices or their footsteps.

"Gone," he whispered, crouching back down beside her. "Heading east, I'd say."

"They're not looking for us," she said, equally quietly. "We covered our tracks well enough. They're on the lookout for Ryan."

"Which way we heading come dark?" he asked.

"Northeast. We shouldn't meet up with them."

"You checked that scanner of yours to see if he's on it yet?"

She reached into her pocket, pulling out the small scanner. Switching it on, she moved it around to see if anything showed up. "Nothing." This time she kept the scanner out and switched on.

"Let's get going," she said, leading the way out of their hiding place.

At last a small blip showed up at the extreme edge. Faint, but there, and when they stopped walking, it remained in place.

"What's the range on that thing?" John whispered.

"A mile or two," she said, getting out the map. "It's a very small scanner, specially made for us so it could be easily concealed. According to the map he should be in Centertown."

"Best get movin' then," Les whispered. "We've only a few hours of darkness left. We want to find him and get well on the road to our exit."

"Agreed." Cassie, folded up the map and stowed it back in her pocket. Scanner held in front of her, she led the way.

The forest thinned rapidly until they were in what had once been farmland.

Voices rang out, sounding not too far away. The four youngsters dropped to the ground, rolling into the old irrigation ditches. Cassie lifted her head just enough to peer over the edge of the ditch and home in on the sounds. They seemed to be coming from their left, heading away from them. She breathed a quiet sigh of relief as she lowered her head back down again.

The voices were more distant now, but Cassie kept them all hunkered down until they could no longer be heard.

"Okay," she whispered, getting to her knees. "They're gone. I was able to make out that they've checked this area. Bad news is they're heading for Centertown, too."

"But they're not going into it," Les said.

"They may well do so this time. Hopefully Ryan knows how to hide himself properly."

Staying low, they crept forward, keeping to the ditches and ruts of the abandoned fields until they could see the outskirts of the town ahead of them. The blip on their scanner was larger now, and positioned more toward the center of the device. Ryan was definitely close.

Cassie called a halt, waiting to see if there were any nearby patrols, but so far it looked good for them. Leading them toward the right-hand side of the town, she gestured for them to move forward. They began a slow crawl toward Centertown. Like their home village, this one was ringed with scanner poles, and a watchtower stood at the entrance.

Les, who'd been taking point for them, held up his closed fist, signaling them to stop. He snaked his way back level with Cassie. "Gate's open!" he whispered.

"You're right," she said as a large spotlight suddenly lit up the town, destroying their night vision. "Dammit!" she hissed, blinking and rubbing her eyes. "It's facing into the town, not outside. They must be searching the houses. Let's get moving before they see us!"

Centertown was the only large settlement the nascent colony had time to construct before the Vess arrived.

A mix of modular prefabricated buildings and those constructed using local materials, it had been a gathering place for the colonists, the main market for staple goods, as well as the few luxuries available.

Like the sensors at the villages, those positioned around Centertown were only there to prevent adults from entering or leaving, not to alert the guards to the presence of any would-be intruders. Only children could safely walk between them, and they were considered no threat.

They skirted the town, looking for an entrance as far from the search parties as possible, then, keeping to the shadows, they slipped quietly into the town.

Hiding in the deep shadows of a doorway, Cassie checked the scanner, working out Ryan's location relative to themselves and the Vess.

"In here," she whispered, gesturing to a building behind them. "We'll be safe here until they clear this quarter."

The others nodded. Les pushed forward, throwing knife at the ready as he cautiously tried the door handle.

It opened with barely a sound. He entered slowly, Cassie following him. Starlight filtered in through the remains of the dusty and dirty windows. She looked around: the shattered glass on the ground was coated in dust, as was the floor. Theirs were the only footprints. It was a coffee shop, judging from the menu boards and symbols inside.

Cassie pulled her water bottle from her pack. She grimaced even as she sucked the tepid liquid down. Dawn was still a good few hours off, they had time to take a quick break while they waited out the search parties. She stuffed the bottle back into her pack.

Signaling toward the bar, she cautiously picked her way across the dusty floor, trying to leave as few signs of their presence as possible. Behind the bar, there was another doorway.

Silently they filed through, Cassie flicking on her flashlight. She spotted the rear door instantly. Crossing the room she tried the handle. It was locked. Reaching into her pocket, she pulled out her lock picks and quickly had it open. Turning the handle slowly, she opened the door a crack, peering through it to see the back alley outside. Widening the gap, she looked carefully up and down, reassuring herself that this exit was safe if they needed one.

Shutting the door, she unslung her backpack. "We're safe here," she said quietly.

Now they could relax for a short while, quiet their frayed nerves, and prepare for the most taxing part of the mission.

"Eat a power bar if you can, you'll need the extra energy," she said, unpacking her lantern and switching it to its lowest setting. She placed it at one end of a worn sofa. "I'll take watch in the shop."

"Where does the scanner show him?" Les asked, following her out. "How far from us?"

Cassie pulled the scanner out of her pocket and fastened it onto her wrist before activating it. "Real close," she said, trying to gauge the distances.

"How close?" Pete asked.

"Distance isn't easy to calculate on this thing, but I'd say he's about a block to our right."

"And the Vess?"

"About the same," she said. "We have to wait 'til they've passed him, or..."

"Taken him," Les said. "Then we get to try and rescue him. Let's hope he's well hidden."

"Let's hope," she echoed. Four of them against up to six Vess would not be easy, even with her training and Les's natural talent with knives. As it was, they would have to kill all the Vess because not to do so would draw attention to the fact that children like themselves were being used as guerilla fighters. The Vess were suspicious, but their universal belief in the sanctity of childhood had so far worked in the humans' favor.

Picking their way carefully across the littered floor, Cassie and Les moved to the largest window and hunkered down to one side of it, watching the bobbing lights across the town from them. Cold air washed over them from the large gap in the glass. Cassie shivered.

Les leaned over and peered at her wrist. "We'll know in a few minutes," he grunted, sitting back down again. "At least they aren't coming near us."

"No, they seem to be done with this sector," she agreed.

A faint scuffling sound came from behind them. "What the hell?" Cassie exclaimed, as she heard a loud scrape then a door banging.

Pulling her gun, she turned and ran for the back room, Les close on her heels.

By the light of the lantern, they saw a body slumped on the floor. Ignoring it, Cassie ran for the door, reaching it just in time to see a figure rounding the corner at the end of the street. .

"Dammit!" she swore. "Who was it?"

"Pete," said Les from beside their fallen friend. "He clocked John a good one on the head. Just knocked him out, nothing worse. We gotta get out of here. Pete knows where we are and has a good idea where Ryan is. This mission's looking like a bust."

"No! We have to get the information Ryan has," she said, reaching for John's nearest arm. "Let's get him onto the sofa. Pete can't speak their language and they might not have an interpreter with them tonight. He could find it a lot more difficult than he thinks to betray us. I can't believe he'd do this!"

"He's scared of being sent to the work camps," Les said. "He might be small but he's older than me and John."

Cassie grunted her agreement as they half-carried, half-dragged the unconscious boy onto the sofa.

"You bring him around, I'll see what the Vess are up to," she said as she moved back to the main room.

In the distance, she could see the Vess's high-powered flashlights bobbing about frantically to the sound of raised Vess voices.

Dammit! She should have seen this coming! Pete had always been just a little too interested in their plans and missions, even when he hadn't been involved.

On the scanner, Ryan's tracker remained static, but glancing up, she saw that the Vess lights were coming closer and their voices were getting louder. In the midst of their guttural speech she heard a higher-pitched voice—Pete's—calling out.

From behind her she heard a low groan followed by a sharp slap.

"The Vess are heading this way," she said, running back to the inner room. "John, we need you to wake up," she said harshly, grabbing the boy's face and turning it to her. "Pete ran off to the Vess and they're heading this way. We have to leave now!"

"M'awake," John slurred, staggering to his feet as she and Les helped him. "Le's go now."

"Back door," Les said, steering John. "Quicker."

They pushed into the back alley and turned toward where the scanner said Ryan was hiding.

"Is Ryan injured?" Les asked as John, the cold air finally bringing him round, began to take his weight off them and run unaided. "Do we know?"

"Unknown," Cassie said as they kept running. The noise the Vess were making now was so loud it covered the sound of their footsteps. "Hopefully not."

A block further on, they stopped to catch their breath, and to try and pinpoint where the Vess were.

"They've gone to the coffee shop," said Les. "Pete must have tried to get us before going for Ryan."

"If I find that little bastard," began John . . .

"Forget him, let the Vess deal with him," Cassie said. "With any luck, we won't see him again. He'll end up in one of those work camps he was so afraid of! Let's just get to Ryan. It'll give us another fighter." She turned to face John. "How you doing? Can you keep up with us and use that catapult of yours?"

John rubbed the back of his head ruefully. "Aye, I can do that."

"War wound," Cassie said with a grin. " Now let's head for Ryan."

Armed, the three of them made their way from shadow to shadow across the main courtyard toward the building where Ryan's tracker showed him to be.

"Hope after all this he's still alive," Les muttered.

"He's alive. The tracker wouldn't show him if he's dead," Cassie said as they dove toward another storefront. "In here. Ryan should be here."

The store had been a grocery shop. Little was left now except empty sacks and boxes.

Cassie consulted the scanner again. They were almost on top of his red blip.

"He should be here," she said, looking around.

"I don't see him," John said, walking behind the counter. "Does he know we're coming?"

"I'm sure he expects a rescue," Cassie said, eyes on the scanner as she walked around the store. "He is definitely here somewhere."

"Hush," Les said holding up a hand for silence. "I think I heard something!"

They all heard it this time, a faint thumping, seeming to come from a distance.

John looked down at the floor. "Is there a cellar?" he asked.

"That would explain it!" Cassie said as they began to search the store. They found the trap door behind the counter. With her flashlight in one hand, gun in the other, Cassie slowly climbed down the stairs to the root cellar.

"Am I glad to see you! I was afraid the Vess would find me before the resistance did!"

The flashlight picked out the regular features of a young man with brown eyes and hair. He blinked in the glare and raised a hand to shield his eyes— a hand covered in blood.

"You're hurt," she said.

"A piece of wreckage got me just before I bailed out. I was able to make it here and hide." He pulled a wry face. "I'm afraid I passed out from the pain."

"Let's get you out of here," Cassie said, putting her gun away and going forward to offer him her arm. "If the Vess get close we need to be able to leave in a hurry. I have a first aid kit, we can patch you up, then we'll have to leave. Are you armed?" she asked.

"Yes, standard blaster," he said, leaning on her as she helped him to his feet.

The puncture wound hadn't hit any major blood vessels. A pressure dressing, some pain pills, and the color started coming back into Ryan's face.

"The Vess are coming," Les said from his position by the window.

"How many? Can you tell?" she asked.

"Looks like six so far, though they'll likely call in more if they can understand Pete."

"Understand Pete?" Ryan asked, unholstering his gun.

"Yeah, one of our number decided to join the Vess," John said bitterly.

"They went for where we had been," Cassie said. "I don't think they have an interpreter with them."

Ryan dug into his uniform pocket and pulled out a slim device about an inch long. "Here, that's the intel I have for HQ in case I don't make it," he said, holding it out to her. "It's all there."

"We're going to get you back to HQ," Cassie said firmly, turning away from him. "Let's head out now."

"I'll take it," Les said, grabbing the device from Ryan and pocketing it.

They slipped out the back door into the darkened alleyway.

"Nearest exit's three blocks to the right," Les said.

Keeping low and dodging from doorway to doorway, they made their way to the end of the block. Ryan was leaning on Cassie as he found the going more difficult than expected. The Vess were nearing the grocery store now, and the bobbing flashlights pointed away from the roadway and into the stores.

Keeping low, Ryan and Cassie limped across the open street and disappeared into the darkness of the next alley.

"How did you get involved in the resistance?" Ryan asked her as they waited for Les and John to make their way over. "I thought it was mainly the youngsters that lived in the villages and Centertown."

"My father was a captain. Our family was caught in one of the villages when the Vess arrived and he trained us all how to survive before they caught him and took him to the mines. He died there three years ago, trying to escape."

"I'm sorry to hear that. It must have been hard for you."

"You deal with it. There's only me left now, my mother and sister died in the flu epidemic a few years back."

"I'm sorry," he said again. Leaning forward he smoothed the frown from her forehead. "It's hard being left alone so young."

She looked away from him and shrugged, rubbing her forehead as the other two joined them at a run. She barely remembered her family, it seemed so long ago now.

"From the look of it, the Vess aren't happy to have Pete," Les whispered from behind her. "They keep trying to ignore him. They're heading this way, though."

"With any luck he'll prove a bigger distraction that anything else," she muttered, looking past him and down the alley. "Too exposed to go forward. Let's head down this alley and cut across to the next block down there a ways."

"Do you need to rest yet?" she asked Ryan as they made their way slowly among the old trash bins and bits of broken stone and wood from the buildings.

"Soon," he said, stifling a groan as they cut to the side to avoid some large pieces of debris. He staggered, pulling her with him into the side of a large trash bin, which screeched and rolled for a few feet, crashing into the building beside it.

In the distance, they heard the Vess yelling to each other.

Cassie stopped, leaning Ryan against the wall as she studied his face. Even in the darkness she saw how pale he was, his eyes enormous black pools of pain.

"Dammit! We gotta get you out of town," she said urgently. "Once we're out, our soldiers can get us. You gotta last 'til then."

"I'll last," he said, taking a deep breath and pushing himself away from the wall. "Let's go."

"Okay. Les, you lead," she said, waiting for the youth to pass her. "He's hurt worse than we thought," she whispered to him.

Les slipped past her. "I got it," he said as he vanished into the darkness ahead. Moments later he returned. "They're headed this way," he said, pulling out a couple of knives and flattening himself against the wall.

"I'm sorry," Ryan whispered, his voice taut with pain. "I didn't mean to be a burden."

"Not important," she said, hauling him upright again. "Getting you back is what matters."

"We're almost at the alley exit," Les said. "We're gonna have to face them here."

With Les's help she dragged Ryan behind a dumpster, stumbling as he tripped on debris and pulled her down too.

"Leave me here," he said. "I have my blaster, I can delay them long enough for you to escape."

"No, we leave together," she said fiercely, pulling her gun free as she helped him brace himself against the wall. She glanced at John who was preparing his slingshot. "You ready?" she asked Ryan.

"Yeah, I can do this," he said, trying to hide the wobble in his voice. "What's your name?"

"Cassie," she mumbled, feeling the blood rise to her face.

"I can do this, Cassie," he said, reaching out to squeeze her arm.

Flustered, she turned her attention back to the Vess. Their pursuers were no longer making any noise, all that warned them of their arrival was the crazily moving flashlight beams.

A faint *whoosh* of air past her face was all the warning Cassie had as Les threw one of his knives at the lead alien. A cry of pain quickly cut off and the Vess collapsed to the ground. Darkness fell again as all the flashlights were quickly doused.

Cassie gripped her gun tighter and aiming at the black mass of figures, let off one round, quickly followed by another. More screams, and more figures fell to the ground. A light flared from just behind her as Ryan let off a sustained blast.

Return fire came in at them, pinging off the sides of the dumpster and ricocheting off the walls.

The group of aliens had broken up now, diving to either side..

"Cover me," Les said, darting to the far wall to slowly inch his way toward the opposite end of the alley.

"What's he doing?" Ryan demanded.

"Outflanking them," she said, taking aim again. "He has throwing knives, he needs to see his targets."

"Right."

They knew Les reached the Vess when a figure on the left suddenly toppled over and hit the ground.

A shot pinged off the dumpster, grazing her arm. She yelped at the shock of it and pulled herself away from the wall, stepping out into the passageway. Now it was personal. Letting off shot after shot, she ran until she found herself standing in front of the fallen Vess with Les grabbing her arm.

"We got them all," he said. "Just need to check they're all dead. Here." He handed her one of his knives before releasing her to go check the bodies.

She pulled her flashlight out, shining it into the faces of the nearest fallen Vess. One groaned and blinked, trying to turn his head away from the light. Without thinking, she reached down and with a swift movement, slit his throat, turning her head aside as the blood gushed over his chest.

Her eyes began to tear, blurring her vision as Ryan came limping up. A sob escaped her. Why was she crying for a Vess? She hated them, they'd killed her parents, tried to kill her tonight. It made no sense.

Cassie's knife fell to the ground as Ryan reached down to press his hand over her shoulder comfortingly. "It's okay, the danger's past," he said. "This is the same reaction everyone has after their first kill."

"It isn't my first," she said, scrubbing furiously at her eyes. "I don't know what's wrong with me." Picking up Les's knife, she got to her feet.

"I think I got one of them," John said.

"You did good," Ryan said before Cassie could.

"Where's Pete?" she demanded.

"He's not among the dead." John said. "Probably ran for it. Never was much of a fighter."

"I got the others," Les said, holding out his hand for his knife. "We better get moving. It's a two-hundred-yard dash to the woods beyond the sensors." He went round to Ryan's other side and took hold of his arm.

"Hold onto me," Cassie ordered him as she and Les began to walk him toward the rear of the alley. "John, you go ahead and keep a look out for us."

"How are you going to get me past the sensors?" Ryan asked as he began to stumble forward. "Can't you just take them out?"

"Don't work like that," Les grunted as they began to trot, then run. By the time they left the alley, they were running as fast as they could go, Cassie and Les almost dragging Ryan with them.

"Keep going!" Cassie yelled as they drew level with the sensors.

Les was jerked to a sudden stop as both Cassie and Ryan suddenly collapsed to the ground.

"Jesus! I knew she had left it too late!" he snarled. "John, help me find that damned box of hers!"

"Which box?" John asked, helping Les to his feet. "What's wrong with Cassie?"

"Sensors got her, same as they got Ryan. We got to bring her back before she really dies."

"I thought we were supposed to bring back Ryan for his information." John stood there, shocked motionless by the news. "She can't be dead..."

"John! Her pocket!" Les yelled, slapping the other boy on the arm to bring him to his senses. He got down on his knees himself and began rummaging through Cassie's left coat pockets.

John bent down to help when Les spoke again.

"Never mind, I found it." He sat back on his heels with the slim box in his hand. Flipping it open, he pulled out a hypodermic with a long needle. "I already got Ryan's information."

"What you gonna do with that?" John asked, taking a step backward as Les began to pull Cassie's coat open.

"She said to put it into the heart and press the plunger," he said, pulling up her sweater and T-shirt until he reached bare flesh.

"You can't do that!" John said in disbelief. "That'll kill her, sticking a long needle like that in her heart!"

"She's already dead, I can't kill her more than she already is." He felt her chest, hoping for a heartbeat to tell him where her heart was exactly, but there was none. It was in the middle of the chest, nearer the small mound that was her left breast, wasn't that right? He hoped it was as he carefully placed the needle tip so it would go between the ribs.

"The Vess are coming!" John whimpered. "Hurry up or we'll all be dead!"

Les slammed the needle into her chest, pushing down on the syringe until it was empty, then he withdrew it and threw it to one side.

"Quick! Grab her arm, we gotta get out of here now! Hopefully they'll stop for Ryan,"

Bent almost double, the two boys began to run, towing the still unresponsive Cassie between them.

They were pulled to a stop as Cassie began to convulse and cough, dragging in large gasping breaths of air.

"Cassie! We gotta run," Les said, pulling on her arm, helping her struggle to her feet. The night around them suddenly lit up with arms fire streaking past them toward the Vess.

"Come *on*!"

Cassie started staggering in the direction he was pulling her.

"This way," an adult voice called out from their right. Les swerved in that direction and John, grabbing for her other arm, began to haul her that way too. Moments later they were at the center of a small group of soldiers with a medic hurriedly grabbing Cassie then settling her on a stretcher and asking questions of the other two.

"You're very lucky," the medic said to Cassie as she got dressed again behind the partition in the small exam room. "I don't know what they were thinking, sending you back into the field at your age. It's a wonder you even made it into the first village!"

"They needed the information that Ryan gave us," she said. The pang of loss she felt for the young lieutenant had lessened now that a week had passed since they'd returned to HQ.

"Let's hope it was worth it," he said. "It cost the life of two good people, maybe more if the Vess had caught up with you." He hesitated. "I'm sorry we weren't able to help Lieutenant Ryan, but he'd been dead too long by the time we reached him. They did try."

"I know they did. I think it was worth it," she said, coming out from behind the screen. "At least we have a way to save those killed by the sensors now, if we can get to them in time."

"A big if, and it's still very crude. We need something that's easier to administer."

"I hear they've found several of the Vess bases on Hope now, and are striking at them directly. We're hitting them where it hurts for the first time."

The medic looked up from his comp pad. "I don't know where you youngsters get your news from," he said. "But if it's true, that's good to hear. The sooner the fighting's done, the more pleased I'll be. Maybe getting a taste of their own medicine will force the Vess to the negotiation table at last."

"Maybe it will."

"Well you should be proud of the part you and your friends played," he said. "Time for some well-deserved R & R. Maybe you can grow up in safety now."

COMRADES IN ARMS
Bud Sparhawk

ACROSS THE COLD, GRASSY PLATEAU LAY SCATTERED DETRITUS WASHED UP ON THE shores of a war that had ravaged the planet since the invasion. The bright mid-day light of the red sun blazing overhead threw the scene into harsh contrast. Jason knew the deep shadows hid as many bodies as were exposed and the remaining tall grass hid even more.

The patterns of the fallen human and alien forces appeared somewhat random. Here and there were overlapping arcs mowed in the plateau's tall grasses where the aliens' ticklers had ripped into the human force. Craters from the human heavy weapons punctuated areas where alien weapons had been destroyed.

After studying the patterns of death and destruction Jason concluded that ISOBEL, the unit's commander, along with the rest of her troops must have been overrun. It looked like there had been enormous costs to both sides and, from where he stood, he could not determine which, if either, had emerged victorious.

But ISOBEL would know; that is, if he could rescue her. They'd given him this search because of his condition: busted head, torn actuators, and deteriorating life support system that made him useless for combat. He wasn't as strong or fast as he'd been, but troops like him were still useful. Right now, searching this recent battleground seemed the best use.

He examined the areas where the majority of the alien and human remains were clustered in grisly detail. It was a scene from hell and one which left him, Cybermarine Sergeant Jason Ponderson, wondering where he could best search for ISOBEL's position.

He'd leave the rest of the battlefield to the Reaper squad to salvage whatever remains could be reused or repurposed.

There was a path across the plateau not far from where he'd been dropped. The hopper hadn't wanted to risk himself on the off chance that some remnant alien still had the firepower to bring him down if he got closer. "I'LL PICK YOU UP IN FIVE DAYS," he'd warned. "THIRTEEN HOURS. WON'T WAIT."

The most efficient path involved crossing ground torn asunder by the battle. Jason struggled to keep his damaged chassis upright. His autonomic balancing systems were barely keeping him from going ass over teacup as he scanned for anything that might present a threat. He kept his weapons ready just in case the hopper pilot's concerns proved valid.

He planned to head toward the site that had seen the most action first. That was the most probable location to find ISOBEL. IF she wasn't there he'd work his way outward for two days then back to where the hopper should be arriving.

There was no sign of movement except for the wind-driven swaying of the plateau's grass near the rise. Most of the marines and soldiers had been rendered into scattered body parts by the aliens' vicious ticklers. That wasn't unexpected, the alien weapons were highly effective and even armored humans so very vulnerable.

As best he could guess, the troops here had been spread wide to reduce losses; but it hadn't done a lot of good. He had accounted for twenty troops by counting legs and dividing by two, as the ancient joke went, when he caught a furtive movement in the deep shadow of a crater that looked to have been caused by an HE round.

His eyes had automatically switched to IR a microsecond before his brain began analyzing the possible threat. He spotted a small heat source in the crater. He drew closer, readying his weapons should it be an alien, and hoping it wasn't.

The hotspot turned out to be a human half buried in rubble, not surprising considering how many he'd already seen, although how an intact human had fallen into the crater and so far from the other casualties was a minor puzzle.

Then the body moved.

Jason immediately began uncovering whoever was on the other end of the arm, tossing dirt aside until he exposed the armor's shoulder, helmet, chest plates, and finally, boots. The only obvious sign that the marine had been hit was a dent on his side. His breathing seemed steady, as was his heartbeat. His exposed skin felt a little cold, which would indicate shock or simply exposure to the chilly winter weather: Jason couldn't tell. He'd screamed as Jason was checking his body.

Jason suspected his injuries might be internal. "Where's it hurt?" he asked.

The marine's fingers fluttered at his dented side: No penetration so it had to be a broken rib or other internal damage, Jason thought, but he had neither the training not the tools to repair him.

"Mfggh. Wha 'append?" the marine groaned as Jason was giving him a sip of water.

"Your squad was mowed down by ticklers," Jason replied. "Why are you *here,* so far from the others?"

"Takin' a piss," the marine answered, "when somethin' hit me."

"Could have been covering fire. There's a ruined launcher nearby."

"No shit? Probably an effing Instance." the marine coughed.

He winced when Jason helped him stand and clutched at his side. "I can give you something for the pain."

"Pain's not bad. Don't need no damn drugs. By the way, name's Kraff, Thirty-second marine combat support specialist. Who, or should I say, *what* the hell are you?"

"Call me Jason. Reaper Sergeant First Class, Cybermarine Division."

Kraff drew back. "You're a damn zombie! I should have known when I saw your ugly face." He spit. "Sorry to disappoint you but my brain's not ready to harvest just yet, ghoul."

Jason ignored the insult. "I am searching for ISOBEL."

"Some brass idiot?" Kraff wheezed. "And why?"

"I can tag you for recovery. Might be a long wait, but your apparent injuries don't warrant expedient extraction. There are likely more serious things that need their attention."

"You're going to leave me here?" Kraff exclaimed with obvious alarm and then lapsed into a coughing fit. "What if some of them damn bugs are still around?"

"I expect no further threat from aliens," Jason replied. "You should be quite safe here while I continue my search."

Kraff reached up to grab Jason's arm. "I think the lieutenant said she was... over there." He waved an arm toward the horizon. "I'll go with you."

If Kraff was telling the truth his knowledge would help the search. "I have a large area to cover," Jason said. "I doubt you could keep up in your condition."

"You're not leaving me behind. I can keep up. Just get me something to eat and you'll see. A live marine's a whole lot better than a damned animated corpse."

Kraff had collapsed after following Jason's unsuccessful search for half the day. "Can't go any further. Let's stop here. Can't do much searching at night, can we?"

"I assure you that darkness does not hinder my vision," Jason replied as the red sun disappeared behind the distant mountains. "But you need to rest."

The smell must have been horrific from the way Kraff had been gagging. Or perhaps that was his reaction to seeing what marines looked like after a barrage of ticklers. Nevertheless, he slept.

Dawn lighted the area when Kraff awoke. Jason had found a few destroyed carriers during the night but none that could have carried ISOBEL. The scattered wreckage of Cybers and Instances compared to the relatively small number of flayed natural human bodies meant this element must have been a heavy mobile strike force. Alien carapaces littered the ground, most blown asunder, their weapons shattered, armor shredded and everything soaked with brown splatter. He could almost admire their bravery for attacking such a heavily armed unit.

"Up early, eh?" Kraff coughed and spit a gob of bloodied phlegm. "No rest for the weary, I guess." With that he struggled to his feet, bracing himself with a WK-24a he'd picked up from one of the dead bodies. Jason looked at the pack Kraff had been using as a pillow and noticed fresh blood stains, indicating a possible punctured lung.

"I'm starving," Kraff complained as he fumbled through the bloodied pack and pulled out two rations of Meals, Tactical,Single Serving and quickly devoured them. "Need to find more of these."

"I have spare rations you may need."

Kraft grimaced. "What: extra lubricating fluid and batteries?"

"I assure you that my rations are more nutritious than those," he indicated the empty wrappers in Kraff's hands. "In addition, mine will provide increased stamina. I can also give you drugs for the pain you are so obviously trying to conceal."

"I don't need any of your drugs, Zombie." Fragg's coughing fit revealed his lie.

Jason said nothing but as soon as Kraff turned to relieve himself, he injected a dose of pain killer into a combat bar. When Kraff was finished he handed him the bar. "For later," he explained.

Kraff accepted the bar without comment and stuck it into his pack. "Let's go find this girl of yours,' he coughed. "Only don't walk so damn fast. I don't like it when you get out of sight."

Jason looked down at the tiny human. "I only have three days before rendezvous and there's a lot of territory to cover. As I said before, I can tag you for pickup. There's no need for you to accompany me."

Fargo shouted: "You're not leaving me to the damn bugs!" when Jason began to walk away.

Jason didn't look back.

It was early afternoon when Jason detected a faint signal on his T-band. He stopped and slowly turned in a circle to pinpoint the direction of the unexpected signal. It appeared to be strongest coming from the direction of a ruined battlewagon lacking its main turret and port side cannon.

Kraff stumbled up and wheezed. "Did we have to walk so friggin' far? Won't that burn our your batteries or something?"

"My energy stores are sufficient for this mission. Do you need drugs for the pain?"

Kraff shook his head. "Marines don't need drugs to keep up, Frankenstein. Pain don't bother me that much."

"You need to eat that bar I gave you. It will strengthen your resolve."

"I thought you zombies ate brains," Kraff laughed as he quickly consumed the doctored ration bar. "I guess I was more hungry than I thought. You have more of these?"

"Consuming a second bar now would seriously affect your health. These bars are quite powerful."

"I'll say. I'm feeling better already! Let's go."

Kraff started striding away when Jason told him to stop. "There's another casualty close by. Keep quiet but tell me if you see or hear anything unusual." He didn't expect any help from Kraff but at least it would keep the suddenly energetic marine from distracting him. Jason's eyes and ears were a magnitude more sensitive than Kraff's.

A short while later, as Jason identified the signal's source as the twisted wreck of a small mobile howitzer, lying on its side, and missing a drive wheel. Nearby one of its treads had been turned into a knot of tortured metal.

The feeble signal was stronger here. WHOIS? Jason queried and listened carefully for a reply. Had there been a wavering in the signal, an attempt at a reply? Or had it only been random noise from the dying howitzer's electronics?

"Why are you messing around with that junk?" Kraff demanded. "Let's keep moving and find your girl."

Jason ignored him. There was a definable variation in the signal now. On a hunch he switched to the k-band used for short-range communications. "*WHOIS?*" he repeated, and paused to listen.

"ABOUT TIME YOU GOT HERE," came the reply. I'VE BEEN WAITING FOREVER FOR A WRECKER."

"*Sorry to disappoint you,*" Jason replied. "*I'm Jason, Cyber Division.*"

"HYPERION IS THE NAME, FOURTH ARMORED. WAIT, DID YOU SAY 'CYBER?' DIDN'T ISOBEL SEND YOU? I'VE BEEN ASKING FOR PICKUP SINCE THAT DAMN ROCKET HIT ME."

"*You've been wasting your time and energy. I couldn't pick up your signal. Matter of fact all I had to go on was the leakage from your electronics.*"

"Why are you staring at that pile of crap?" Kraff shouted. "We need to get moving if we're going to find what you're looking for."

"This is HYPERION," Jason answered. "He's an Instance who's been taken out of action."

"Screw it. Pull its plug and let's get moving. We don't have time to mess with busted up equipment."

"*My accomplice just said that we should deactivate you. Do you agree?*"

HYPERION's reaction was instantaneous. "HELL NO! I HAVEN'T BEEN BACKED UP FOR OVER A YEAR. YOU'D BE KILLING THIS VERSION OF ME. DON'T YOU TADPOLES HAVE ANY SYMPATHY FOR US POOR INSTANCES?"

The tadpole remark stung. "*Kraff's not a Cyber. He's a Natural,*" Jason shot back. "*Injured but functional.*"

"A DAMN EPHEMERAL? SHOOT HIM INSTEAD. I'M SURE THAT WOULD BE LESS OF A LOSS THAN ME."

Jason didn't reply, even though the suggestion did have a bit of appeal. "*He says he knows where ISOBEL might be.*"

"HOW DOES HE KNOW? WHAT IF HE'S LYING?"

That was a very good question.

Kraff wasn't happy about sitting around while Jason attempted to repair the broken howitzer. As night fell he clutched his scavenged rifle tightly against his vest and stared into the darkness. "Would you stop banging around?" he yelled. "The damn bugs might hear you and come calling in the dark."

"Just as they would if they heard your shout," Jason replied. "Darkness doesn't bother me and I can assure you that no live aliens can approach without being detected."

What concerned him about Kraff was the amount of drugs he'd been consuming. He'd already used Jason's spare supply, leaving barely enough to last until he reached the pickup point.

"HOW ARE YOU DOING?" HYPERION inquired. "IS THE EPHEMERAL INTERFERING? WHY DON'T YOU PUT HIM OUT OF HIS MISERY."

"*I am working as best as I can,*" Jason assured the howitzer. "*There's only so much that I can do without help.*"

"AFRAID YOU'LL DAMAGE YOUR TITANIUM BONES?"

"*My internal structure is as strong as your armor, thank you. Why don't I tag you for later pick up when the Reaper crew gets here.*"

"AND WHEN WILL THAT BE? MY POWER SUPPLY IS NEARLY DEPLETED AS IS. I HAVE ONLY FIFTY HOURS REMAINING."

"*I've queried for an update on their estimated arrival time but have not yet received a reply.*" The Reaper crew's lack of an immediate response could mean that they were encountering difficulties. There were more than enough skirmishes taking place up and down the mountain chain to keep them busy.

He continued working with no success. "CAN YOU DOWNLOAD ME INSTEAD? WOULDN'T MIND LEAVING THIS COPY BEHIND."

"*I have little memory capacity for storage and I am as anxious as you to preserve my essence.*"

"A little help would be appreciated," he told Kraff.

"Yeah, like with a broken rib that's starting to hurt again I doubt I'd be much use working on that useless hunk of metal."

Jason fumed. "You can still use your brain to think of something that will help us get HYPERION back in action, Kraff."

Kraff sneered. "It's just a damn machine, not a person. Besides, without treads on its left side how the hell could it move?"

That was a very good point that neither he nor HYPERION could answer.

"Hey, these machines have a computer that runs them, don't they?" Jason could not see where Kraff was going with this. "I'm thinking that they must have some way of moving the box from one machine to another so why don't we just pull the computer and carry it with us?"

"TELL THAT MEATHEAD THAT I AM NOT AN EFFING COMPUTER. NEVERTHELESS, THAT'S NOT AN UNREASONABLE IDEA," HYPERION replied when Jason relayed the idea. "I AM LOCATED AT THE BASE OF MY TURRET." He then went on to describe the field extraction process. "REMOVAL WON'T DAMAGE ME. I CAN RETAIN TWENTY HOURS OF EMERGENCY POWER."

Which, Jason thought should give them barely enough time to reach the rendezvous.

Jason completed extracting HYPERION just as brown dawn lit the clouds above the mountains. He'd intended to have Kraff carry HYPERION but the awkward two hundred kilogram unit was more than even a healthy marine could have managed. The oddly shaped weight presented few problems for him, although it would slow him to Kraff's stumbling pace.

"I HAVE NO OPERATING SENSORS, TADPOLE," HYPERION said. "HOWEVER I DO RETAIN TACTICAL MAPS OF OUR DEPLOYMENT AND CAN IDENTIFY THE LOCATIONS OF OTHER INSTANCES YOU SHOULD CHECK. THERE SHOULD BE TEN IN THE NEXT FEW KILOMETERS."

That information would be helpful, Jason thought. One of those locations might have COMMAND's carrier. *"But what about the Cybers and Naturals?"* he added.

"WHO CARES? THE MEATS ARE PROBABLY DEAD AND ANY TADPOLES WOULD BE TOO DAMAGED FOR YOUR HELP. SEARCHING FOR THEM WILL DELAY REACHING THE RENDEZVOUS."

Which meant HYPERION would be of little help. "Pick up your stuff," he told Kraff. "We're moving out."

Kraff grumbled as he stuffed things he had gathered from a fallen kit into his mouth. He had some difficulty getting to his feet but did not ask for help as he gathered his scavenged supplies.

Still heading toward Kraff's pointed location, Jason had come across more bodies, Cyber, Natural, and one Instance so heavily damaged that he could not tell what it had been. "AUXILIARY MORTAR UNIT." HYPERION said, which was informative but hardly helpful.

The repeated bloody carnage had not, could not bother him, but it was having a profound effect on Kraff who stayed away from the ruined bodies. Twice he had thrown up, a waste of drugs and rations, but managed to struggle through.

Toward evening, as the fading sun softened the harsh scenery of death and destruction, Jason detected movement about half a kilometer ahead of them. "Down," he ordered. Kraff dropped immediately and brought his WK to his good shoulder. He appeared confused as to where he should be pointing it.

Jason lowered his heavily loaded body carefully, trying to balance HYPERION as he dropped. "Movement ahead. Half a klick." He pointed.

After a few moments he raised his head and used his IR sight to find a heat source. Nothing. Had he been mistaken? "Shift to your left. Large boulder. Stay alert." As Kraff shifted Jason caught a sudden flare; too cold to be human, too small to be a Cyber, and certainly not an Instance's exhaust.

"Is it a bug? Kraff whispered and quietly shoved a round into the breech of his WK.

"WHAT IS HAPPENING?" HYPERION demanded.

"Possible hostile half a klick ahead. Identity uncertain."

"NO INSTANCES WERE IN THAT AREA," which again was informative but unhelpful.

A sudden darting movement appeared to the right of the first sighting. It had the usual lack of detail IR provided. It had been moving quickly away. "Just an animal," he said as he got to his feet. "We need to keep moving."

Kraff groaned as he came to his feet. "I sure hope those ugly eyes of yours can see in the dark because I certainly can't."

Jason didn't wince at the insult. He knew the Naturals' aversion to the multiple eyes that adorned his nose-less face, just as they accused Cybers of being cold-blooded resurrections that were more machine than man. So what if he'd had to practically die before he became a Cybermarine. He was faster and stronger than the toughest Natural and probably the best fighter a squad could have, that is, until the advent of the Instanced.

HYPERION's "tadpole" insult had been all too true because that was the next progression after being a Cyber. There was a certain beauty in the progression of being a natural human to becoming an augmented Cybermarine, and finally an installed Instance. The only drawback was...

Something heavy suddenly struck, sending him toppling to the ground, and HYPERION tumbling away. He began to turn when there was a sudden loud burst from Kraff's WK. Jason leapt to his feet and saw half of a bug smoldering beside him.

"Glad this baby's got tracking capability. I've had it on full automatic since you spotted the boggie." Kraff boasted as he patted the side of the WK. "Saved your ass."

"That was incredibly stupid," Jason shot back. "I was in no danger and the sound from that model can be detected from kilometers away. You may have put us at unnecessary risk." He mentally kicked himself for not having Kraff shut off the WK's tracker earlier.

The cold rain that had been threatening since daybreak finally began descending in torrents, turning the plateau into slick mud, and making forward progress difficult. Kraff had fallen multiple times and was coated with mud and things he probably didn't want to think about. He slipped each time he tried to retain his footing.

The time for rendezvous was approaching and he had nothing to show for the time he'd been given except a damaged Instance and a wounded marine.

In the last day Kraff had become surprisingly energetic and, although he'd frequently fallen behind, always managed to catch up. Jason thought the drugs in the combat bars must be having a more significant effect than expected. Or maybe Kraff hadn't been as seriously damaged as he'd thought.

Kraft had indicated that ISOBEL had been on a slight rise. If she had she'd have made a better target. The area around the rise was tormented. Overlapping craters were witness to the intensity of fighting. Jason carefully examined every possible wreck for some indication of COMMAND's location.

He spotted Kraff busy searching the gear of the fallen and, as he watched, saw the marine rip open a medical packet. Was he self-medicating? That was dangerous if he was supplementing the measured dosages Jason had been administering. Supporting himself on emergency drugs for more than the short term they'd been designed for carried a heavy penalty. No wonder Kraff had been so hungry; his body needed to replace what the drugs were draining.

It wasn't difficult to determine that the heavily damaged communications van had held ISOBEL. The vehicle's undercarriage was separated from an armored body that had been scattered as random pieces over a sixty square meter area. Fused components that once housed ISOBEL, none larger than Jason's hand, were indistinguishable from each other. The case that had once held COMMAND's Instance and memory banks looked torn and twisted as if by a giant's hand into a pretzel of silicon and metal. He knew without further examination that there would be no recovery of the battle data, no possibility of rescuing the genius level commander.

"I WAS HOPING FOR SUCCESS," HYPERION remarked when Jason informed him of the extensive damage. "BUT ISOBEL IS ALWAYS BACKED UP BEFORE AN ENGAGEMENT. THERE WILL ONLY BE A LOSS OF THIS BATTLE DATA."

Jason swore. *"Yes, but we've also lost whatever went wrong. ISOBEL should never have been placed at risk."*

"I SUSPECT SOME DAMNED EPHEMERAL WAS RESPONSIBLE. THEY CARE LITTLE ABOUT WE INSTANCES."

Jason wondered about that. It did seem that the caravan had included more Instances and Cybers than Naturals. But....

"Are we finished here?" Kraff interrupted. "I thought you wanted to find your woman commander, not stare at rubbish."

"This," Jason said slowly, indicating the wreckage that surrounded them. "This was ISOBEL."

"She's just some stupid machine?" Kraff wheezed. "I thought you were looking for a dead woman's remains, not more trash. Where are your priorities?" He abruptly fell to the muddy ground and began coughing. From his appearance Jason could tell that the drugs were finally taking their toll.

"Kraff, can you continue? I cannot leave you here. Your only chance for survival is reaching the rendezvous."

Kraff struggled to his feet but after three hesitant steps he collapsed again and began breathing heavily. It was half a day's march to the pickup point and he doubted Kraff could make it. "You'll have to carry me," Kraff wheezed. "I can't go another step."

"I cannot carry both of you," Jason replied and wondered about his options. If he tagged and abandoned Kraff he doubted the marine would survive until the retriever team arrived. His own reserves were nearly exhausted and any additional weight would further tax his body.

"Why don't you dump that computer you're carrying," Kraff suggested.

"How long could you last if I left you here?" he asked HYPERION.

"YOU CANNOT ABANDON ME." HYPERION replied. "I HAVE ONLY A FEW HOURS REMAINING, LEAVE THE MEAT. WE ARE JUST TWENTY KILOMETERS FROM YOUR PICKUP POINT."

Jason was nearly exhausted; he'd given Kraff all of his spare rations and some of his own. Worse, carrying HYPERION was making him burn through his reserves.

"Can you give me a little help," Kraff requested. "The pain's getting worse." The marine's dragging steps gave witness to his failing energy.

Jason had only one drug dose left to keep Kraff from total collapse. He knew Fragg's body would crash and pay dearly for the drugs, that is if he made it to a field hospital.

HYPERION announced. "I HAVE IS ONE POINT FIVE HOURS BEFORE SHUTDOWN. CAN YOU PICK UP THE PACE?"

"Not without abandoning the Natural. He appears to be on his last legs." Kraff was sitting wearily on the carapace of a dead alien, breathing heavily and shivering so hard that his teeth chattered. He'd lost the WK somewhere along the way.

Jason coldly debated his next actions. He didn't have the strength to continue carrying HYPERION, but if he abandoned the Instance he'd expire. He *knew* HYPERION wouldn't really die; somewhere they had a backup that could be resurrected to fight again. Nobody wasted a trained and combat-tested Instance. Sure, the restored HYPERION would not recall anything of his life since his backup date, but that would be a small price to pay. All HYPERION would lose would be the terrible memories of this failed battle.

Nobody would know if Jason left him to expire. He'd just be another broken machine among a field of too many.

If he abandoned Kraff, on the other hand, he could easily die. His injuries were not so life-threatening that he'd be transitioned into a Cybermarine nor had he the combat experience that would make him effective. Besides, Kraff had been nothing but a burden since his rescue. Bigoted, opinionated, and dumb he'd matter little to the Force after his recovery, that is if he didn't get retired to breed another generation of slow and stupid Naturals. But he owed the man for helping. He had saved him from the surviving alien.

As to himself, no one would mourn his passing. Most Naturals tolerated the Cybers only because of their utility. He'd backed up just six months earlier so his own instance, his essence, could be used as an Instance like HYPERION. As a already damaged Cyber, he was expendable.

Considering all that, the decision was easy.

"Eat this," Jason said as he handed Kraff his last doctored ration. He hoped the drugs and meagre nourishment would get the marine the rest of the way.

He lifted Kraff to his feet and, supporting him, began heading for the waiting chopper.

Kraff woke. Bright light came through a nearby window and illuminated the soft blue walls of what was obviously a hospital room. He ached all over, worse than the hangover he'd had after his last bender. As he tried to remember how he had gotten here fragments, little more than snapshots came to mind; a hulking monster making him eat disgusting and distasteful rations, a ruined howitzer machine, and firing a WK.

"Awake at last," a nurse said cheerfully as she came through the door. "You've been unconscious for weeks, soldier, and no wonder with the amount of drug residue in your system. It was lucky you stumbled on that extraction chopper. Tell me, how did you survive when so many others died?"

"Good living, but I think I used one of those animated corpses. I tell you, the sooner we can get rid of those monstrosities the better."

The pretty nurse smiled. "The war's almost over. I'm sure we'll get rid of them soon."

A previous edition of this story was published in
The Intergalactic Medicine Show, June 2018.

MEDICINE MAN
Robert E Waters

CAPTAIN VICTORIO "TOMORROW'S WIND" NANTAN, SQUADRON COMMANDER OF THE Devil Dancers, 3rd Sol Fighter Wing, expected the worst from Vice-Admiral Hector Pal-Marbary.

He got it.

"I'm sorry, Captain," Pal-Marbary said, fiddling with a tactical fleet tablet at his desk. "Your request to keep your second in command out of Operation Gold Javelin has been denied."

Victorio gritted his teeth, biting back the words he wanted to say. "Sir, with respect, it is my decision, is it not, being squadron commander? Personnel decisions are mine and mine alone, is that not true?"

Pal-Marbary nodded and set the tablet down. "Under normal circumstances, that is correct. But this is not a normal circumstance. Your squadron is flying under-strength already with your recent casualties, and as far as I can see, there is nothing in Blue Bird's most recent psych eval and physical panel to suggest she isn't fit to fly. And let's be honest: you know as well as I do that the Gulo are coming at us with everything they've got this time. We need all asses in the seats, and Blue Bird is one of the best pilots in the Union. She *can't* sit this one out."

"I—" Victorio swallowed, cleared his throat, loathe to speak the next words, "—I have a hunch, sir. A feeling. If she flies, she dies."

Those last two words stuck in his throat, though he tried holding back the emotion. It did not do to show such emotion in front of a superior officer, especially one as upwardly mobile as Vice-Admiral Pal-Marbary. The man was on the fast track to becoming the supreme commander of the entire Union fleet.

The Vice-Admiral stood slowly, letting a long, exasperated breath escape his thin lips. "I respect your skills as a squadron commander, Victorio. You are one of the best captains in the Union. Your Devil Dancers are, without a doubt, the best *Radiant* squadron in the fleet. Which is all the more reason to countermand your decision." He paused, glanced at his tablet once more, then continued. "I have tried to respect your cultural beliefs, and I have given you and your squadron latitude to practice your rituals and ceremonies as you see fit here on the *Star Chariot*. But you know perfectly well that I cannot make operational decisions based on your *visions*, as it were. If your rituals and customs give you and your pilots courage and strength in battle, so be it. But at the end of the day, I have to look at the numbers, Victorio, and the Gulo have more. With a pilot as skilled as Blue Bird in the fight, our odds improve. I'm sorry, Captain Victorio, but the decision stands: Blue Bird cannot stay out of the next fight."

Victorio handed the amulet to Blue Bird. She accepted it reluctantly. "Why are you giving me this?" she asked.

She had a right to know, but the vision in his dreams was too strong, too... horrifying to tell her. Besides, Blue Bird was never one to believe whole-heartedly in *di-yin* power. She believed it in her own way, but when it came to embracing visions in the manner that Victorio did, her beliefs fell more in line with Pal-Marbary's: they were valuable only in the way in which they gave a pilot strength. Nothing more. No matter what Victorio said to her, she would not believe her own death was imminent.

"It is made from the hardwood bookend that my father gave me," Victorio said, "before Naiche and I left Earth. Wear it during flight, so that you may draw strength from it."

Blue Bird turned the amulet over in her hand. It was a small thing, no larger than a coin. Round, smooth, Victorio had cut it from the lightning-charred piece of wood that he displayed proudly on the mantel in his office. Wood struck by lightning was powerful medicine, and he had shaped it himself and then sanded it down by hand for hours until it was as smooth as glass. His third in command, Lieutenant Red Moon, had carved the symbols into it afterward, those symbols to ward off evil spirits that might invade Blue Bird's mind during operations to confuse her judgment and drive her to mistake.

Blue Bird palmed it, smiled, and handed it back to Victorio. "No, I will not wear it, unless you tell me why."

Victorio huffed and turned away from her. "Goddammit, woman! Can't you do what I ask you to do without question? I'm your commanding officer, for Yusn's sake. I order you to wear it."

There was a pause and a silence that bothered Victorio. With such silence, he expected Blue Bird to grow angry, turn and walk away. Instead, he felt her hand on his shoulder. "Dear Heart," she said, in that soft voice that always ran a chill down his back. "Come now. Are we not beyond such commandments? Do you still not feel free to speak truth to me?"

It was forbidden for officers of The Federated Union to fraternize, and fall in love with, pilots under their charge. It was a sound policy, and in principle, Victorio agreed with it. But life was life, and Blue Bird was the most beautiful and most skilled woman that Victorio had ever met. She was his equal in many ways, and there was never any doubt that they would find reassurance in each other's arms. In the cold vacuum of space, that mutual love and respect had given them strength to endure, and so long as the Devil Dancers piled victory upon victory, the Admiralty looked the other way on their forbidden relationship.

Victorio sighed, lowered his head, pinched his eyes together. "Okay, here it is..."

He told her everything he saw in his dream. He told her about how the squadron flew Raven pattern into a full flight of Gulo *Wasps*. He told her about how she was swarmed by enemy craft such that there was too much interference to get a good lock on her position. How he and their remaining pilots tried to break through the chaos of swirling Gulo fighters, only to see the cockpit of her much larger *Radiant* fighter burst into flames. How he had managed to finally regain contact only to hear her final screams as the fire took her. By the end of his story, Victorio wiped a tear from his eye. "And it will happen, Blue Bird. The vision was too strong not to be true. I know that you do not hold stock in my dreams, but I am di-yin. I understand these powers better than you. It will happen. The vice-admiral has refused my request to keep you out of this fight. See, the spirits are already working against us. You will die, Blue Bird, and there is nothing I can do to stop it."

"Then why give me the amulet?" Blue Bird asked as she ran her hand down his back to comfort him. "If my death is inevitable, no tiny, polished piece of wood will change that."

"There is always a chance," Victorio said, turning to her and looking deep into her precious face. "We can always change the odds a little. We can try at least."

Blue Bird smiled and took his hands. She opened his palm and removed the amulet. "Okay, my love. I will wear it for you, and for the squadron. But if what you say is true and we can change the odds, then let's change them even further."

Victorio raised a brow. "What do you suggest?"

"If this is to be my last fight, then it is my right to fight it in the manner of my choosing."

A Clown!

He was a fool to let her talk him into it, but Blue Bird's rationale was tactically sound. If his vision had seen her become separated from the main squadron, and then destroyed in fire, why not change her position in the squadron? Why not have her fly as the Clown?

In a Devil Dancers squadron, the Clown was a fifth fighter that flew independently from the main four, acting as a kind of rogue asset capable of exploiting weaknesses behind enemy formations while the main squadron of four Ganhs attacked from another position. In Apache folklore, the Clown was a comical member in a Ganh dancing troupe, making children laugh and causing amusing disruptions in an otherwise serious ceremony. In the cold vacuum of space, Captain Victorio Nantan had used the Clown to great effect. A Clown was deadly, but the position was dangerous, and Blue Bird had never flown as Clown before.

But he agreed, allowing her to be so because giving her agency over her own fate was the right thing to do. If he were in her position, he'd demand the same from *his* commander.

All five Radiant fighters in the Devil Dancers' Alpha Squadron moved in Hawk pattern toward the Gulo fleet line. Victorio was on point in tight formation. Blue Bird flew three kilometers behind, hidden from view, and would remain so until released. Hawk pattern allowed for a serious blanket of firepower to be delivered to target, plus the ability to change formation quickly to compensate for Gulo fighters trying to exploit gaps in the line. And the battle line stretched for hundreds of kilometers, with other Union fighter squadrons and gunboats moving steadily forward to meet the Gulo threat.

"Steady, now," Victorio said, pitching to the right to close up the formation. He tapped his dashboard to activate his rocket packages. "The swarm is coming."

On radar, the enemy forces looked like a cloud of stardust, an amoeba-like creature floating through space. In a way, they were, and that's how the Gulo liked it: messy and chaotic. They had won many battles with this tactic, but Victorio, and the Union, were determined not to let it happen this time, but one could never tell how things would evolve against the mass of a Gulo fighter wing.

Victorio swallowed and fought against saying the next word. He knew he had to say it. Blue Bird knew as well. "Say it," she whispered to him through a private comm. "Say it."

He swallowed again, then said, "Go."

He watched her on radar break from the pattern, up and away, until she flew out of range and disappeared. Victorio mouthed a prayer, for he knew that she would not be in radio contact, again, until the end. *Oh, please, Yusn Life-Giver, let me hear her voice once more.*

"Fire!"

He'd given that order so many times that it felt reflexive, almost comical. But all four Devil Dancers still in Hawk Pattern let loose their first sortie of rockets and waited, waited, until the Gulo fighters were in range, and the swarm didn't even try to evade.

Twenty-four *Wasps* took rockets and exploded, causing collateral damage to other Gulo fighters nearby. That forced the swarm to divide momentarily, and the Devil Dancers took advantage, changing their pattern to Raven and flying into the divide with energy weapons on full auto. Victorio hated the cliché, but he couldn't think of anything other than fish in a barrel. The thin *Wasp* hulls just peeled away under the torrent of laser fire, and another thirty Gulo pilots found death in the void.

But now they were in a tight situation, surrounded by the *Wasp* swarm with no chance of escape. Round and round the Gulo fighters rolled, peppering Devil Dancer hulls with mini finger rockets and laser fire. The Union had met this kind of barrage many times in the past and had reinforced their shield technology and armor strength, but there was always one rocket or lucky laser strike that found a seam, and thus, Victorio ordered a new pattern.

"*Gahn* pattern!"

The *Gahn* were the mountain spirits that Yusn Life-Giver had sent to earth to teach the Apache people how to be good citizens, good human beings. The pattern itself was new, something Victorio had only experimented with in simulation. It was more erratic and less uniform than the bird patterns that his squadrons typically used, but it served a greater purpose: it allowed the Clown to move into formation with the rest of its squadron, and yet remain independent from the squadron's movements.

Where are you, Blue?

She should have attacked already, come barreling in from above with double-packed rockets boring holes in Gulo hulls. She hadn't returned, and time was slipping away. Was she already dead? No. Victorio would have known that. Their comms might not be linked at the moment, but her *Radiant* heat signature was still alive and active on his dash. She was out there. *What are you waiting for?*

Red Moon's fighter on the left of the pattern wavered under intense rocket fire. Victorio responded with a barrel roll, came up mere feet away from his number three in the pattern, locked on enemy targets, and showered them in another sortie of rockets. The explosions pushed both Victorio and Red Moon out of the pattern, and Gulo fighters pounced. Victorio fought to realign his fighter, but he kept flipping over and over from the rocket impacts. He laid on the stick, letting laser fire fly in a vortex from his wings. It helped cut a path through the thicket of *Wasps*, but there was no denying the blood-red warning blips on his dash: a half dozen Gulo finger rockets were closing fast.

I am going to die, he thought as he fought against his rolling fighter. He never once considered his own death to be the result of this affair, so fixed he was on protecting Blue Bird from her end. But it was okay. He could accept his own death, so long as she lived. Blue Bird would take over the squadron, the Devil Dancers would go on, and he would finally find that peace that he sought.

Victorio took his hand off the joystick, closed his eyes, and waited for the rockets to come.

Instead, his *Radiant* was bumped hard to stern. He opened his eyes and fought against the inertia in his cockpit, tried grabbing hold of his joystick, but couldn't find it. He straightened himself in his chair and refocused his dash radar to what had hit him.

It was Blue Bird, the Clown. She had come into the fray and had pushed his fighter out of the way. And now there she was, taking strike after strike from Gulo finger rockets, laying hard on her point-defense to minimize the damage. But Victorio could see the scorch marks and the fissures from the Gulo rocket fire burst across her hull.

"What are you doing?" Victorio screamed over his reconnected comm. "Get out of here. That's not what a Clown does. She fires from a distance, pulling the enemy away, forcing them to divide their attack. You are too close. Get away... now!"

"I cannot leave you to die," Blue Bird said, but her voice wavered, her words stuttered. Victorio laid again on his laser to cut a path to Blue Bird, but it was too late.

Another sortie of Gulo finger rockets struck Blue Bird's hull and tore her *Radiant* in half.

"You brought her to me. Why?"

It was a valid question, but Victorio was in no mood to explain. He stared at the grey-haired man who sat near a fire in the center of his wickiup, looking at Victorio with deep brown eyes and a cold expression on his face.

"I have not brought her all the way to Earth," Victorio said, "to argue, or to justify my decision, Juh. You are the best, most qualified, to save her."

Juh stood, his old knees creaking as his thin, emaciated frame wavered in place. Victorio suddenly had his doubts about this man, this *di-yin*, who many claimed was the best, most experienced Apache shaman alive. His frail body told another story.

"But you are *di-yin* as well," Juh said, trying to maintain his balance on feeble legs. "And surely you understand her wounds better than I. You are in a fight with the Gulo; not me."

Victorio fought the urge to grab the man and offer support, but he knew that would be an insult, especially in Juh's own home. He readied himself, though, if the old man should collapse. "Do you remember the story of Wind and Lightning?" Victorio asked. "Wind said to Lightning, 'See that mountain over there? If I want, I can split it in two pieces.' Lightning answered, 'I also.' They both had the power to do the same thing, but the power of the wind is not the power of the lightning.

"We have powers that are similar, Juh, but I am the lightning, and you are the wind. Blue Bird needs the wind."

Juh nodded, straightened, and found strength in his old body to walk. Victorio stepped aside and let the man out into the warm light of the afternoon sun. The light gave him strength, and Victorio soaked it in as well. He hadn't stood on solid ground and felt the real heat of a star in ages.

They walked over to Blue Bird's body, air-locked in a suspension chamber, submerged in green stabilizing gel. The machine that she was in hovered four inches off the ground and hummed lightly. Juh was almost too small to see into the observation panel that revealed Blue Bird's naked face and shoulders, but he forced himself up on tip toes and held the machine's railing with both hands. He stared at her face for a long time. Victorio gave him space and patience to assess.

"She's a lovely woman," Juh said, resting back on his heels and turning to face Victorio.

Victorio nodded. "She is a warrior, a Devil Dancer, and the love of my life." He sighed. "The gel will heal her burns in time, but the internal damage, the bleeding… Union doctors do not know if she would survive surgery and are loathed to try until she has spent adequate time in the chamber. But that it not enough. She teeters on the edge of the sand cone, Juh, staring down its vortex and into the afterlife. She is dying. She needs more than surgery."

"What do you want from me?"

Victorio stepped up to Juh and placed his hand on the old man's shoulder. He tried to smile, to put on a brave face. The tear forming in his right eye belied his positive stance. "I want you to perform a curing ceremony for her, and I and my Devil Dancers will do anything you ask to help."

Juh walked away, his head low, his shoulders slumped. He shook his head. "It would be a dangerous endeavor. She is in a very bad place, Victorio. Her wounds may be too severe. There is a sorcerer on the other side of the cone, and he calls to her. I may fail."

"I would not hold you responsible if she dies."

"Like you hold yourself?"

The question stung. Victorio tried looking away from Juh's deep, imploring eyes. *He may be feeble in body*, Victorio thought, *but not in mind*. He swallowed and bit back his tears. "I've done enough damage, Juh. Blue Bird deserves someone better than me."

A long silence fell between them. Then Juh nodded, his withered face growing grave and serious. "I will try, Victorio, as you request. The wind will try to fix what the lightning has wrought."

Her body had to be cleansed, and this required that she be removed from the suspension chamber. Life support itself was kept in place. A rebreather mask covered her mouth, so Victorio could not see her face adequately to kiss it, to wipe it clean so that he might whisper his final goodbye if the ceremony failed. She bristled with tubes, wires, as if she were cybernetic, alien. It wounded him to see her in this condition, and he did not want anyone else to see her like this either, lest they consider her weak. She had been so strong in life, so confident. To see the burns that roped her body like red lava, the oozing blood and bile from her tender skin, was too much, and he almost turned away. But Juh's steady demeanor, despite his meager frame, made Victorio stand firm.

She was transferred from the suspension chamber to a soft white blanket in the middle of a circle made from those who would witness and participate in the ceremony. Medical staff stood nearby, keeping a nervous eye on her vitals should they fall to unacceptable levels. She was placed in a sitting position facing east, her back braced against a metal half-chair that supported her weight, her head supported by pillows so that she would be as comfortable as possible. Juh was there, of course, and so too Victorio. He had also ordered the entire Devil Dancers to be in attendance, including Beta and Gamma squadrons, which did not normally participate in ceremonies, but this was different. Their second in command lay on the edge of death; they had to be here.

Several of Juh's assistants were there as well, including an old woman who had already begun to dance around a small bonfire nearby. She had on a mask. Not a *Gahn* mountain spirit mask like the ones that the Devil Dancers used in their ceremonies and the ones the squadron were wearing right now, but a more modest cover, one of long black hair fixed to the top to flow down in front of a wooden face painted in deep blue and brown earthen clays. The mouth of the mask was red and puckered as if it were blowing wind. The woman wore a bedraggled shift of splattered green and black and white paint, and danced like she was deranged, as if her muscles were involuntarily writhing in directions that they could not normally go. There was a madness in her movements, and Victorio understood them well. She was the conduit through which evil spirits would flow out from Blue Bird... if such a thing were necessary.

There were eight children positioned around the circle so that a pair, one boy and one girl, stood at each of the four cardinal positions. The boys held hoops; the girls crosses. Their faces were painted in red clay.

The Devil Dancers wore their ceremonial attire and were ready to move into the circle when required. All but Victorio. He would sit this one out. For he was Blue Bird's commanding officer, and if she passed, it was his duty to help her into the Hereafter as her commander, not as her lover, though he wished it. Now was not the time, however, for such sentiment. Now was the time for strength and courage, and he tried showing that to her in his stance, his demeanor, as he waited with everyone else for the ceremony to begin.

Juh moved slowly into the center of the circle, waving a feather fetish and humming words that Victorio understood. *Di-yin* words. Shaman words, to call forward the wind, the spirits, to come and wrap themselves around Blue Bird and to pull the evil from her body. There was much evil there, and the old medicine man was doing his best to exorcise it. He even found the strength to hop as he moved, trying to, in his fashion, match the violent motions of the woman who still danced around the bonfire. Juh stopped in front of Blue Bird, stared at her for a long moment, and then pulled dried herbal leaves from the small pouch coiled on his hip. He chanted and then sprinkled them over her head, letting them trickle down her body, to cascade through all the tubes and wires that kept her alive.

Then he pulled back, and the eight children standing in the circle came forward, still in pairs, dancing, singing, holding their hoops and crosses forward toward their patient. Victorio watched as one of the boys lifted his hoop high, shouted something Victorio couldn't quite catch, and then laid the hoop over Blue Bird's head, letting her life support tubes and wires cradle the hoop and keep it in place atop her shoulders.

The girl who stood beside the boy now moved forward and touched Blue Bird's forehead with her cross. She held it there delicately so as not to move or harass Blue Bird in her repose. And then the girl pulled the cross away quickly and twirled backward in song. The boy removed his hoop and did the same.

On and on it went, one child after the other, placing their hoops around her neck, touching their forehead with crosses. When they were done, they returned to the circle, the four cardinal directions, and waited.

And waited, and waited... and nothing. Victorio wasn't sure what would happen at this time, not overly familiar with the healing ceremony that Juh employed. It was a bit of a conglomeration of many different methods and procedures from the various Apache tribes. Victorio waited with everyone else, anticipating what might come next.

Nothing.

They performed the ceremony again. Juh called others from the circle to perform his ritual dances. Everyone worked hard to make their presence known, to call upon the spirits to bring Blue Bird to full health. Victorio waved his Devil Dancers into the fray, and they danced, like they always did before battle, to draw strength from the *Gahn* Mountain Spirits. That's what Blue

Bird needed right now: the familiarity of her squadron, of her co-pilots, and Victorio was proud of them as they danced around her, letting the brightly colored, sharp edges of their headdresses reach into the sky to call upon the Cosmo to bring their Blue Bird back.

Bring her back, Victorio cried silently into the sky. *Bring her back.*

The bonfire lady now came into the circle to add her dance to the ceremony. She worked her body hard, flinging her arms left, right, casting her head in all directions. Juh joined her, trying to work his body in the same manner, their voices high, lilting, making a direct appeal to Yusn Life-Giver. It was a beautiful tableau for Victorio, and he wanted it to go on forever. This community, this *Apache* community, worked together again to save one of its own, though Blue Bird had been gone from it for years. Gone to space to fight and, yes, to die if necessary, for the betterment of The Union. And look at her now.

In the midst of his joy, Victorio's heart sank, for nothing happened. All the singing, all the dancing around Blue Bird, and there she lay, limp and non-responsive. Even the wires attached to her, which monitored her blood pressure, her pulse, her O_2 saturation, her temperature...all the same, if not a little worse.

Victorio walked into the circle, through the chaotic dancing, his eyes fixed on Blue Bird. He knelt beside her, took her burned hand in his, raised it carefully to his lips, and kissed it. He did not fight back the tears this time. He let them flow, to drop onto her mangled skin as a light rain began to fall. Distant thunder and lightning drowned out the clamor of the ceremony. Victorio wiped his eyes dry and shouted, "Enough! Stop!"

The chanting and the dancing stopped. "Enough," he said again. "There is no use. She is gone. She's gone."

The rain grew stronger. Victorio stood and motioned for the suspension chamber to be brought forward, but Juh stepped into its path. "It isn't over yet, Captain. There is still one person here who has not danced for her health."

"I cannot," Victorio said, weeping. "I'm the reason she is in this place, why she will die. My dance would be an insult to her and to the spirits. My dance will do nothing to bring her back, do nothing to—"

"Dance!" The old man's voice rang forceful, full and alive. "Remember, Captain, you said it yourself: the wind and the lightning can break the mountain in the same way, but the power of the wind is not the power of the lightning. Blue Bird does not need the wind. She needs the lightning. Now dance... before it's too late!"

Victorio hesitated. Then Red Moon stepped up to him and placed a headdress into his hands.

Victorio danced, as the rain fell harder and the thunder and lightning cracked in the sky. He never danced so wildly and so vigorously in his life, not even when his brother Naiche died at the hands of the Gulo. He danced, and his spirit left his body and soared above him like a hawk. He could see himself dance around Blue Bird as if she were a bonfire. Her body glowed with power and he took it in, lifting his own spirit to meet hers and they danced together through the haze of rain and mist. He did not care who stood nearby, who watched. He let his body move like the old woman had done. It was an undignified display for a Captain of the Union, but he did not care. On the white blanket before him sat his Blue Bird, his life. She deserved it all.

Finally, he stopped as the rain became a torrent. The tubes and wires from Blue Bird's body echoed the sound of the rain, but held up well under the wet barrage. He knelt beside her again, took her hand like before, and waited.

Nothing.

Then Juh raised his arms into the sky, uttered a plea to Yusn Life-Giver, repeated the words twice, and then waited. Victorio turned to stare at the old man when the lightning bolt struck.

Juh fell immediately as the high voltage leeched through his body and cooked his flesh. Those gathered fell back, but Victorio held his ground, not letting Blue Bird's hand fall. The ground around them popped with residual static shock as the force of the bolt began to dissipate. But the damage was done. Juh, the old medicine man, lay dead at Victorio's feet.

Blue Bird squeezed his hand. Victorio jumped at the surprise of it. She squeezed again, and his heart leapt as he squeezed back. He reached up to her covered face. Her eyes were still shut, her body still weak from all the trauma. "I feel you, my love," he whispered to her. "I can feel you."

Victorio could see a tear well in the corner of Blue Bird's eye. He smiled, for he knew what that meant: she was alive. She was alive, and Juh was dead.

"Juh gave his life for me," Blue Bird said months later. "It was the only way to save me."

She had to stay another full month in the suspension chamber for her burns to heal, but they did heal, and so too the internal damage. All of it.

There would be many months of physical therapy, skin grafting, surgeries, but she would live.

"A *di-yin* will sometimes do that," Victorio said, "when the evil spirits are so great that they demand a sacrifice. Death does not like to be cheated."

"You helped," she said, standing up with assistance and reaching for the handles of the treadmill. "Without your dancing, without your call to the lightning, I would have died."

"Then it is my fault that he is gone."

Blue Bird smiled, shook her head. "You merely called it. You did not direct the strike. No. Juh knew what he was doing, and for that, I'm forever grateful. Someday, I wish to return to his village and thank the people properly."

"You will," Victorio said. "We all will."

Victorio gave her a small kiss on the cheek, and then turned away so that she might train. She had a long road ahead of her to return to fighting condition. The thought of it both pleased him and frightened him. Someday, and sooner than he wished, Blue Bird would be back in a cockpit, fighting alongside them all, and what would happen then? How much more damage could she possibly take? And what medicine man would be there to sacrifice himself for her next time?

I, Victorio mouthed silently to himself as he walked away, *I will be there, and I will die for her.*

SYMPATHETIC

Eric V. Hardenbrook

YMPATHY NURSE JO HOVAN PRESSED HER CHEEK INTO THE DIRT MAKING EVERY effort to 'get small', as the troopers called it. Not the first time she'd been in this position. United Global Forces were making a push to drive the enemy back and out of... she couldn't remember the name of the blasted collection of buildings they were in this week. She was tired. It wasn't the running or the perpetual adrenaline surges and crashes; those she would have been fine with. It was the weight of her work. It tugged at her, dragging slowly at her wrists, her ankles, her lower back. On a bad day, she stooped as much as a woman twice her age. Today looked to be a bad day.

Jo glanced back at Nurse-In-Training Wilson. The trainee squirmed and wiggled like a worm caught out on the sidewalk after the rain dried up. Clearly, she'd never been in combat before. It was Jo's job to get her in shape to take over a Sympathy Nurse post in another triad.

"NIT Wilson!" Jo shouted at her and got no reaction. "April!" she shouted again. That got through. Wilson raised her head, her eyes wide and panicked.

"When the shooting slows down, we move. Do you hear me, Wilson?" Jo turned her head back toward the line of troops ahead of them, laying in the dirt behind a barricade of burned out vehicles. The troopers seemed to have fared well so far. She ducked her head down instinctively as shots hit near her. The impacts had an almost musical quality to them if you listened long enough. The Liberty Earth forces had developed high-velocity weapons that had been nicknamed needle guns. Mini, rifle-mounted rail-gun-type weapons with slender metal rounds that looked like needles. Those needles blasting against her barricade sounded a little like a rainstick she'd seen in a museum once.

As the barrage slowed Trio Commander Felix Harris shouted for his troops to move forward. Harris was an angry man. Jo should know. She was his assigned Sympathy Nurse. As part of his direct support, she spent far more time around him than she really wanted. Jo would have preferred to stick around the Trios and work more directly with her subordinates. Unfortunately, her talent was rare enough that she couldn't avoid the position she was in. Rapid advancement was far too easy when those above you are continually killed in the fighting.

"Wilson, follow me," Jo said as she got to her hands and knees, crawling forward to see if anyone had been hit when the shooting started. She glanced back to see Wilson still trying to look smaller and stay down.

"Hey! Let's move, Nurse Wilson! There's work to be done!" Jo resisted the urge to swear. The single, worst part of her entire military career was taking scared kids like April who had talent but no experience and forcing them to take a hard look at the reality of the front lines. Far too many were too gentle, overly sympathetic, and just couldn't handle what getting shot did to people. They would crack, break, or shut down and become a liability in the field.

"If she won't move, leave her!" Harris was almost standing at this point. His features were twisted and ugly as he looked down through the dust at where Wilson lay. "You've got work to do."

Jo scrambled backward, latched onto Wilson's medic harness and dragged her a couple of steps. Pulling her from what she felt had been a 'hiding place' seemed to do the trick. She began to move along in a waddling run, keeping her head down. They could stand up again once they reached an intact building a few yards beyond the edge of the barricade. Triple Lead Sergeant Washington was there. Jo knew him as Reggie. He was normally a quiet reserved man, but on days like today, he could shout commands with the best. She admired his control.

"Jo." Reggie nodded in her direction. "You doing okay so far today?"

"Another pleasant stroll down main street... where are we again?" Jo replied.

Reggie chuckled and then pointed down the next alley. "I've got a trio in the lobby, one sneaking down the alley, and one trying to find a way around to the left, in case we need it."

"Are you in touch with...?" An explosion rocked the building they were sheltering behind, cutting off her question. Jo never got to finish. Dirt, concrete chunks, and scraps of metal showered down around them. Wilson dove screaming onto the sidewalk and huddled next to the wall. As soon as the first rumble stopped another began. Rather than dragging Wilson away, as the shelling continued, Jo joined her on the ground next to the building. She looked up for Reggie. Reggie lay motionless in the open. That was never a good sign.

Jo rapped Wilson on the helmet. "Listen to me! What is the worst pain? Is it the acute but anticipated surgical cut, the lingering repair from an unexpected injury, or is it the fear of either of those?" Wilson's eyes remained wide, but they were at least focused on Jo now. There was a reason training was mostly repetition. Do the same thing over and over again until you don't have to think about it. That way when things went to hell, you could still function. Repetition would get through to her. Jo started again.

"Remember your training! What do we do?" Jo moved toward Reggie's still form, drawing Wilson with her. "Repeat the explanation, NIT Wilson! What do we say to those who don't know us?"

Instead of responding, Wilson flinched at the continuing rain of debris. The shelling was going on far too long. The rain of debris was distracting.

"Answer!"

Wilson began to speak. Jo didn't hear the greeting portion but as Wilson went through her trained response she started to relax. Her motions grew steadier as they crawled up to Reggie's unmoving form. "Members of the Sympathy Corps can, by way of touching the skin of another, slide into their senses and feel the pain the way the person experiencing it does. We feel what you feel. We know what you mean when you think, '*Hmm, something is causing my leg to drag...*' We learn that pain. We absorb that pain and we can then direct doctors, surgeons, and specialists to the best possible treatment. We are like a doctor or a field surgeon, but we do not practice in the same way. Please let us help you. We can take some of the pain away."

As they came up on Reggie, Jo noticed blood dripping from one of the downed sergeant's nostrils. She saw no other evidence of injury but his helmet was off-kilter, the chin strap clearly loose and not broken. Reggie hadn't buckled his chin strap. No matter how many times she saw that she would never understand. Such a simple thing as buckling a strap meant the difference between a headache and severe trauma.

Wilson reached up and laid a hand on Reggie's cheek. She flinched as she got the first dose of whatever had knocked the sergeant to the ground. Slowly, she slid her fingers around to the back of his head and lifted it gently. Reggie's eyes fluttered and he looked around him.

Jo smiled as she pulled on her trainee's sleeve. "Well done, Nurse Wilson." With contact broken, Wilson startled and reached up as blood trickled from her nose. "Stuff some gauze up there. Remember to find the place in your self to store that pain away. Keep yourself from the pain while you work. We'll work on letting it all go later." Jo turned to the patient. "You, Sergeant, need to buckle your chin strap. Are you good to go?"

Sergeant Washington grimaced and shook his head slightly as if still expecting it to hurt. He glanced around him and then focused on the nurses. "Thank you, Trainee Wilson. Good to go, Nurse Hovan." He reached up and did as she suggested, then clicked his helmet mic. "Trios, report."

The three of them scrambled back to the shelter of the wall as Sergeant Washington got the sitrep from his teams. While they were hunkered down, the shelling slacked off and eventually stopped. "Wilson," Jo ducked her head to make eye contact with the trainee. "How are you doing?"

Wilson's head came up slowly. "My head hurts."

Jo nodded.

"That's part of the deal. Remember your training. How is Reggie?" This was not the way to gather information about wounded soldiers. Jo diverged from the standard reporting protocol, trying to be gentle with her charge, just as she would with anyone else injured on the battlefield.

"He..." Wilson started, then hesitated. "His head will be fine but he's got at least three other wounds that he's been nursing along on his own."

That did not surprise Jo at all. Soldiers didn't make it to Triple Lead Sergeant without being tough as nails. He was in charge of three Trios, or ninety-nine people. Each of his Trio Sergeants, controlling teams of thirty-three each, were just as tough. She hoped they had all managed to find shelter when the shelling began.

"Sergeant Washington, where are your trios?" Commander Harris yelled as he ran up to their position. "I have word that the L.E. troops are surging."

Little chunks of wall ripped apart over their heads moments before the sound of the gunfire reached them. Dust rained down from above. Those weren't needles! Not with that kind of structural damage. Apparently, the rumors that the Liberty Earthers were also using old-fashioned lead throwers were true. Nobody knew for certain what other weapons they'd dug up to use against the U.G.F., but the possibilities made Jo cringe.

Commander Harris didn't wait for his Triple Lead to answer him. He keyed his mic and started, "Trios, this is Harris. Bring your teams to position beta. Bring them in and get them in this building. We need to shelter!"

"NO!"

Reggie was a veteran of city warfare. Jo had served with his unit a long time as a Sympathy Nurse. She'd seen enough to know that he shouldn't be ignored.

"Sergeant Washington, you will gather the heavy gunners and put them on the high corners," Harris rolled on ignoring his primary advisor. He keyed his mic again. "Lee, Johnson, Huff, let's move. Get your people over here."

Another volley shredded the corner near Harris and he slid closer to the ground. Jo noticed that he stayed on the opposite side of Reggie from both herself and her trainee. More rounds ripped past and now some of the other team members were pulling back up the alley trying to keep some kind of cover and failing. She saw at least three soldiers being dragged backward rather than running with the others.

"Lee, hold your position behind the barrier there to your right." Reggie keyed his mic as he scrambled to see where the others were.

"Sergeant Washington, I don't want them there, I want them in this building with us!" Harris yelled again.

Reggie ignored Harris. "Huff, where are you? Report."

Jo spied soldiers behind and off to her right but didn't get a good look at them. Moving on pure instinct, she grabbed both the sergeant and Wilson and flopped flat to the ground. More shots ripped across the building, shattering their hiding spot. Harris jerked and fell to the ground. At least her trainee wasn't screaming again.

"Johnson, fall back to my position. We are taking fire and need support!" Reggie keyed again from the prone position. He rolled over and dragged his rifle into a firing position. He was still talking as he sighted in and fired.

Jo turned and crawled back toward Harris, leaving the maneuvers to Reggie. The commander was bleeding, but he was sitting up and working on his own care. Harris wasn't supposed to perform medical treatments, but he had produced a small med-pack and had already pulled out a shot stick. The palm-sized tube, a combination of anesthetic and sealant, wasn't supposed to be used by anyone except trained medical personnel. Properly administered, it would stabilize a wound until better medical facilities were available. Properly being the operative word.

Jo grimaced. At one time, shot sticks had been issued with each trooper's equipment. Due to a variety of misuses, they had been discontinued. The average troop didn't know enough about a wound that would require medical treatment at that level to decide when to use it. They would panic and use them on lesser wounds and run out of shots before all the wounds that required them had been seen to. Others didn't care. They used them, injured or not, just to get high. No matter how advanced the equipment there would always be some enterprising soul that would figure out how to take it apart. She had to wonder where Harris had gotten his.

"Commander Harris, please allow me to help you." Jo started to reach for him.

"You keep your hands to yourself, Hovan!" Palpable anger rolled from Harris. "I know you're backing the sergeant in his attempt at mutiny!" His eyes rolled as he stuck the shot into his wounded shoulder.

"Commander, I assure you..."

"I said BACK OFF!" Harris brought his sidearm up.

Jo raised her hands in surrender. She glanced back at the others. Wilson had gone back to cowering. Reggie gestured to one of his troops, attempting to direct him visually rather than verbally. Harris noticed as well.

"Sergeant Washington, you will direct all the remaining troops here to position beta and instruct them to take position INSIDE this building and that's an order!" Harris crouched and shuffled through the remains of a nearby door frame.

Washington glanced back at her and Jo shook her head slightly in the negative but then shrugged her shoulders. She moved toward her trainee and guided her inside the building. Washington followed.

"Sir, we can't all cluster here in one building. The L.E. forces will just bomb our location and we'll be done. We *have* to stay mobile and spread out." As Reggie spoke Trio Leader Johnson came jogging into the building. His troops moved in behind him looking for windows to aim out of. Much to their credit, they all moved with efficiency. They might not like or understand their orders but they clearly followed them.

"Johnson! It's about time you got here!" Harris continued to yell. "Where the hell is Lee?"

"She's pinned down two blocks from here, sir." Johnson seemed caught off guard by the commander's question. "You should have her on tactical..."

"I know that!" Harris hollered. "I want to hear it from my people, not tools! Get your soldiers upstairs so we can rain fire down on anybody coming at us."

Johnson paled. "Yes, sir." was all he said and dashed back to his troops.

"Where the hell is Huff?" Harris spun around. "Washington, get some more men over to this back corner in case the Earthers try to sneak up on us!" As Harris turned back toward the troops filtering in from the forward side of the building Jo spotted another shot tube in his hand. Before she could say something he jabbed himself in the thigh. She couldn't see any wound there, just a thin spot in the uniform pants behind the side cargo pocket. She had a bad feeling about this.

"Sergeant Washington," Jo said remaining formal. "Have either Trio Leader Lee or Huff checked in?"

Reggie looked harried as he turned back to her. "Lee can't break out. No word from Huff at all."

"I think we're going to need at least one of them, along with Johnson, as soon as you can get them here." Jo turned and strode toward Trainee Wilson. "I'm going to assist Nurse Wilson for a moment. Please inform me as soon as we have two of your trio leaders here." Jo tilted her head in her best impersonation of looking over her glasses. Washington's eyes narrowed as he seemed to realize something was up but had enough sense not to ask. He just nodded.

"Nurse Wilson, please come with me for a moment." Jo strode toward the sturdiest looking wall she could find. It looked like some kind of building support. She hoped she would be in time.

"I'm sorry, Nurse Hovan. Have I done something wrong?" Wilson looked scared and pale. She seemed to have come to some level of personal equilibrium. That was good because things were going to get a lot worse before they got better.

"You're doing just fine, April." Jo reached out and put her hand on Wilson's shoulder. "The first actual combat action is one of the most difficult times in our training. There is so much going on and so much pain swirling around, it can be very overwhelming." Jo gestured toward the men and women at the front of the building. "These troopers are going to need more of your help. Remember your training. You did excellent work bringing Reggie up quickly, but don't spend too much of yourself on any one patient. Remember to move and store. Don't keep the trauma, box it up. There will be a great deal of need. If a medkit will do the job, use it."

"Yes, ma'am."

"I might need to do something here that wasn't in your training. Whatever happens, understand that you must maintain your demeanor and stay steady on for the troopers. Do you understand?" Jo had just finished speaking when something large hit the building, shaking the walls.

"I understand," Wilson's voice faltered.

"You stay solid and render aid to any you can. You will not be a trainee after today." Jo did her best to smile. She shuffled back to the command group just as Trio Leader Huff stumbled through a side doorway with one of her troopers helping her along. Her helmet was scorched on one side and her communications equipment was nowhere to be seen. Neither was her communications man. One side of her uniform had patchy burn marks mixed with bare spots where blistered skin showed through.

"Commander Harris, Trio Leader Huff reporting."

Harris spun on her. "Where have you been? Get your troops around this side and start returning fire!" He didn't even glance at her long enough to recognize the burns.

Jo sidled around one of the troops and moved in beside Huff. She gently placed a hand on the same shoulder that was giving her support. "Olivia, would you like me to help you?" Jo held her other hand just off from touching exposed skin.

"Thank you, Nurse Hovan." Huff looked as if she might cry with relief.

"Hold tight, dear." Jo grabbed her patient's exposed hand and reached her other hand up to hold the back of Olivia's head. Jo closed her eyes. She slid into darkness. She mentally spun and flipped and then she was looking hazily back at herself. She tilted her head to one side but couldn't hear anything but ringing from one ear. She slid and flowed away from sight and down toward the chest, the arms, the ribs, along the sides and over the hips. She slid down the legs and all the way out to the toes. She was burned. She was bruised. She wasn't sure if the one knee was attached with mangled tendons or just too sore and swollen to function. She'd need to sort that out later. She steadied herself then began to gather. She pulled a little of the swelling. She pulled a little heat from the burns. She pulled some of the ringing away from the ear and the building pressure from behind the eyes. There was always a little bit of a headache lurking from stress and dehydration. Some of the worst things seemed better if you didn't have that little bit of pain. She swirled and gathered and then slid back toward herself. She dragged the pain and the hurt she had gathered along with her. She pushed and shoved and then yanked all that she could back to herself. She mentally swam and flipped once more, staggering slightly. She opened her eyes and let her hands fall away.

Jo had learned over many sessions like this that she needed to stay steady on her feet. She swayed ever so slightly and then stopped moving.

She watched as Huff's eyes cleared and she stood up straighter and taller, her trooper's support no longer needed.

Huff smiled. "Thank you!"

"Well, now that the hugging and squeezing part is done, there's still shooting to do!" Harris's eyes bored into Jo's. She didn't flinch. Her focus was on managing the damage that she had soaked up from Huff, packing it away into little boxes deep inside herself that she used to store pain. She glanced down at Harris's hands. He cupped something in his right hand. She expected she knew what but couldn't see it clearly. She needed to be certain. She motioned to get her trainee in close.

"Wilson," Jo whispered. "Step up to Harris and ask him if you can give him aid. When you're done be sure to salute him."

Wilson looked startled. "We're not supposed to salute in the field..."

"I know that," Jo whispered again. "We're doing a reflex test." She nudged Wilson in the commander's direction.

Wilson did as she was told. She walked up and got directly into the commander's line of sight. "Commander, may I render you aid?"

"What the hell are you doing? Get back to whatever you're supposed to be doing! Can't you see that I'm busy here?" Harris leaned close enough that Jo almost felt sorry for having put Wilson into the spittle zone.

Just as instructed, Wilson fired up a sharp salute. On reflex, Harris brought his right arm up as if he was going to salute. He stopped abruptly with a scowl, but it was enough. Jo clearly saw the tube in the commander's hand. The tube was fresh and used. While Harris was distracted yelling and berating Wilson for trying to get him killed by saluting him in the field, Jo moved forward. She stepped between the trio leaders, past Reggie and laid a hand on the back Harris's bare neck. She closed her eyes and her essence surged forward into Harris catching him off guard. He jerked taut, clearly not expecting her to swoop in from the side. *Silly*, she thought, *a good commander would have considered the risk of being outflanked.* It was only then that he began to resist. He tried desperately to push or pull or do something other than just stand there stunned, but Jo was no trainee. She'd entered directly at the spine, the control network of his body. While she held him immobile, she whirled and pushed as she had with Huff. She began to reach for his pain but encountered only numbness. Suddenly that haze began to break as Harris's emotions surged, overpowering the massive amount of chemicals he'd dumped into his body. She watched as his fear transformed into a surging red tide of deep, deep anger coming right at her.

Her spirit stood steady, unflinching. Jo knew anger as well as she knew all the assorted horrors that came along with war. She'd seen troopers without legs, without arms, worst of all without hope. She still held within her fresh shards of the pain, suffering, anguish, and loss gathered from every soldier she had ever aided. She retained so many of these remnants from her years in service she was almost out of boxes to store them all in.

His anger was like nothing compared to her own! She risked her life to care for these men. She took their pain into herself to heal these troops, only to have this one man risk them all on a bad strategy driven by fear and too many numb shots. He was not fit to command. He endangered all of his troops and the mission.

She was required to act. So she did. She gave back.

Jo envisioned herself grabbing various boxes. Small ones, large ones, dark and battered boxes... She released the locks and let the lids fall open. Without holding back, she emptied every box into Harris's soul until all either of them felt was agony and anguish. She was used to it. Harris was not. The numbness he'd dosed himself with shattered. The red swell of his anger broke apart under the fury of this onslaught. And still, she dumped more. She reached deeper into herself than she had in a very long time. Then she felt what she was doing. How close Harris was to breaking. Her shame swamped the pain. She stopped herself before she unleashed total devastation upon him. She wasn't here to be judge or jury. She was here to help. Drawing her essence back, she released his neck and opened her eyes.

Harris shook where he stood. His eyes rolled back in his head and foam flecked the edges of his mouth. As soon as Jo took her hand away he collapsed to the floor, his body wracked with spasms.

Despite the yelling and shooting in the background the little command group stood silently staring at Jo. She ignored them, needing to finish what she had started. First, she leaned down and pried open the commander's hand. Then she held up the empty shot stick. She pulled three other empty tubes from the commander's side cargo pouch. Standing, she held the empty tubes out toward the others, while she addressed the man on the ground at her feet.

"Commander Harris, you have jeopardized your troops and are unfit for command. You are relieved." She closed her hand around the empty shot sticks and tucked them into her own cargo pocket. "Triple Sergeant Washington, please take command of the triad and get us the hell out of here."

Reggie stood for just a moment and stared at her. They all did.

Though weary to the bottom of her soul, Jo stood straighter than she had in a long time. She felt lighter, too, as she addressed the command group.

"The Sympathetic Nurse Core does *not* take the Hippocratic oath," she told them, her voice firm and steady. "We make no vow to do no harm. Our duty is to get our troopers healed and ensure as many of them make it home as possible, to the best of our abilities... no matter what that takes. The empathy we use to take away your pain and find your injuries also works in reverse. We can give it all back." She glanced down at Harris. He was still spasming. The rest of the group was still stunned. "I do not wish harm on anyone. As soon as we are clear, please restrain him so I can withdraw what I have given him. Let's get our troopers home."

That seemed to be the signal they were waiting for. Washington took control. Huff raced back to her group faster than anyone who had suffered her injuries had a right to. Wilson just stood and stared.

"Remember this, Nurse Wilson. We are responsible for more than just the physical health of the troops we are with. We have a responsibility to them mentally as well. War triggers many different responses from people. Our job is to lessen the pain and heal what we can. That can be physical or mental. Sometimes that means it needs to hurt more before it gets better. Let's go see who else we can help."

NO MAN LEFT BEHIND

an Alliance Archives Adventure

Danielle Ackley-McPhail

ERGEANT JUSTIN KROUGLIAK OF THE 428TH RECON WOKE WITH A START, confused as someone delivered a powerful kick to the cot he lay on. If not for the pong of drying blood surrounding him, he would have expected he was late for PT or duty. He opened his eyes and struggled to sit up. The first thing he noticed was a Dominion officer staring down at him, his icy blue eyes brimming with hatred. (The man wore no rank, but the uniform and posture were unmistakable.) The second thing Justin noticed was that his own uniform was covered in blood—mostly, from what he could tell, someone else's. The third thing he noticed— and the most troubling—was that his radio-frequency tags were missing from around his neck.

Justin fell back on the cot and just stared up at the enemy, saying nothing.

The officer pivoted and walked out, calling back to two soldiers Justin hadn't noticed until now, "Bring him."

He didn't resist, but he didn't exactly cooperate, as they came to either side of the cot, gripped him by his upper arms, and hauled him to his feet. Justin's head swam and if not for their rough hold on him he would have fallen. Maybe more of the blood was his than he'd thought. He struggled to regain his balance as they marched him from the cell, having no doubt they would drag him otherwise. They led him outside and across a barren compound to a Quonset hut that seemed to serve as temporary command of the makeshift camp. Though the bright sunlight caused his head to pound violently, Justin forced his eyes to stay open, doing his best to scan the terrain without seeming to. Not that the grunts hauling him around were paying any attention. Other than the blockhouse they'd held him in and the hut, there were no permanent structures. There were, however, plenty of soldiers bivouacked beneath the towering old-growth trees. He nearly slumped in relief. Not at the soldiers, but at the landscape. It appeared they were still on Demeter. One point in his favor, anyway. If he could just disappear up into the canopy...

Memories began to surface. He and the 428th had been securing a new sector. Coop was running Treybot, their bomb-detection robot, with the rest of the unit following behind, dealing with any explosive ordnance discovered. As they cleared the treeline, they encountered a company of Alliance infantry pinned down by the enemy. The last thing he remembered...well, that would be the last thing he remembered.

They must have joined the fight and, clearly, it hadn't gone in their favor...or at least not in his. He had to assume some soldier had stripped him of his RF tags when they'd snatched him from the battlefield. The absence of their slight mass resting against his chest weighed heavy on him. With those tags and the right codes, the enemy could learn pretty much anything about him. Nothing critical, just his personal details. Given time they could learn more if they had resources inside Alliance territory. But nothing right now. Nothing that would endanger his unit.

How had they faired...? He shut down that line of thought fast. He couldn't think about Coop and the others. They were either out there or they weren't. He chose to believe they were, but he couldn't depend on it and worrying would only mess with his head. With deep, centering breaths, he shut down his emotions and focused on the shit-basket he was currently in now...and how to get out of it.

The guards let him trip over the doorframe he wasn't paying attention to. Justin kept his expression carefully neutral and picked himself back up, standing at attention (out of habit) and seemingly staring at nothing as he assessed the room: A desk, a single chair (occupied by the officer from earlier), and nothing else. No help there. The guards remained outside, but a medic filed in and started laying out his kit on the desk: bandages, tear-tape, alcohol swabs, liquid sutures, a white transdermal pain patch. That's it, nothing usable there—though the pain patch was a surprise. They must have plans if they were wasting that on him.

"If you would sit on the edge of the desk," the medic instructed him, his tone businesslike and impersonal. Without hesitation, Justin complied. He didn't know why they wanted to patch him up, but he sure as hell wasn't going to miss the opportunity to improve his chances of getting free. Justin watched closely as the guy treated his wounds. He frowned.

There was a ring on the medic's finger. A simple, silver-tone band. Flat and kind of thick. A wedding band? That's what it looked like. Most soldiers—on either side—abstained from such open signs of attachment. Why hand the enemy a tool to use against you? Anything was a source of intel during wartime. Of course, he could be conscripted. Justin kind of envied the guy, his own finger never felt so bare as it did now. A fleeting image of his wife Kelly rose in his memory, wearing her trademark smirk and her flight gear.

Again he shut down his emotions, hard.

Justin watched closely as the guy treated his wounds. His motions were quick and confident, but relaxed, as if he was just another patient, not an enemy soldier. The guy was good. Efficient. Not too rough, though there was a time or two before the pain patch kicked in where Justin couldn't help but hiss. When the medic was done he rested his hand on Justin's wrist, the cool metal of the ring pressed against his skin. Justin started to tense and pull away, feeling a faint prick as the medic tightened his hold.

Something wasn't right. Justin's breath came faster as his body tingled. Every impulse shouted at him to get clear, to break the medic's grip. By then, of course, it was too late. He didn't know what they'd done but his blood began to burn and every muscle in his body went stiff and unresponsive. If he could have, he would have screamed. All he managed was a grimace and he'd had to fight to manage that. A memory surfaced from his childhood of his mother warning him not to make faces: *If you're not careful, it will freeze that way.*

What do you know? Justin thought. *Mom was right.* Silently, he laughed, but even in his mind there was an edge to it. He knew when he was fucked.

The medic quickly stepped back, his hands falling to his side. Justin met his gaze and saw regret reflected back before the man looked away. With haste, the medic packed up his kit and left. For untold agonizing moments, Justin and his captor sat in silence. He had no idea how long, but his need to scream in rage increased exponentially. His grimace slowly shifted into a snarl as the muscles of his face relaxed. Or fell back under his control, at least.

"If we wanted to kill you," the officer said in a cold matter-of-fact tone, "we could have done so on the battlefield, Sergeant Krougliak. But let's just say we're reserving that option for now."

He pulled open one of the desk drawers and tossed a new uniform in Justin's direction. Then he took something else out. Justin couldn't move his head to see what it was but then he didn't have to. The officer stood and walked around the desk to stand in front of him. In his one hand were Justin's name tape, rank marker, and unit patch. In the other was a circular object.

"Your demolition skills are useful to me," the officer said as he held up the patches, "but I am not a fool." He then held up the object, a metal band much like the ring the medic had worn, only larger. Bracelet-sized, large enough to fit a man. Knowing what was coming, Justin struggled to move. His jaw clenched and his fingers twitched, but the rest of his body betrayed him as the Dominion officer secured the manacle snug around Justin's wrist. He had regained enough sensation to feel the tiny pinpoints just touching his skin. "You've had a small taste of the neurotoxin from Corpsman Pierce's ring...just enough to appreciate the severity of its effects. This..." The officer tapped the metal band. "This will kill you outright; don't give me a reason to activate it.

"I'm through losing men and territory because of Allied soldiers. You work for me now, Sergeant. Krougliak...or for your life...however you care to think of it. Once you can move, change. My men will escort you back to your new quarters."

The medic showed up the next morning before dawn to change Justin's bandages. He looked like he wanted to say something, but all he murmured was, "I am Anatoliy, I did not enlist."

The man had a faint Czech accent that reminded Justin of *Děda*... his grandpa. Taking a calculated risk, he responded *"Ano,"* 'yes' in the man's language. Anatoliy's eyes widened, but he said nothing more, his shoulders tense. As he worked he seemed almost poised to speak, then his eyes would dart toward the door and his lips would press thin again. Justin remained patient and cooperative. What choice did he have?

Just before he left, the medic seemed to make up his mind. He leaned in close and, barely moving his lips, he whispered in Czech, "The lieutenant, he lost his younger brother to an Allied mine. It would not take much to convince him to set that off." Anatoliy dipped his head toward the manacle, though there really was no need. Justin nodded as the man hurried from his cell.

Lieutenant, huh? Justin filed the information away. None of the Dominion soldiers wore any markings he could identify. Safer in a war zone, he supposed, but not very convenient for him. And that is when it hit him. *He* no longer wore identifying marks and his RF tags were gone. As far as the Alliance was concerned he was another faceless Dominion soldier.

And Sergeant Justin Krougliak was dead.

Which meant he was on his own.

The rest of Justin's day, along with the next and who knew how many more after that, disappeared into a fog of exhaustion as he went from one shit job to another around the camp. They worked him hard and long and watched him closely. For everything from shitting to shaving to slaving, some Dominion grunt was his shadow. The only time there wasn't someone standing over him was when he slept and even then he was sure someone stood outside the door.

So far he hadn't done a thing with his demolition skills but the lieutenant's words ricocheted around Justin's thoughts any time the fog cleared. What would he be asked to do against his own forces? Against innocent civilians caught between their two armies? And how could he avoid it? The only way he could think of was to refuse and take his poison. After all, the Alliance already thought he was dead...which meant Kelly had been informed he was dead. What did his life matter if he couldn't get back to her?

He clenched his teeth and mentally kicked his own ass. Rising from his bunk he ignored the throb of his injuries—joined by a few new ones—and dropped to the floor in a set of punishing pushups, gritting through the pain. The transdermal patch had long ago lost its effectiveness and had not been replaced. It had done its job, snare to their trap. Fucking thing should have set off a red flag. Like the Dominion ever did anything benevolent toward an Allied soldier. On each upward stroke of the pushup, Justin held the position for a count of five before lowering down and holding for another count of five. His muscles screamed but did their job, just like he would, if not in the way the Dominion expected. His wife was a bad-ass fighter pilot, one of AeroCom's legendary Morrigans, she would kick his ass herself if she could hear his thoughts, if she even suspected he'd given up hope of getting back to her.

When his body began to quiver, Justin lowered himself to the cool concrete of the floor. It felt good but what he needed now was some sleep.

Without rest, he would be useless to react when his opportunity presented itself. Rest was the difference between life and death on the battlefield. He would get back to his wife. He climbed to his feet and lay down on the cot, barely more comfortable than the floor had been. No matter what the Dominion put him through, he planned to be ready to take the fight to the enemy.

Within moments he drifted off as any seasoned soldier could, no matter the conditions.

Justin came awake instantly as the door to his cell slammed open. He leapt from his cot just moments before the guard flipped it over, nearly crashing it into his legs. He held himself very still, not showing any aggression, but more than ready to evade, for whatever good it would do him. From the open doorway, where he stood limned in moonlight, the lieutenant spoke, "Time to earn that air you're breathing, Sergeant. Krougliak." The tone of his voice was akin to a death knell. Something happened. Something bad. And Justin expected he wasn't the only one going to pay for it.

One of the guards thrust a helmet and basic tactical gear at him. They waited as he suited up, then marched him from the blockhouse what had to be only hours since he'd lain down to sleep. He followed them to the command hut, bypassing the entrance to the lieutenant's office and circling around to the back side where an open door led to a munitions bunker. Three men waited inside in full oobleck—or liquid Kevlar—body armor with night-vision gear perched on their helmets. Four demolition kits sat at their feet.

"Meet your new team. You don't need to know anyone's name," the officer said, before pausing and pointing at the massive soldier in the middle. "Well, except for his. We're calling him 'Kill Switch' for now."

Justin hardly heard the words, his eyes locked on those kits. Knowing they meant only one thing. Then what the lieutenant said sank in and Justin's gaze lifted to the man before him, center of the pack. He kept his expression neutral and hooded his eyes. The significance of the man's handle wasn't lost on Justin, even without the soldier's evil leer. Kill Switch lifted his hand in a mocking salute, baring a metal band on his wrist similar to Justin's, only one with a clear pressure switch on the exterior.

One of Justin's guards gave him a shove toward the men. Without a word, he shouldered one of the kits and waited for the others to do the same. All the while, his mind worked furiously to find a way out of this circle of hell.

As the four-man unit headed for the forest past the soldiers' tents, a form rose from the nearest one. The Dominion soldiers went on alert, but relaxed as the man spoke with Anatoliy's soft tones, "Wait, allow me to check his injuries before you go, so he does not slow you down."

Kill Switch's eyes narrowed until the whites were but a sliver as he looked from the medic to Justin and back again. He gave an abrupt nod. The medic ducked back into his tent and came out with his kit, quickly and efficiently going about his task before the soldiers could change their mind. Old bandages came off and the wounds were cleaned before new ones went on. While he worked he avoided Justin's eyes but kept up a steady murmur of Czech words too low for anyone beyond their immediate sphere to pick up. "This is all I can do for you now..." the medic said as slid a length of tempered steel into Justin's boot under the cover of darkness. Then he pressed a clear transdermal patch on Justin's wrist right above the manacle. Justin snarled and started to draw back as the skin grew warm and began to tingle in an almost familiar way, but not quite. Anatoliy risked looking up for a fleeting moment and just barely shook his head. "It is a ruse," he said, his fingers settled on the patch and trailed over the metal band as he drew away. "Remember...it is a ruse." And then the man was gone before the soldiers could order him away.

Justin watched the medic duck back into his tent. Dare he trust him? This wasn't the first time Anatoliy had warned him, but his words conflicted, then from now. Had he truly understood the man's hushed whispers? Which was the truth? Justin was still conflicted when Kill Switch grabbed him roughly by the arm and yanked him into motion. That decided him. There was only one group these ordnance packs could be intended for and Justin would be damned before he helped make that happen. Either Anatoliy told the truth or Justin would die. Either way, he was out of here.

As they made their way through 'undergrowth' taller than most Terran forests, Justin stumbled with the grace of a lumbering bear while the others moved like jaguars through the grass. Of course, they wore night-vision goggles. He had to feel his way in the dark. After about an hour's march, they cleared the treeline and paused at the edge of a war-torn field.

At this distance, in the faint moonlight, it was difficult to tell the terrain from the bodies.

Bile crept up Justin's throat. His jaw and every other muscle clenched. This wasn't the battle he'd been taken in. Too much time had passed. But it might well have been. So many lives sacrificed to the Dominion invasion. And they had the gall to blame the Alliance for their losses.

A hand reached out and yanked Justin down into a huddle.

Kill Switch glared at him. The promise in his expression one of death. The soldier's gaze then traveled to each of his men, clearly making sure all of them paid attention as he opened his kit and extracted the contents.

"Deploy the hydras in the open spaces where the enemy forces are likely to transit. The claymores place beneath the bodies." Here his gaze locked back on Justin, his expression one of venomous satisfaction. "Allied wounded first; carcasses second. Make them pay in blood and body parts."

Outwardly, Justin refused to react. Inside, his blood boiled and all he could picture was plunging the knife hidden in his boot deep in the man's eye socket.

These weren't just random Allied forces that would fall to the Dominion traps. Recon would be sent in first to clear the field for the medics. Very likely Justin's own unit, the 428th. What if they missed one of Kill Switch's little surprises? There was a reason the Dominion forces were called Demons by the Allied troupes. This was a new low even for them.

The unit leader repacked his kit with efficiency, then turned and motioned each of his men in a different direction, all but Justin. The two of them watched as they scurried off to wreak their havoc. Kill Switch then turned and shoved Justin ahead of him into the unassigned zone.

"You're with me, sunshine."

Justin tamped down his rage. He scanned the field, calculating the distance between the other men and their location. Then their location and the treeline. Could he make it? His fingers itched to grip Anatoliy's blade, but the odds were not yet in his favor. He had to wait until the others had begun their reprehensible efforts.

Kill Switch yanked him to a stop beside a crumpled mount in an Allied uniform. Justin looked down into a face way too young to be bathed in blood and battle grime. The kid's eyes fluttered briefly as his head rolled fitfully from side to side, but he didn't wake.

"Get cracking, you know what to do," Kill Switch ordered.

Sonofabitch! Justin's right hand flexed. That kid's momma didn't deserve to receive a letter from his CO. Not like this. Not ever. But definitely not like this. When Kill Switch shoved him to the ground Justin reached into his boot and pivoted, bringing his arm up in a single, fluid motion only to have the Dominion soldier block with a solid grip to Justin's wrist.

Rather than resist, Justin pushed into the hold, bearing the Demon to the ground. Any moment he expected a bullet to the brain as they grappled, but if the other soldiers noticed they didn't interfere. He twisted his arm and tried to use his momentum to drive the blade into his opponent, but Kill Switch rolled and thrust Justin away as they both scrambled to their feet.

Silently they circled one another, Justin trying not to trample the wounded kid, but Kill Switch didn't bother. Justin lunged and shoved the Dominion soldier away, reversing his thrust to swipe with his blade. The tip of his knife scraped over the liquid Kevlar and just nicked the edge of the soldier's wrist, drawing a single drop of blood.

Kill Switch bared his teeth and continued to circle, his eyes taking on an unholy gleam. The metal bands at each of their wrists glowed faintly in the twilight but the soldier didn't reach for his. Instead, he drew his own blade. For some reason, the man wanted this fight. He wanted it bad. And he wanted it personal.

Justin met his steady gaze and that is when it clicked. Icy blue eyes stared back at him brimming with both rage and hatred. Then he remembered what Anatoliy had told him way back that second day of captivity: *The lieutenant, he lost his younger brother to an Allied mine.*

Well...this guy was clearly related. But Justin had to wonder who they lost this time because this was a whole other level of escalation.

He heard a sound. The other soldiers converging? Or something closer? Justin dare not take his attention away from Kill Switch long enough to figure it out. They continued to circle and feign. Then suddenly the Dominion soldier stumbled and looked down. The kid...the wounded soldier, he'd feebly reached out and grabbed Kill Switch's leg throwing him off balance. In that instant of distraction, Justin lunged forward, his knife aimed just below the ribcage and angled for an upward thrust. His weight and momentum pressed it up into his opponent's chest to the guard.

As they fell to the ground, Kill Switch sneered and slammed his wrist against his armored thigh.

Justin tensed as the light slowly went out of his adversary's eyes.

For a moment nothing happened, then the skin beneath the patch on Justin's wrist began to tingle and his muscles locked up. His whole body burned with betrayal as the toxin took hold. It didn't matter that he was prepared to take this particular bullet by his own choice. He'd gambled, wanting to believe in Anatoliy. Allowed himself to hold hope in seeing Kelly once more. Not in this lifetime.

His only satisfaction now was that he'd taken Kill Switch with him.

Faintly, he heard the other men yelling, and even fainter yet, he heard approaching transports. Dominion or Alliance? It made little difference now...

He lay there collapsed atop the Dominion soldier's corpse. He couldn't move. And then he couldn't breathe. He barely felt it as the rest of the unit pounded up and rolled him away to retrieve their leader's body, leaving Justin in the dirt to stare upward as dawn lightened the sky.

Until his heart stopped. His back arched off the ground as that last muscle seized.

Then his world went black.

Sergeant Justin Krougliak of the 428th Recon woke with a start, confused as someone delivered a kick to the bottom of his boot.

"Wake up, Sleeping Beauty!"

He opened his eyes and struggled to sit up. The first thing he noticed was an Allied sergeant staring down at him. The second thing he noticed was the big-ass grin on Coop's face. The third thing he noticed—and the most perplexing—was he was still alive.

He didn't know how, but he was still alive.

Coop gripped him by the forearm, hauling him to his feet and right into a bear-hug. "Aren't you out of uniform, soldier?"

"Don't tell my wife..."

The whole unit laughed as they piled on to hug and slap his back, one of their own returned from the dead.

As he shook and laughed and delivered a few half-hearted punches at his team as they ribbed him, Anatoliy's words came back to him: *Remember...it's just a ruse.*

BUCKET BRIGADE
Jeff Young

C ERTAIN EXPERIENCES CAN HAUNT THE OBSERVER FOR A LIFETIME. FOR SASHA Anderev it was not an image, but a sound. On hearing it, he could not place the scrape of metal mixed with the dragging noise of a knife through meat. He could hardly distinguish that the sound repeated over and over, in quick succession, before the in-rush of air and the pounding impact overloaded his senses.

Pulling himself groggily awake, Sasha searched the HUD overlay for any of the other passengers' call sigils. The data feed from the Combat AI and comm chatter from the others was missing from the sides of his vision, but the comms still showed open channels. Seconds before, they were all chattering about ground-side leave, while the shuttle brought them down through the cloud layer. He shook his head. The overlay glitched and his vision blurred. As he stabilized, he realized the floor slanted hard to his right.

We've been hit and we're down, he thought, becoming aware of the gravity. It was a struggle pulling himself free of the rear lockdown, or baby seat, as experienced soldiers called it. Standing, he slid his linear-accelerator rifle into his hands. Then he made his way across the canted floor. As he moved his combat armor fiddled with his inner ear until it felt like he was on level ground.

His armor, officially the Smart Suit—among the enlisted, Soldier Suit, or usually just Suit—linked to implants throughout his body. Its

AI amped his vision, balance, and even mental state through chemical or electrical impulses. Everything he saw and heard filtered through his implants. It gripped every inch of him like a jealous lover. Stasis gel covered him in a thick cocoon, but in the Suit, it was his second skin. Sasha trusted the Suit with his life and right now, he had no doubt it had kept his ass alive.

Whoever shot down their shuttle was coming to finish the job. It was likely rebel forces were out to sever the Federate's fuel supply line. They often targeted tritium refineries like the one in orbit about their destination, Minos, the small moon circling Akenar. Then the Suit hit him with the IDGAS. The combat drug dropped over him like a shroud. It cooled all his nerves; it made his focus hyper-fine and the mix brought him to knife-edge readiness.

The shuttle lighting flickered as Sasha worked his way over to his gear pack and slammed it onto his back. He paused for a moment launching his minder drones. Three microdrones lifted from his Suit and he set them on search mode looking for signs of survivors. A sigil appeared on his helm. A small blue cross. He focused on it and the Suit brought up the shuttle manifest, expanded to display a woman's photograph and basic stats. Conroy, the medic. One of the staff members being transferred to Minos base. Things were looking up. They needed a medic. Well, what they *needed* was a miracle, but a medic was a good start. If Conroy made it, perhaps there were others. Another sigil came into focus, this time in red, a pair of crossed tools. Uraius. The mechanic would be helpful too but considering the state of the shuttle that was probably one miracle too many. The choice was commonsense. Sasha set out to locate the medic first. He would find the flight mechanic as soon as he could. His HUD overlay shifted back and forth as he triangulated Conroy's position.

Scrambling along, Sasha fought his way through the loose debris on the decking. The wall paneling had popped from its mooring and loops of optical cable hung like jungle vines from the ceiling and walls. As he rounded the turn ahead of him, he realized being strapped into the baby seat was likely the only reason he was still alive.

The main bay door had taken the strike. The back end of the shuttle had disintegrated into jagged shrapnel, which bristled from the wall before him. The remainder of the door had sailed across the room and was embedded in the wall. It sliced through most of the troop rack seating like a blade. The fore part of the rack remained attached to the ceiling but canted at an angle. One suit was still locked in, but unmoving. He couldn't see the rest of the unit. They had to have been carried along by the momentum of the flying door. Their Suits would have locked up rigid as soon as their AIs detected the incoming impact trying to brace and protect their occupants. A futile effort, given the sheer mass of the door. Inertia would have made any impact deadly.

Glancing to the left at the gaping hole left by the bay door, Sasha at first saw nothing but darkness lit by occasional flickers of flame from the burning wreckage. He kept his view on the darkness until the Suit compensated for the lack of light. The shuttle came down in a valley. Debris was strewn in their wake like a trail of burning breadcrumbs leading right to them. They had to get out.

Conroy's sigil hovered over the still figure at the fore of the troop rack. She was one lucky devil. The door had missed her by a mere foot. Shouldering his lin-acc, Sasha made his way to her.

From what he could see, Conroy's Suit appeared intact. A gold bar appeared above her sigil. Damn, the Combat AI flagged Conroy as command. Every other ranking officer was dead. More IDGAS hit him, hit him hard and everything in his perception tightened yet another notch.

"We're not looking good here, Sasha, not good at all," Conroy stated, her helm coming around to face him, voice shaking. "The pilots are gone. I've picked up a signal from Flight Mechanic Uraius. The other passengers, well, we'll talk about the others when I get done arguing with this damn C-AI."

"Sir, we are a stationary target for active hostiles. If we are going to survive, we need to move," Sasha stated. He gave her Suit a quick once over. How badly hurt was she? When the IDGAS hit him, he couldn't stand to sit still. She wasn't moving. That was a bad sign.

"Straight out of the book. Glad to see they hammered that into your head. Got a few loose ends to tie up first and then we can talk about evacuating. Link your drones with mine. See if we can find Uraius."

With six drones, Uraius was quickly located. His seat broken free from the troop rack, was spun around and its back slammed into the wall. The mechanic stumbled to his feet, one hand against the tilted wall, the other grasping his weapon. His gear pack was already attached.

Initial objective achieved; Sasha ordered his minder drones out into the night. Gradually, they began building a terrain map of the crash site. The Combat AI dutifully superimposed it over a map of Minos. The image spun until it aligned with terrain mapping. 38 klicks to the Base. A long walk in the dark with injured personnel and hostiles.

The ground wasn't too bad, but the only cover was clustered around the waterways. There were no trees, but rather large fungus growths, which occupied that ecological niche. Animal life was confined to the rivers and seas. None of that would help them with cover or speed along their trip.

"Uraius, you're on watch," Conroy ordered.

The flight mechanic hesitated for a second and then walked over to the gaping hole in the hull.

Conroy took a breath before continuing, "The Suit's already patched up a number of Uraius's problems. Sasha, you're just damn lucky. Stay that way. You can help the rest of us when we need it."

She was quiet for a moment and when she spoke again there was a different, more determined tone in her voice. "One of the things they probably don't mention to anyone who serves is not only does the C-AI have a suite of medical programs helping me deal with all of your injuries, it also has a triage program. It will not direct me to treat someone it deems will not survive ahead of someone else who has a better chance. Command doesn't spread that around. Right now, the program was only telling me to help you two. It wasn't telling me to help the other nine survivors because it considers them dead. However, since I am in command, I overrode the AI."

Uraius let out a sharp cough. "Buckets," he said.

Sasha felt a chill run down his spine. He glanced over at Uraius and eyed the raised bar on the back of his Suit's helm. Old hands liked to joke it was for hanging up the helm when the Suit wasn't in use; others knew it had a more sinister purpose. That was the point at which Sasha identified the sound he'd heard upon waking. The sound of nine helm guillotines sliding across and severing the heads from their occupants since their bodies were damaged beyond recovery. In theory, the head could be kept cryogenically preserved until a new body could be grown from clone stock. The theory didn't consider there was a limited amount of power in each helm keeping the head cooled. Nine ticking clocks. Before he could start doing the math of how much they weighed and consider how to carry them, the Suit hit him again with the IDGAS.

"Hold on there, Sasha," Conroy said, and he felt her connect with his Suit. The razor-fine quality of his attention wavered and then leveled out. "That stuff is good, but too much makes you likely to only follow AI commands. You will be most helpful focused but still thoughtful. First, I need you to ready us to go. Find the 3'printer. Start off with three all-purpose gear packs with a larger capacity than our regulation ones. Then set it to make more minder drones. Run off as many as you can until the feed bin's empty."

Sasha turned back to the rear section where the 3'printers were housed. He watched on the overlay as Conroy gave control of her minder drones to Uraius, who added his own to the search pattern. Their grid extended farther and farther. Fortunately, they hadn't encountered any hostiles. So far. With the 3'printers rolling, Sasha worked his way back to the front. "We'll get about thirteen more drones before the feed stock runs out. The gear packs are almost done printing. The 3'printer's bin is punctured, and I wasn't sure we had time to try to run another line. The backup 3'printer was completely destroyed," he reported. When he reached Conroy, he was surprised to find her still strapped into the remains of the troop rack.

She turned her helm, looking up at him. "Gonna need some help, Sasha, but first, could you pick up my arm from over there?"

For a moment, the request threw him. Then he bent down for Conroy's arm, the Suit fibers and actuators still rendering it rigid from the impact. His fingers closed around the limb; his eyes took in the shiny metallic join where the guillotine blade's mono-atomic whip had sliced it free. A gash ran up from her elbow, breaching the tough Suit matrix. The Suit had detected the breach and reacted immediately to save her. He was stunned at how she'd sat there the whole time running things, calmly getting them going. However, she hadn't trusted herself to click free of the troop rack. She'd waited for his assistance.

"Help me get that re-attached. Then we'll hit the road," Conroy ordered. Then she continued, "Put all of the drones out on patrol. We're breaking protocol, but they will give us advance warning. Uraius, I need you collecting the buckets. I know it's not an easy task, but I need Sasha's help first. Once you have all of them, gather up any additional ammo or supplies you can salvage. I'm setting our clock to 15 minutes. Then we move."

"Yes, sir," Uraius replied as he clipped the lin-acc rifle to his back and began climbing over the remains of the troop rack.

Sasha spared the three bags on the floor by the 3'printer a brief glance, concerned. 15 minutes wasn't much time.

Conroy's left hand clapped him on the shoulder. "Come on, Sasha, focus here. Take my arm and seat it over the seal until the interfaces lock up. There, see that was the easy part. This is the bit where you're going to hate me for a moment."

She reached out from her Suit AI and took control of his Suit. He stumbled closer and the Suit reached down for her left hand. His fingers worked without his own accord detaching the bush-glove covering Conroy's Suit-encased hand. Then she was clamping the glove to his. A rapid series of commands raced through the overlay when Conroy booted up the glove. The glove consisted of hundreds of small manipulators, each branching out and downward in size. Like a bush, each limb grew yet more branches until the manipulators were microscopic. Conroy turned him toward her seat and through him began the task of re-attaching her arm.

"Uraius, anything on comm?" she said with a sigh.

"I haven't received anything other than the standard beacon from the base. That's a good sign. I'm setting up a burst transmission to fire off when we destroy the shuttle advising the base of our situation," the flight mechanic replied. "The silence from the hostiles could mean they missed us going down," Uraius continued as he pulled forth another dented helm from the wreckage around the troop carrier. So far, he had recovered five of the shuttle's passengers. "Sir, what are we going to do if I can't recover all of the buckets in the time you've given us? I'm all for helping my fellow soldier, but we're inviting trouble by staying here." Uraius stood on the pile of debris looking down at them.

"Is there a problem, Flight Mechanic?" Conroy asked as the glove manipulators hesitated.

"No, sir. No problem." Uraius turned back to his work, his tone sullen.

Sasha refocused on Conroy's arm as the delicate work began again. He wasn't ready to assign faces and memories to those scratched and dented helms. "That's just plain weird, sir," he commented watching his left hand move deftly about as the bush elements closed the metallic joins around Conroy's shoulder.

"Trust me, Sasha, it's plenty odd for me, too." She finished the repairs covering the breach with a thick sealant. Then she moved his hands away, pulled off the bush glove, and relinquished control. Her right hand reached out and took the bush glove back, fitting it on. Conroy ran her right arm through a quick series of motions, the Suit musculature standing in for her real arm. "That's better than strapping it across my back until I can get my arm re-attached. Never know when you might need another hand," she joked.

Finally, Conroy reached up and released herself from the troop rack. Sasha could tell she wasn't completely pleased with the result. Taking the first step down, she staggered and caught herself with her good arm on the frame. Sasha raised a hand in case she pitched forward and then she righted herself with a shake of her head. He studied her for a moment, hoping that the Suit AI would compensate for any other issues she might have. Eventually, she waved him out of her path, moving forward.

Conroy stepped over to look at the helms Uraius had retrieved. After examining them, she put two on the bottom and stacked the third on top. Reaching into her gear bag, she pulled out some quick-setting air gel sealant. She quickly sprayed the three helms together, encasing them in a globe of the spongy material. Taking one of the gear bags Sasha had 3'printed, she placed the resulting mass inside, pushed it down as far as she could and added a little more air gel on top, tamping it down. Conroy appropriated one of the passenger's gear packs lying loose on the ground and cut three circles from it. She laid one of these on top of the gel so that it wouldn't adhere to anything additional placed in the pack. Satisfied with the result, she moved on to the next set of three helms.

"Sasha, dump your gear pack. Put as much gear as you can carry into this one. Focus on ammo and armaments first. Uraius, how much more time?"

"Got the last one, sir. On my way back."

Emptying his pack and refilling the new one, Sasha glanced at the helms. The sound he'd heard when he first awoke played again through his mind. He flinched as he imagined that brief instant before the mono-atomic whip separated the others' heads from their bodies. How much had they realized? he wondered.

At the thought, he started gasping for breath and his neck muscles twitched. He wanted to tear off his helmet and hurl it as far away as he could.

Then Conroy's voice came over his private channel. "Your heart rate is spiking, Sasha. Stop dwelling on your cargo. Right now, they are not dead, no matter how much they suffered. And neither are you. Yet. Get your head back in the game so you can keep it attached. We all have a long way to go."

Conroy was right. Sasha wasn't just responsible for himself now but three others. He had been responsible for the others in his unit before, but they'd worked together. Here those depending on him weren't going to make it without him. He was glad the timers on the helm power units weren't visible to him.

The futures of three people lay inside his gear pack. His Suit AI brought up their Sigils: Comm Specialist Arianne Felton, Corpsman Delton Pierucci, and LT Patrick Donnelly. People they could have used right about now, especially, the LT. Not that Conroy wasn't doing a good job, but the LT got things done, done fast and people snapped to it. Sasha hadn't hesitated when Conroy took the lead. But he'd noticed Uraius's reluctance at Conroy's first few orders. The mechanic had training, but Uraius's focus wasn't the field, unlike Sasha and Conroy. From what Sasha remembered, Uraius was a smaller man who often joked he was just the right size to fit inside vehicles.

Conroy built another stack of helms and loaded her gear pack. When Uraius arrived, his burden went into the final one. As Sasha watched their go-clock wind down, Uraius took a moment to pry open the weapons locker and exchanged his medium-range lin-acc for a long-range sniper model.

Uraius turned toward the wall and reached for the panel where the CAI was secured.

"We won't be needing that," Conroy said.

Sasha swung around to face her, shock tightening his gut.

"Right now, the Combat AI is constantly making assessments of our survival and almost all of them are based around the common theme of abandoning our fellow soldiers. We're not going to do that. Its recommendations are going to become less and less relevant as we go along since it's not going to let go of the idea of us leaving the others behind. I've overridden it once. I refuse to have to do that every step of the way."

Conroy's statement caught both Sasha and Uraius off guard, but the latter was quick to respond.

"If we're not following the CAI, then why are we assuming that you're still in charge?" Uraius challenged.

"We do not have time for a pissing match, Flight Mechanic. You, yourself have pointed out how limited our time is. I'm in charge because I have the most field experience and right now there's a lot of field between us and that base. What I need you to do is take over control of the drones since we won't have the CAI helping. You're good with machines, so you get to handle them. I'm good with people, so I get to deal with them. Are we all clear on things now?"

"Yes, sir," Sasha responded. Uraius echoed him a moment later, his tone grudging.

When they walked out into the night, Akenar, with its oily blue cloud layers, covered half of the sky. Overhead, the minder drone swarm spread out further and accelerated forward. Uraius laid out a course for them on the overlay. Down the valley to the river, follow the shoreline downstream and cross over before the flat plain where the base was located. Conroy gestured Uraius to point, Sasha to their six and called for them to move out.

Sasha glanced up. Somewhere up there was the station harvesting the tritium for military ships' drives. Stars scattered across the remainder of the heavens. Uraius repositioned their minder drones so they could see farther, but now they were also visible to the enemy. It was a risk they would have to take.

Uraius looked back at the shuttle. "We were hit twice. The first took off the tail assembly and the other hit the bay door. That's why the pilots couldn't control the descent. They kept the bird in the air long enough to put some distance between our attackers and us. It was ground-based weaponry. I've seen that damage before and even repaired some of it. We're lucky to be able to walk away." Then he set off at a brisk pace down the valley. Ambient light from Akenar colored his Suit like a bruise.

"Nice night to walk away from a crash—" Conroy never completed her thought as shots came at them from behind.

Sasha jerked as an impact spun him around. I'm hit, screamed through his mind, the IDGAS fighting with his nerves and working to slow his panicked breathing. He was looking at the HUD trying to determine if his Suit was breached when Uraius shoved him off his feet onto the edge of the shoreline. Fire from their unseen foes hammered around them. Uraius quickly brought around two waves of minder drones into their attackers in a kamikaze dive. During the distraction, Sasha and the others crawled down the slope to the river. One moment they were among the fungus tree analogs and then they were splashing into the edge of water. Sasha fetched up against the rocks, struggling to turn back toward where they almost died.

"Sasha, to me," Conroy ordered, and he crawled toward her through the shallows over slippery rocks. Conroy caught him, spun him around, and crouched over his back.

He felt her digging in the gear sack. He hadn't been hit; one of the helms in his charge had been hit. The only reason he was still walking was because one of them took a bullet for him.

The clacking of Conroy's bush glove sounded over the rushing water. She worked swiftly pulling him this way and that as necessary. Her breath was harsh and ragged. Finally, she slid back into the water, the branches of the bush glove folding up.

"Felton ... I think ... I think I saved her ... I just don't know. The slug hit then ricocheted off your suit and hit the vulnerable underseal of the helm," Conroy gasped.

"What do you mean?" Sasha asked, turning to her.

She clamped a hand on his shoulder and held him still while she resealed the gear pack. "I stabilized her, Sasha. There's a slug in her brain. It's frozen in there with her. How much will she lose? I don't know. How much does she need, how much does it take to be her?"

Without even trying, Felton saved his life. Sasha gasped, his arm shaking, the IDGAS fighting the reaction and losing ground.

"Get under the water, we're still vulnerable," Uraius cried. Then the sky lit up behind him and a thunderclap rolled down the valley as the shuttle exploded. "I'd say they know we're here now," Uraius snapped as he pushed away from them, diving deeper into the water. "The message burst went out. So, the base knows about us, too."

"Sasha, move it," Conroy said wearily, pulling at his shoulder. "You're not just risking just your life; you're risking three others who have no choice in the matter. Follow Uraius out into the current."

Built to withstand vacuum, the Suit had no problem with water, but the swift current made it impossible to stay together. Uraius came up with a good solution using their EVA tie offs. Strung together, they drifted in the silty river.

Conroy's voice broke through, "Uraius, get me a count on the remaining drones."

"We have eleven, seven were lost during the attack," Uraius replied.

"Send three out as decoys."

"I'll put the remaining drones in a cordon around us."

They drifted onward in silence. Sasha could see little in the darkness of the river. He flipped through the optical enhancements until the waters became layers of gray. Now he could see the bottom and his compatriots. Conroy's voice came over the comms, "Our drift is about five klicks an hour. We're about 6.75 hours from the base. We need a better current or should consider leaving the river and slogging through the fringe jungle."

Something huge appeared behind Uraius. The flight mechanic thrashed at the end of the EVA cord until the creature passed over him. It rolled through water like a submersible. Sasha glimpsed a gaping maw, three lines of strangely glowing lights, a series of paddle-like projections, and a pair of fins. The whole thing was half the size of the shuttle. Then it was gone, vanishing as quickly as it appeared.

"What the hell was that?" Conroy shouted, turning around in the water in case there were more incoming.

"Hukhuk," Sasha blurted.

"Also known as big damn fish apparently," snapped Uraius, fumbling his lin-acc into his grasp.

"They're migrating this time of year. Heading back to the sea since it's becoming colder inland. That was a small one. There's plenty of other life here in the river. Fortunately, there are few predators in these waters," Sasha stated. He pulled his weapon into his arms anyway, peering into the gloom.

"A small one? Damn, let's avoid the big ones then," Uraius snapped.

"When did you become an expert on the biology of Minos?" Conroy queried.

"I got bored on the ride down. While the rest of you were talking, I was reading," Sasha answered.

"We've got another problem." Uraius sent them a map created by the drones. Ahead lay a blinking line. The hostiles had set up a makeshift detection net, positioning their drones across the river and the surrounding land.

Conroy cursed softly. "How the hell are we getting through that?"

As they drifted in silence, a thought occurred to Sasha. As he considered it, the others began to argue.

"We need to make a break for the shore and find cover in the trees," Conroy said.

"No, what we need is someplace to hole up underground until the net passes over us," Uraius disagreed.

"What if we use the remaining drones to break the net?" Conroy countered.

Sasha's own idea seemed so outrageous he hoped Conroy wouldn't immediately dismiss it out of hand. Finally, he blurted out, "They are only looking for us, right?"

The others stopped their discussion and he leapt into the conversational gap. "They are only looking for us. You said the river is full of life, so—"

"We strap a transmitter to a fish and throw them off?" Conroy posited. "Not bad, I kind of like it."

"No," Sasha insisted. "We hitch a ride inside a hukhuk."

"Damn insane that is," Uraius commented.

But Conroy, Conroy hadn't said anything. Sasha could sense her rolling the idea around in her head. "That's so ridiculous the other side would never consider it. Damn it, Sasha, I knew we brought you along for a reason. Okay, boys, find us a big one!"

With the minder drones, Uraius found one of the largest hukhuks upstream and tracked it. The team dropped out of the current and crawled along the bottom until they were in the area where the hukhuk would pass. Their ride came out of the gloom like the prow of a ship. Conroy timed their release and they drifted upward. The maw of the beast was a black void as they fell inside. Then they were pulled further along the dark hall of its gullet.

"The good news is I still have contact with the drones. I've also brought a drone down and had it latch to the outer skin of the hukhuk. We can keep it powered down and contact the base when we're ready for extraction," Uraius said.

"Put the others up as high as possible. At least one should over-fly the net without detection," Conroy ordered.

Sasha watched her suit spin about as she considered the interior of the hukhuk. Ahead of them the water surged with slow peristaltic pulses. Large flaps of a valve pulsed open and closed in a languorous rhythm.

They sailed through the opening and into a strange cathedral-like space lit by weirdly glowing algae and bacterium. Then the relative calm disappeared as sudden currents ran through the surrounding water. They tumbled together until Uraius latched onto a rounded projection halting their forward motion. Vibrations shook the space as debris shot past them.

Sasha dug at the Suit's tool belt until he found the service knife. He slashed at the skin until something like cartilage showed under the bluish flesh. A jet of inky blood jetted out obscuring his view. When it cleared, he dug a hole through the tough material and threaded another EVA cord through it to tie himself off. He was surprised by the lack of reaction from their host. Then he realized, they were so small compared to it, sticking it with a knife was like poking him with a hair. Uraius had done something similar, digging in behind the spike of cartilage. Together, they reeled in Conroy and helped her attach her Suit to the wall of the passage.

Uraius looked down at the passing water and flotsam. "Why is there so much current?"

"Just a thought, but Sasha did you read anything about these fish having a gizzard?"

He didn't immediately respond to Conroy. "I might not have gotten that far."

"Well whatever it is, we don't want to go through there," Uraius stated.

Conroy laughed tiredly. "Looks like our ride is going to have some unexpected surgery when we arrive."

The inrushing water slapped them repeatedly against the walls of the throat. After a while Sasha the motion lulled him. Every half hour, he woke from his daze to recheck the integrity of their tie offs. Twice already he'd needed to drill a new hole. Then just as he was starting to fade from consciousness, everything went sideways. Uraius's tie down snapped suddenly. His flailing form passed before Sasha and he instinctively reached out scrabbling for a handhold. Catching a hold of Uraius' gear pack, Sasha clamped down and held on.

The hukhuk rolled. Down became up and they were all thrown about. Uraius managed to catch hold of the EVA line between himself and Conroy before the hukhuk floundered again. "It's been hit. The enemy detected something in our drone on the hukhuk's skin and targeted it. Right now, the only thing that's keeping us safe is how much fish there is between them and us," Uraius gasped out.

The beast thrashed again, and they were once more tossed about. Water surged through the entry valve above them with a tidal force. Sasha saw a massive array of grayish intermeshing spines grinding together below them and their orientation changed yet again as the wounded hukhuk foundered. This was the source of the tugging they'd felt as the water and food passed through those grinding surfaces, and he was very glad they'd secured themselves. Gradually, the agitation lessened as the fish's struggles slowed. When things went quiet, Sasha imagined them floating slowly down to the bottom of the river never to be seen again. But instead, another sensation of movement came to him. They were rising.

It took the defending forces from the base an hour to raise the corpse of the hukhuk. It was even longer before the survivors were freed from its embrace.

Air on his face was always the strangest sensation after peeling off his Suit. Sasha luxuriated in it for a moment. Scents poured into him: disinfectant, something sharp and acidic that might be hukhuk bile, river water, the staleness of the recycled air of the base. Beside him, several medtechs were prying the helms he had rescued out of his gear pack. The techs began fitting the helms with new power sources. They handled Felton with extra care, packing her helm into a special case. Only then did Sasha relax.

Conroy sat nearby on a camp chair. Her helm was off and by her feet. Medtechs clustered around until she shooed them off. She gave Sasha a look and then broke out into a grin. Her face was lined with fatigue and her kinky, coiled hair glistened from the stasis gel.

Sasha finally felt the IDGAS let go of him. His shoulders slumped. He wondered if the combat drug was what kept him going throughout their escape. When he looked over at Uraius, he saw the flight mechanic having the same reaction. Then it sank in. He swung around to Conroy once more. No reaction. She caught him staring.

"Figured it out, didn't you?" she asked.

"They don't dose you?"

"I can't be dosed. The medic is always fully responsible for her actions."

Damn, she'd gone through all of that. Dealt with every bit of it. Led them through hell and done it without any combat drugs. "What are you?" he asked before considering what he'd said.

She leaned forward a little and said, "I'm a doctor. I can't let the AI's make my choices for me because I always choose in favor of life. My choices are always how many I can save, rather than how many it makes sense to save. I make the tough calls. Me, with no machines or drugs influencing me."

She pulled herself to her feet. Sasha watched her walk over. She bent down and laid a hand on his shoulder. "You did good today, Sasha. You did good." Then she pulled herself upright and walked over with the other medtechs. Back on the job as usual, ready to start saving more lives.

SLINGSHOT

Aaron Rosenberg

LET'S MOVE, PEOPLE!" CALLIE GUNDERSON SHOUTED AS THE DOORS SLID OPEN allowing them to pile into the launch room. "Sling in five!" Her team poured in behind her, each of them racing to their assigned post with the ease of long practice and the haste of necessity. Every second was precious but they'd done this enough times, both live and in simulation, to know that as long as they each stayed focused on their given tasks they could hit the launch window without any problems.

"I've got an anomaly here," Heaven sang out, their voice clear and smooth, even melodious, despite the potentially dire pronouncement. "Weight is nearly 250 kilos over norm." Their job was checking the allowances, making sure everything was within standard operating parameters.

"Are we still within tolerances?" Callie asked. She was over at her own station, which was medical, gathering the tools and medicines they'd need. This was an emergency evac so the goal was to get there, grab everyone, and get back, but there would probably be some patching up needed, either before bringing wounded onboard or once they were under way.

"Well within," Heaven acknowledged. They tapped their screen. "And we can still fit the full crew complement for the return."

"Then leave it," Callie ordered. "We can check it in flight, see if there's anything that got left behind by the last team—I'll bet it was Havoc, that lazy ass—but as long as we won't be over limit, it's fine." Going over limit was a serious issue, since the sling was carefully calculated for the established tolerances—add extra mass and the difference could change their angle, their velocity, their braking speed, or all of the above. Often with disastrous consequences. "Station check, sound off!" she called to the room at large.

"Allowances, check!" Heaven replied.

"Sling, check!" Django answered.

"Compartment, check!" came Bev's response from within the capsule.

"Gear, check!" Tomas acknowledged beside Bev.

"Supplies, check!" Callie finished. She checked the countdown clock mounted on the wall. They had exactly two minutes left. "Launch positions!" She raced for the capsule, trailing Django but leading Heaven, and once inside the three of them joined Bev and Tomas, who were already buckling in. Django took the pilot's chair and, as team lead, Callie claimed shotgun beside him, while Heaven took the first of the side seats on Django's side, facing Bev and Tomas. Then it was just a matter of waiting for the clock to reach zero.

"Sling in five, four, three," Django declared, finger hovering over the launch button. "Two, one—sling!" He jammed down on it, and all of them were slammed back into their seats as the capsule erupted from its launch pad. There were a few moments of intense pressure, a loud roar filling the capsule, and then that vanished, leaving behind only the rushing sensation of immense speeds. "We're in sub-space," he announced, though they all knew that from the change. "Begin braking in exactly forty-seven minutes. Transition back to target in ninety-four." It never failed to amaze Callie how fast they could get where they were going—even though this target was nearby, on a galactic scale, it was still more than two hundred light-years away. But the sling shot them forward at incredible speeds, and sub-space distorted distances and wasn't subject to Einsteinian physics. Combine those two facts and they could reach in hours what had once taken humanity thousands of years.

Beside her, Django had pushed back from the console and swiveled around to face the rest of the team, reaching for the pocket on the outside cuff of his pants leg. "Who's up for some cards?"

"Not a chance," Heaven replied, adjusting their posture to a more comfortable position but remaining belted in, as per regs. They were always a stickler for rules—unless they had the opportunity to pull a prank, in which case anything went. "Last time, I wound up owing you a week's wages—and my favorite shirt!"

"It looks good on me," their pilot pointed out with a shrug, tipping the cards from their box and shuffling them in mid-air. "But I'll play you for it back. Double or nothing."

Callie laughed and, rotating as well, leaned back, stretching out her legs to prop her crossed feet on the seat inches from Bev's leg. "Count me out too," she warned before the man next to her could start in. "I aim to catch a little shut-eye while we're in transit."

"Long night?" Tomas asked, smirking beneath that trim little mustache he was so proud of.

"Something like that." She didn't see any reason to share details about her night with her crew. Especially since she knew how much that annoyed them.

Bev started to add something to the conversation, but cut off mid-sound as the door to the rear cargo bay slid open. Callie blinked and looked that direction, ready to snap at Bev. That door should have been secured! She froze, though, as someone stepped through into the capsule proper. It was a man, an unfamiliar one.

And he was carrying a pistol, which he had aimed in their general direction.

"Don't move!" he shouted, and the others glanced up, all staring, all too stunned to speak. Especially as two women followed the man into the compartment, also armed. Clearly, this was where their extra weight had been! Bev had checked the main compartment, of course, but the cargo bay was supposed to be handled by the prep team, not her crew. Someone had gotten careless, or been paid off, or something!

"What the space is this?" Callie demanded, unbuckling and rising to her feet. "Who the stars are you, and how did you get onboard?" Two long steps brought her clear of the chairs, meeting the man halfway. "You can't be here. This is an emergency sling!"

"Shut up!" He waved his pistol in her face, and she could see that it was old and battered but looked to be very much still functional. The same could be said of its owner, who was shaggy and surly and whose sunken cheeks and shadowed eyes suggested a lack of proper nutrition. "We're stealing this ship, and everything in it!"

"Stealing—?" Django piped up, cards still clenched in one hand. Then he burst out laughing. "Oh, stars, that's good!"

"What?" That was one of the women, a tall, lean, hungry-looking lady with angular features and wild black hair. "Why're you laughing? We're in control!" She looked around a little wildly. "Do I need to shoot one of you to prove it?"

"No!" Callie slid between the woman and her crew. "Nobody needs to shoot anyone," she urged, holding up both hands and speaking in as soothing a voice as she could manage, given the circumstances. "But— sorry, do you know what you're in?"

"A ship," the other woman, who was shorter and broader with darker skin and buzzed blue hair, replied, her tone making it clear she thought the answer was obvious. "*Our* ship, now."

"This isn't a ship," Callie said, speaking to all three of them. "Not really. It's just a sling." Their blank expressions told her that hadn't gotten through at all, and she sighed.

Django reached out and tapped her on the arm. "I've got this," he stated, and she nodded, shifting out of his way as he rose to his feet, though he didn't step away from the pilot's chair. "We don't have an engine," he explained, "and no real navigation. We're flung from the launch pad at our designated target, the exact angle and velocity determined by computers beforehand. Once we reach it we lock on using magnetic grapples. When we release those, we get tugged back to base. That's it." He shrugged. "It's like we're in a tunnel between those two. We couldn't escape the path if we tried." That wasn't strictly true, of course—throwing off their weight would send them spiraling out, for example—but Callie wasn't about to bring that up.

Their three would-be hijackers looked at each other. Then the man scrubbed at his forehead with his free hand. "So we can't pilot this thing?" he asked.

"Not really, no," Callie answered. "Django keeps an eye on our trip but if there's a problem all he can do is report it." Beside her, he nodded. Again, it wasn't a whole truth—he could manually start braking early, or delay the brakes past the prearranged activation point, which would result in them coming out of sub-space farther or closer than originally planned, but he couldn't change their heading.

"We can get out once you land, though, right?" the second woman wanted to know. "Is there a ship there?"

"Oh, absolutely," Heaven told her. "The Quantum Four. Explorer class, galaxy-level drive, full crew complement of ten, supplies for up to one year's travel."

"Fine," the man responded, grinning to show uneven, yellowed teeth. "We'll take what we can from here, board them, and take *their* ship." His two companions nodded, all three of them looking far more relaxed now that they had a new plan.

"Swell." Callie glared at them, then returned to her seat, dropping into it with a defiant plop. "Might as well take a load off, then. We've got about ninety minutes before we reach it."

All three of them studied her, then let their eyes be drawn to the counter on the front console beside her. "Thanks, but I think we'll look around a bit," the man told her. He smirked. "Do a little shopping."

"Whatever." Now that she was almost sure they wouldn't shoot her or anyone else, the letdown from her adrenaline surge had left Callie even more wiped out than she'd been before. She propped her feet back up, crossed her arms over her chest, and closed her eyes. Either she'd wake up or she wouldn't, but at least she'd get a little sleep beforehand.

A faint shudder woke her, and she cracked one eye to peer at the clock. Ninety seconds to target, which meant they'd transition back to normal space in one minute. She'd always been good at waking up right on time for that.

"Any trouble?" she asked Django, keeping her voice low.

"Less than you'd think," he answered just as softly, tucking his deck of cards back away. "They pawed all the meds, of course, and took the heavy-duty stuff, but that's about it." Which made sense—they always slung light, after all, just what supplies they figured they'd need. And most of the medicine and tools wouldn't appeal to anyone who wasn't in the healing business.

As she studied their three unexpected passengers, the capsule shuddered again, making them all stagger like drunken sailors. "Better grab a seat," she warned them. "We transition back to normal space in thirty seconds, right at the *Quantum Four.*"

"Good." The leader waved his gun at her and the rest of the crew. "Stay out of our way and we won't have any problems, clear?"

She nodded. "Clear." She couldn't resist adding, "Stay out of ours, too. We're here to save lives, and we can't do that if we're tripping over you." He considered that but finally nodded, which was a relief. She'd been worried that they'd be too focused on turning a profit to care about lives.

Of course, these three were about to have other problems, but that was entirely on them. And Callie had her mission to worry about. That and her crew's lives were all that mattered.

"Prepare for translation," Django warned, spinning his seat back around so it locked in forward position and buckling in. Callie did the same. Behind her, she heard the three hijackers hurrying to sit as well. Had they been strapped into something in the cargo bay during launch? she wondered. Or had they rattled around in there like pebbles in a shoe? Well, if they had, it was their own damn fault.

Another shudder, followed by increased noise and pressure, indicated the return to normal space. Their capsule slowed rapidly, the momentum pressing down on them like a stone weight as natural laws once more claimed them. Then there was a loud clang and they jolted to a halt. "Locked on target!" Django called.

"Right!" Callie hit the strap release and leaped out of her chair, grabbing the med kit from its secured position at her side. At least the stowaways had put it back after they'd gone through it! "Let's go, crew!" The others followed her to the hatch, each grabbing their respective gear. They waited impatiently as the light beside it winked red, red, red—green. The instant the color changed she hit the release button and the portal irised open, allowing her to charge into the *Quantum Four*, her team right behind her. Only Django remained in place to monitor their systems. On the console before him, the new countdown clock appeared, its readout mirrored on the wristbands each of them wore.

As Callie hurried forward, a heavy hand grabbed her arm, halting her run and yanking her around. "Where are the stores?" the man demanded, shoving his face so close she could feel his breath warming her cheek. "The equipment and other supplies?"

"One flight down, rear compartment," she replied, wrenching her arm free. "Now if you'll excuse me, I have a job to do." She hurried away, tapping her comm unit. "Django, life signs?"

"Straight ahead, then to the left," he answered in her ear. "Two there. Two more to the right. Three one level up and right above us." That was the ship's med bay, she knew. All the explorer-class ships had the same layout. Ahead and to the left was navigation, to the right was the ready room.

"I've got med bay," she called. "Bev, with me. Tomas, you take nav. Heaven, you're the ready room." Her teammates confirmed that as they split apart, Bev hurrying to her side as they raced for the lift. The man and his two companions barreled past, however, shoving them aside and claiming the small compartment for themselves. Not pausing long enough to curse, Callie veered to the right and the emergency stairs instead.

She and Bev were both out of breath by the time they reached the upper deck and staggered across the hall to the med bay. There they found the captain, the ship doctor, and two crew members. The latter two were in sickbeds.

"Ah, thank the stars," the doctor, a tall, robust man in his later years with graying bushy hair, said as soon as he saw them. "We need to get everyone back to base, stat!"

"They're infected?" Callie confirmed, reaching into her med kit and pulling out the auto-syringe. "I can inoculate them long enough for the sling back." At the doctor's nod she jammed the device against first one crewman's arm, then the other. Then she repeated the gesture with the doctor and the captain, just to be safe. Bev was already hauling the first crewman to his feet—he was woozy but able to walk with her help. The doctor grabbed the second one, and Callie led them all back to the lift. Fortunately, it seemed the hijackers had already reached their own destination, and the lift came at once and was empty when it arrived.

"The first two started showing symptoms a week ago," the doctor explained during the descent. "I tried to quarantine them, but there just isn't enough space onboard. We're all starting to show symptoms." Callie nodded. *Yersinia pestis*, once referred to as the Bubonic Plague, was nothing to sneeze at—cases were almost unheard of anymore, but the disease had killed millions back in Earth's early history, and it reappeared from time to time, often in a slightly mutated strain resistant to whatever cures had stopped its previous incarnations. The first cases in recent memory had sprung up roughly a year ago, and it had taken almost five months before a cure had been developed. She and her team had been inoculated as soon as it was ready, as had all space crews and support personnel, but the *Quantum Four* had launched over eight months ago—a few weeks before the cure had been ready. And this latest strain of plague could have up to an eight-month incubation period.

"We'll get you all back and treated," she promised, leading them down the hall to their capsule. Tomas emerged from nav leading two more crew, both of whom looked feverish. Heaven popped out of the ready room and waved desperately for help.

"They're both out of it," they reported as Callie joined them. "I can grab one but not both."

"Got it." Callie followed them into the small, round chamber and chose the closer of the two people slumped over the table there, a slender woman with bright red hair shaved on both sides. The woman didn't even moan as

Callie hauled her up, and she was forced to shift to a fireman carry, draping the unconscious crew member over her shoulders.

"Figures you'd take the smaller one," Heaven groused, using a similar technique on a big bear of a man with silvered hair. Tomas met them at the door and took the big man's other arm, which sped up the process considerably. That was good, since the countdown clock showed only a minute remaining.

They were just getting the crew settled—Callie had asked the doctor quietly about the two missing members, and received a sad shake of the head in reply—when the hijackers appeared in the lift. "Where do you think you're going?" The man demanded, raising his pistol. But he was still a good fifty paces away.

"Home," Callie replied, and hit the door panel. It slid shut, and a moment later the man's face filled the hatch window as he banged on it with what must have been his gun.

"Open this door!" he shouted, his words muffled by the layers of metal and insulation.

"Not a chance," Callie answered. She wasn't too worried about him trying to shoot his way in—the capsule had been built to withstand the rigors of a sling launch and the pressure of sub-space, it could handle a little pistol fire.

"We'll disable your ship!" That was the tall woman, who must have joined him though Callie couldn't see her. "We won't let you launch!"

Django laughed from the pilot's chair, and the rest of them smiled. Callie didn't bother to answer as she took her seat and strapped in, just as the countdown hit one.

There was no return launch, of course. Their capsule was tethered to base by a string of baryons, which were played out like rope during launch, just far enough to be able to reach the target when stretched to their limit. Every second the capsule stayed there, the tension increased, until finally the strange particles exceeded their threshold and reverted to their normal shape, yanking the capsule back in the process.

That's why it was called a slingshot. Because they were the bullet, and the tether was the sling, stretching and stretching and finally firing them back home.

"Sling in three, two, one!" Django stated, and Callie felt the shudder as the clamps disengaged, followed by the pressure as they were tugged back toward home. She'd send a security detail back to collect the hijackers and pick up the crewmen's bodies.

At some point, maybe in a day or two. Of course, if there were any plague particles still loose in the ship, those three might be in for a rough time of it, but again, that was their own fault. Still, Security would bring the cure with them when they came back. If the hijackers were still alive by then, they'd live to stand trial.

In the meantime, she turned and looked around at her team. "Job well done, crew," she told them. "Time for home."

Django glanced her way and held up his deck. "Maybe a quick game or three along the way?"

SOMETHING TO LIVE FOR
Christopher M. Hiles

CHIEF DAVID STERNBACH SETTLED INTO THE THIN CUSHION THAT SERVED AS HIS BED. He closed the hatch that provided him the only privacy to be found on the station. A lot of personnel considered the bunks claustrophobic, like a coffin. Sternbach considered his a comfortable refuge.

Leaning back into his pillow, he pressed a button. A small monitor popped out near his head. The screen displayed a short list of messages, all of them work-related. The top message was flagged as "unread." It was from his mentor, Commander Theodore.

Sternbach pressed the monitor and a video began to play.

The commander's face filled the screen. Stubble bristled his chin and his gray hair floated in zero gravity. "Hey, Chief," Commander Theodore said. "We're about to get into the sleepers and make our way back to the station. We were able to rendezvous with the ship but those aboard were long dead. They didn't even have time to get to their pods. We'll be bringing back their remains so have Steve prep the morgue for seven bodies." The man looked away from the camera for a moment. "There's another thing, Dave. I received notification about your application to the warrant officer program. I'm sorry, but they passed you over, again. I know this is a blow, but you'll still have one more go next year. I'll be putting you up for promotion in a couple of months. Between that and your test scores, there's no way they'd reject you. Keep your chin up, Chief. We can talk more about it when I get back next month. See you then."

The screen went blank. "Shit," Sternbach said, smacking the button to retract the monitor. He threw a blanket over his legs and turned off the light. Commander Theodore had been his mentor for nearly a decade. The Commander had welcomed his enthusiasm to learn more about surgical interventions in low- or zero gravity and taught him enough technique to perform minor procedures with minimum supervision. It had motivated the Chief to become a surgical physician's assistant. He had applied three times only to be passed over because he was in a "mission-critical position."

Floating around in a metal dumbbell waiting for a distress call hardly classified as "critical." Most calls became recovery missions long before a search-and-rescue (SAR) team ever arrived on scene. Most of the patients he'd seen over the past few months were of the "I need a physical" or "it hurts when I pee" variety.

He heard movement in the room outside of his bunk. In a stern voice, he said, "Petty Officer Raditz?"

"Umm, yes, Chief?"

"Unless someone is dying, I'm not in the mood for any news."

"I totally understand, Chief," Raditz replied. "But Commander Nelson needs to see you."

"Is he sick?" Commander Nelson was the administrative lead for the station. He was nice enough, but he generally stayed on his side of the station.

"No, Chief, he wants to see you on the secure side."

The station was divided into two halves; the medical suite and the vault. Medical was open-access. The vault required a security clearance. Sternbach had no idea what went on in there. He hadn't stepped foot on that side since it had been converted from a medical lab a year earlier.

Sternbach slid the shell open. "Did he say what he wanted?"

"Negative, Chief. Just said he needed you now." Raditz was a short man as it was; but, Sternbach got the feeling that the petty officer was trying to sink into the floor. "This is a first," Sternbach muttered as he swung his legs off his bunk. He threw on a jumpsuit. "Let's go."

The duo walked toward the center transit tube, their steps becoming bouncier until they began to float. The center of the dumbbell-shaped station did not revolve to generate gravity. The intentional zero-g made it easier to unload cargo or move patients. The transition could be a little rough on the stomach; but, once you got your space legs, you were good to go.

At the end of the tube, they oriented themselves to transition back into gravity. A stocky young Marine stood in front of the hatch.

"Matt," Sternbach said, giving a small nod.

"Chief," the Marine replied. "He's in the Ops Center." He opened the hatch and stood aside.

"Any idea what's up?" Sternbach asked.

The Marine shook his head. "Way above my pay grade, Chief."

Raditz moved to follow Sternbach but was stopped the guard. "Sorry, Mikey, just the Chief."

Sternbach nodded and entered the hatch. He made his way down the corridor and stopped in front of a bulkhead marked "Ops Center". Another Marine guarded the door.

The Marine gave a curt nod. "Chief."

Sternbach nodded and handed his identification card to the guard. The Marine pushed it against a panel which turned green and displayed his face and information. The Marine unlocked the hatch and swung it open. He handed the ID back and waved Sternbach into the room.

The Operations Center took up a long stretch of the interior side of the wheel. The back wall curved and held a long window with a view of the inner ring and central hub of the station. Scattered around the room were several clusters of workstations filled with banks of monitors. Personnel stood around them discussing what was being displayed in hushed tones. Near the center was a gaggle of officers, including Commander Nelson, who looked up and waved Sternbach over.

"Welcome to the dark side, Chief," he said.

"Literally," Sternbach said as he accepted Nelson's hand. "Happy to see you, sir."

"I heard you got screwed out of medical school."

"Warrant Officer Surgical School, sir," Sternbach replied.

Nelson nodded, "Right, right. Well, their loss is certainly our gain. I have a mission for you."

Sternbach's eyes scanned the room. "Sir?"

Nelson handed Sternbach a datapad. "I need to send you to Phobos."

"Sir, we have a response team nearby—"

"There isn't a patient, Chief."

"I'm confused, sir."

"There is a woman on Phobos that needs to be extracted... quietly," Nelson said.

"And she is not injured, sir?"

"Not as of the last data stream. You're going as emergency backup. You'll be accompanying Lt Edens." he nodded to a young, lanky man with a short buzz cut. "He'll be in charge of the mission. You'll act as his corpsman."

Sternbach and Edens shook hands. "Nice to meet you, sir."

"Same," Edens replied.

"So, this is a pick-up mission," Sternbach said.

"In a manner of speaking," Nelson said. "You're going in by way of a replenishment drone."

"An ARD, sir?"

Nelson cut him a sharp look.

"Right, sir," the Chief said.

"You're being *inserted*, Chief. Nobody can know you are there, except your target, of course. An ARD arrives every three weeks. The next four are going to crash due to a 'programming error'. You're about to board number three. It's set to impact Phobos with enough force to destroy the ARD but not your pods. Those will blow after you've been on the deck for ten minutes, whether you're in them or not. Chief, can a person recover from sleep and exit a pod within ten minutes?"

They'd rather blow us up than have us—, Chief thought.

"Chief?" Nelson said.

Sternbach startled. "Um, sorry, sir."

"Chief, I need you to focus. If things go bad, your expertise may be the difference between success and failure."

"Yes, sir," Sternbach said, standing straighter.

"Can you recover from the juice and clear your pod in ten minutes?"

Sternbach shook his head. "No, sir. Most people won't remember their name at the ten-minute mark."

"What kind of timeframe are we looking at?" asked one of Nelson's staff. "We have to blow the pods at ten minutes."

"On average, thirty minutes before you're awake and mobile. You can shorten that by five or so minutes with stimulants; but, it's rather dangerous." The group grunted in disapproval. "Why does it have to be ten minutes?"

"That's about how long it will take for someone on the surface to get to the crash site," the woman replied.

"Ah," Sternbach said.

"We'll wake you forty-five minutes prior to impact," Nelson said. "That'll give you a wide enough margin, right?"

Sternbach had only ever been "juiced" once during his medical training. It was not a pleasant experience. "Forty-five minutes should be sufficient, sir."

Nelson nodded. "Alright, then. Once you land, you'll hook up with the objective here." He pointed to a map of Phobos projected on the wall. One area had a small red circle labeled "L2" and a blue one labeled "Objective". Seeing as Sternbach had zero experience with Phobos, he'd have to trust Edens to get them there. "You'll hunker down until a military supply ship lands with 'emergency rations'. That's your route of egress.

"Lt. Chavez will be your contact," Nelson continued. "He's responsible for getting you to the shuttle. He is leading the quick-reaction team. Their primary objective is to get the package onboard. I'll be frank; you and Mr. Edens are secondary objectives."

Nelson waved his hand in front of the projection and the map was replaced with two pictures. The first was an image of a small, dual-deck shuttle. The second was a photo of a United States Space Force Lieutenant. He was surprisingly nondescript. Medium build, white complexion, and close-cropped black hair. He wouldn't stand out in a crowd.

Probably why they chose him, Sternbach thought. Aloud, he asked, "Who is this woman?"

"Glad you asked, Chief." Nelson brought up a new image. The picture was a headshot; probably from a government identification badge. Her blue-green eyes complimented her burnt sienna hair that was cut into a short bob. She had a broad, warm smile. "She will confirm her identity using the code word 'bingo'. Your response is 'joker'. Her codename is 'Janet'. Why she's being extracted is highly classified and not germane to your mission. Questions?"

"Does she have any known pre-existing conditions that might complicate things?" Sternbach asked.

"None that we are aware of, Chief," Nelson replied. "She is being hunted and it's going to take you a while to get there. Situations can change and command has stressed that whatever she has is of prime importance. If she is injured or ill when you get there, she needs to live long enough to pass it on to Chavez." Nelson turned to Edens, "I cannot overstress the importance of this mission, Mr. Edens. Bad actors are trying to get to her first. If you run into them, you are authorized to put them down. Don't hesitate."

"Roger, sir."

"That goes for you, too, Chief. Anyone gets in your way, drop them as quietly as possible. Got it?"

"Yes, sir."

"Good. Get to work, gentlemen."

Sternbach looked at the woman's picture before following Edens out of the room. *Who are you?* he thought.

Sternbach sat on a stool in the medical supply room. It was a cramped u-shaped closet. The stool in the middle put the user in a perfect position to reach the neatly organized boxes that covered the walls and ceiling. Best of all, the stool had a seat-belt. Having the supply room in the zero-gravity section made moving supplies a bit easier once you got used to being able to set a bottle or box in midair while rummaging for something else.

There wasn't much room for Sternbach's medical gear. It was going to be a tight fit. At least food and water would be stored on his vacuum suit. He stuffed every pocket with as much gear as possible. The rest of the tools were carefully placed in his bag.

It was hard deciding what to take and what to leave behind. Sternbach and Raditz had lively discussions about the problem. Sternbach generally yielded to Raditz. The kid knew how to pack a bag.

Sternbach rotated to face Raditz. "Should I bring an extra oxygen tank?"

"Can't you just use your main suit tank?"

"There's some concern that I may need every molecule out of the tank."

"There a specific concern, Chief?"

"I'm worried that I won't have enough air for me if I use it to treat another person."

Raditz looked down at his pristinely packed bag. "Hmmm... we'll have to remove something sizeable. Stand by one, Chief."

Raditz floated out of the room with an oxygen pack in tow. Several minutes later, he floated back. "You'll have to wear it, Chief, but..."

"But?"

Sternbach blanched. "It's a tight fit, Chief, you in your suit, plus the pack, will barely fit in the passenger part of the pod. Of course, it's not like you'll be able to move around, anyway."

Sternbach narrowed his eyes. "Not helping."

"You'll be asleep the whole way," Raditz offered more as a question than a statement.

"Let's go." Sternbach grabbed the bag and oxygen pack as he kicked off toward the dressing room.

While Raditz loaded the gear, Sternbach and Edens took a trip to the small cafeteria adjacent to the crew quarters. Getting juiced slowed down metabolic processes to a crawl; but, it didn't stop them. Eating a high-carb diet washed down with a lot of water would keep their systems fueled enough to make the trip.

The two men sat at a table that folded up into a slot in the wall. Each had just finished a mound of pasta. "So, how'd you come to be stationed here, Doc?" Edens asked.

"I was stationed at Luna out of A-school. I met a doctor and we seemed to work well together. When he transferred to a SAR team, he sent me to rescue training and I've been following him ever since."

"How long have you been in?"

"A little under thirteen years."

"Isn't making chief as a corpsman pretty hard?" Edens asked as he stabbed at a piece of "chicken".

"It wasn't that painful. You just have to be willing to stay on stations like this for long periods of time."

"And the time away from your family isn't an issue?"

"Not really, no. I'm an orphan. My parents were killed in a shuttle accident."

"I'm sorry," Edens said as he diverted his attention to his tray.

"Don't worry about it, sir," Sternbach said. "I grew up in orphanages so you're going to have to do a lot worse to upset me."

"Fair enough."

"If you don't mind me asking, what's your story, sir?"

"I'm a military brat and fourth-generation Marine. My great granddad was part—"

The overhead blared, cutting him off. "Lt Edens and Chief Sternbach to the EVA Prep Room. Repeat, Lt Edens and Chief Sternbach to the EVA Prep Room."

The two men made their way to the Extravehicular Activity Preparation Room. From there, they'd be loaded onto the ARD. *Just like cargo*, Sternbach thought. A chill ran down his spine.

The helmet clicked into place giving Sternbach a good field of vision coupled with a twinge of claustrophobia, *And the faceplate isn't even on yet*, he thought. *Happens to everyone. Deep breaths.*

He stood there while Raditz tugged on straps and checked that his suit was properly sealed. Across from him, Edens had put his own gear on in half the time. He probably had done it a million times in training. *Hell, he probably had to live in it for a semester,* he thought.

Raditz slid the faceplate into its groove and snapped it in place. A breeze moved across Sternbach's cheeks as the air started pumping. He gave Raditz a thumbs-up. The petty officer tapped Sternbach's helmet and ducked out of view. Edens took his place.

"How ya doing, Doc?"

"Living the dream," he replied with a forced smile.

Edens chuckled. "Yeah. It's probably my dream, though."

"You can have it," Sternbach said. "I'll stick to handing out anti-inflammatories and telling people to drink more water."

Edens smiled. "The universal cure! I have another cure for you." He held up a handgun and two magazines. "This is going to be your sidearm. It uses a mass driver to scrape off a little but of the block tungsten in the magazine and accelerates it at a target. Almost no kickback."

"I've never used a mass driver weapon," Sternbach said.

"Have you ever shot a traditional weapon?"

Sternbach nodded.

"Same principle. Just put your booger hook on the bang switch and you're in business. Be careful about what's behind your target. The gun intentionally causes the projectile to tumble so it bounces around in the bad guy instead of zipping straight through 'em. Still, it is possible a round could punch through and hit whatever he's standing in front of." Edens slid the gun into Sternbach's holster. "Just remember to turn the safety off when you're ready to fire."

"Got it," Sternbach replied.

"Don't worry, Doc," Edens said with a smile. "I'm bringing a boom-stick of my own." He held up a compact rifle. "My goal is to make sure you're not in a position to have to use your weapon. Better safe than sorry, though."

Edens disappeared and Raditz returned. "Time to go, Chief."

"I hate this part," he muttered

"Don't worry, Chief, I checked the suit myself," Raditz said giving him a thumbs-up.

"I thought you were supposed to make me feel better."

"Have I ever failed you before, Chief?"

"Just tell me that I'll be asleep before I'm loaded into that thing."

"Should be...." Raditz said with a smile.

"*Should* be?" Sternbach felt a jolt as his pod's cover locked into place. His pulse began to spike.

"I didn't program that bit, Chief."

"Shit!" Sternbach said as the suit jabbed a needle into his arm. The pod moved him to a supine position. "I'm still awake, Raditz!"

"Injecting now, Chief!"

Sternbach felt a wave of warmth run through his body. *The easy part,* he thought. As his pod slid back into the vessel, darkness surrounded him. Only the dim glow of his HUD gave him an idea of just how small a space he was in. A cold sweat covered his body.

"I'm still awake!" he said as he futilely fought the restraints.

Another wave of warmth surged through him and he tasted something bitter in the back of his throat. *There it is,* he thought. His muscles relaxed and he quietly giggled, a normal response to the medication.

The glow of the HUD dimmed as machinery clicked and hummed all around him. His giggling stopped as he felt a brief spike of pain at the base of his spine before his HUD clicked off and darkness swallowed him

"Chief?" said a calm, male voice.

Sternbach's eyes slowly opened. All he saw was darkness. He tasted and smelled bile. He attempted to move his arm. Nothing happened... and he couldn't feel his arm, either. *Am I dead?* he thought.

"Where am I?" he said. His speech slurred and his mouth felt as dry as Martian soil.

"We are on our final approach to Phobos," his suit's AI replied.

"I think I'm going to throw up," he said.

"You have vomited twice already. There is sufficient tank space for more, Chief."

"Good to know you're keeping count," he said before drawing a mouthful of water from the tube protruding from the lower left rim of his helmet. He swished it around his mouth and spit it into a second tube on the lower right rim. "What's our status?"

"We are thirty minutes from contact with Phobos's surface," the AI said. "You were awakened fifteen minutes ago.

"That's good. Have you been assigned a name?"

"Negative, Chief."

"Going to have to change that. You're Bert from now on."

"That parameter is now set to Bert, Chief."

"Mush better," Sternbach slurred, still feeling the effects of the sleep drugs.

"I should tell you that we are going 1% faster than projected."

"One percent doesn't sound too bad."

"The difference is enough to cause an impact that would flatten the entirety of you and your pod."

"Could have led with that," Sternbach mumbled.

"We have enough fuel left in the thruster system to slow us down to the desired velocity. However, we must be careful to not do a burn that would lead to suspicion."

"Bottom-line it for me."

"I will ignite the thrusters in ten seconds. We will slow down; but, it will appear that the pod has lost attitude control."

"Why?"

"Because we will have lost attitude control," the AI replied.

"What effects will that have on the Marine?"

"I have lost contact with Lieutenant Edens' pod. His AI may have disconnected his pod from the capsule once it realized we were traveling too fast."

Sternbach felt his stomach jump into his throat. "And you have no contact with his pod at all?"

"Negative, Chief," the suit AI replied. "If I attempted to send a transmission at this time, it will be picked up by the station."

"Would a narrow laser communications burst—"

"Initiating burn," the AI said, cutting him off.

This time, it felt like his stomach was actually trying to enter his throat and, perhaps, make an escape as the pod's thrusters burned. The capsule entered a slow spin that was picking up speed while the walls vibrated. He grunted against the strain, blood rushing to his head. He tried to speak but no sound came out.

Sternbach's vision blurred and bile forced its way into his throat. *This is it,* he thought. Then, in one motion, the taste disappeared and his vision cleared. There was nothing but darkness and the residual pounding of his pulse in his ears.

After a few moments, he said, "I'm not supposed to have a headache if I'm dead."

"I'm happy to say you're alive, Chief. I have successfully slowed us to a survivable landing speed."

"I can still feel the spin."

"I do not have enough control over the propulsion system to manage the spin. However, it is unlikely to cause any complications in our landing."

"Says you," he muttered. "What's our impact time, now?"

"Eighteen minutes, Chief."

"Great. Can you give me an exterior view?"

"Yes, Chief."

He worked to control his breathing. The previously blank view screen barely changed but for the occasional prick of light.

"Any chance you can knock me out again?"

"Negative, Chief. You would not be able to recover before the pod detonates. I can change the view to something more pleasing."

"More pleasing?"

"A country field, a tropical beach…"

"I'll stick with mostly black inky darkness for the moment, but thank you."

"As you wish, Chief."

They continued in silence. He reviewed what he would encounter on the surface of the rocky moon. He had seen pictures of Phobos. As far as he could recall, the base was strictly scientific with a small water-mining outfit.

"Two minutes, Chief," Bert brought him back to the issue at hand. "I will need to do one more ten-second burn."

"Roger."

"Burning."

Sternbach was ready this time. He braced himself, pumping his legs to assist his suit's gravity mitigation system. Still, he felt himself blacking out. Then the pressure was gone and he returned to normal nearly instantaneously.

"One minute, thirty seconds," Bert calmly stated.

"How bad is it going to be?"

"The impact, Chief?"

"Yeah. How violent is it going to be?"

"You will experience a force equivalent to 10 g's over a period of less than one second. The system is designed to reduce the strain by crumpling. You are restrained to a point where you do not need to brace. However, you should, anyway."

"Right," Sternbach said. He reviewed the sequence of events after landing. *Pod hits ground, I get out, open lower cargo stowage hatch, grab medical bag, and get out of there,* he thought. *I got this.*

"One minute."

"Any luck detecting Edens' pod?"

"Negative, Chief," Bert replied. "I have seen signs of another vehicle engaging in burns. However, I cannot be sure it is from his pod."

He can't be far, Sternbach thought.

"Thirty seconds, Chief."

"Can you show it to me?"

"Yes."

Sternbach's view of space blinked and he was staring at Phobos. The moon was getting very large, very quickly.

"Ten seconds, Chief. Try to stay loose."

"It really does look like a potato," he mused before his world was filled with the sound of collapsing metal. He felt the ARD tumble across the surface before it hit something big causing it to come to a sudden halt. The violent stop threw him against his restraints. His head slammed into the capsule wall hard, knocking him out.

His head was screaming at him when he awoke. He felt something warm collecting in the sweatband built into his helmet. He attempted to move his arm up to inspect his head, but it wouldn't move.

"Where am I?" he muttered.

"Chief! You need to wake up as quickly as possible!" Bert shouted; the sound caused another jolt of pain in his head.

"Where am—?" his head cleared enough for his memory to kick in. "Shit."

"Four minutes until detonation, Chief. I've transferred my files into your suit's computer."

"Release the hatch," Sternbach ordered.

It moved a few inches, then screeched to a halt.

"Why isn't the hatch fully opening?" Sternbach said.

"The pod is partially on its side. I assume there is an object blocking the hatch. Your restraints are released, Chief. Attempt to push it."

He pushed against the pod's hatch with no success. "Doesn't this thing have explosive bolts?!"

"Yes, but if the hatch is too obstructed, detonating them will likely kill you."

"Great," he muttered, throwing his shoulder into the hatch. It felt flimsy as it gave another couple of inches.

"Three minutes, Chief."

"Not helping," Sternbach said.

He leaned into the upper portion with all his strength. He felt the plastic crunch. He crouched and, with as much strength as he could muster, he launched against the hatch. It gave way and Sternbach felt two sets of hands yank him out of the pod. The spare oxygen pack caught a moment on the hatch before popping free. Sternbach fell to the ground. He fumbled for his sidearm and managed to get it out of its holster.

"Whoa there, cowboy!" Edens' voice came over his headset as the gun was snatched from his hand.

Sternbach finally got a look at his rescuers. One was Lt Edens and the other was their contact, Chavez.

"Two minutes, Chief."

"Come on," Edens said, helping Sternbach to his feet. "Get your shit. We need to get out of here."

Sternbach moved to the cargo hatch and extracted his bag, still in its immaculately packed state.

"One minute, Chief," Bert warned.

"I got the bag," Sternbach radioed to Edens.

"Great, time to go!"

The trio made short bounces away from the pod with Chavez on point. Bert projected a waypoint on Sternbach's HUD by way of a red dot. The words "safe minimal distance" sat below the marker. When they reached that distance the dot would change green. "Forty-five seconds, Chief."

Sternbach did his best to keep up with the others. Edens and Chavez moved almost graceful. Sternbach pictured himself lumbering his way across the jagged edges, impact craters, and the occasional smooth grooves of Phobos' surface. "Fifteen seconds, Chief."

"Fifteen seconds, aye," he repeated.

"Jump into the groove and get small!" Chavez said. All three men dove into the groove letting their suits do most of the work.

The ground shook as if they were standing on top of a balloon filled with rocks. Small jets of dust and rock were flung into space. Sternbach looked back toward his pod, now a quickly dying fireball and a geyser of rock.

Before he could say anything, Chavez grabbed the back of his helmet and pushed it against the ground. "Stay down!" A flurry of rocks shot over their heads. Only then did Sternbach notice that the dot identifying a safe distance was still red. The groove acted like a foxhole.

When the moon's grumbling settled down, Edens handed back Sternbach's weapon, "Here you go, Doc."

"Thanks," he replied, holstering it and turned to look at Chavez.

"I thought you were a part of the extraction team."

"I am," Chavez replied. "Janet was late for two check-ins. They sent me to see what the situation was. I'm glad you're here, doctor."

"I'm a corpsman," Sternbach replied. "Joker."

Chavez replied, "Bingo. Please tell me one of you is a physician."

"Sorry," Edens said. "The Chief, here, has some surgical skills."

"I found her two days ago with the help of a young lady who is a resident here."

"What's wrong?" Sternbach said.

"Someone beat the shit out of her and left her for dead in one of the shallow mines," Chavez said. "I did the best I could to stabilize her then called for emergency transport; ETA about eight hours... I'm not certain she's going to live that long without some serious help."

"Take me to her," Sternbach said.

Chavez pointed down the smooth channel to an area that was slightly brighter than the surrounding crust. "She's that way."

It wasn't a long walk; however, moving quickly in nearly zero gravity was tricky. The entrance Chavez had pointed at was more of a tent than a proper airlock.

There was only enough room for one person at a time. Chavez went first, followed by Edens. When it came to Sternbach's turn, he waited for Edens to give the thumbs up through the clear plastic windows. He unzipped the exterior seal and stepped in, closing it behind him, making sure that the flap was totally sealed. Through the window, Edens motioned for him to open a valve at the top of the interior door. There was a hiss as the room filled with atmosphere. A light at the top of the internal flap blinked green. Sternbach opened the hatch and went in.

The area behind the airlock was cramped. There was barely room for the two cots inside. On one lay a woman, her face so battered her eyes were swollen closed. Blood and dust matted her hair. Chavez or someone helping him had inserted an intravenous catheter in the antecubital space of her left arm. On the other end of the tube was a black bladder jacketing an IV bag. The bladder had a small hand pump that was used to put pressure on the bag so it would still feed downward into the patient.

Hello, Janet, Sternbach thought, suddenly feeling more comfortable. This was his element. Making his way to her side, he placed his gear bag next to her cot. He pulled out a small, flat object made of gray plastic and placed it around her wrist. Numbers immediately filled a space on his HUD.

"Her blood pressure is quite low, Chief," Bert said.

"Yeah, I see that and so is her pulse ox," he replied.

"Who is he talking to?" a tiny voice asked from the corner of the room.

Sternbach jerked a look over his shoulder. A short child stared back at him, her unkempt auburn locks floating in the low gravity. Her face was covered with dust and freckles. She couldn't be more than twelve years old. *What the hell is kid doing on Phobos?* Sternbach thought.

"That's JD," Chavez said. "She's the one who found your patient."

"Hello, JD," Sternbach said. "Can you tell me what happened to her?"

JD looked at Chavez who nodded. "It's okay, JD. They are the good guys I was telling you about."

"She was chased by two big men I never saw before. She almost got away but they caught her and punched her and kicked her until she stopped moving," JD said, her eyes locked on the woman. A tear stuck to her lower eyelid.

"Did you know her?" Edens said.

The girl nodded and wiped her eyes and nose with the sleeve of her tattered shirt. "She was nice to me. I helped her steal food packets from the miners. She's going to be okay, right?"

Sternbach hesitated but, eventually, nodded and forced a smile. "We'll take good care of her."

"Bert, please use the internal and external suit speakers," he said.

"Very well, Chief."

JD stared at his suit.

"Bert is a computer AI that will help me take care of your friend," Sternbach explained as he turned his attention back to the patient.

"What did you intubate her with?" he asked, looking at Chavez.

"Combitube."

"Haven't seen one of those in a long time."

"I'm not exactly stocked with the best gear," Chavez said.

Janet's mouth bit down on a thick, plastic tube that went down her throat. The top of the tube glowed green telling Sternbach that the tube was placed correctly. Had it gone down her esophagus, the chemicals the stomach put off would have turned the top of the tube red. It was an old, but effective, technology.

The tube connected to a silver box with a grill on each side. *This is newer tech,* Sternbach thought as he checked the seals. The box drew in air, separated out the oxygen, and pumping it down the tube. "What did you use to paralyze her?"

"A triquanoxazine drip," Chavez said. "Not much of it left."

Sternbach nodded and placed another sensor pad on Janet's head. Several alarms went off.

"Shit," Sternbach said.

"Chief, her intracranial pressure is dangerously high," Bert said.

"I can see that!" he replied as he dove into the bag. He rummaged through, pulling out equipment and allowing it to hover in the low-g. "Dammit!"

"What do you need, Doc?" Edens said.

"I need to relieve the pressure in her head. I'd usually do that with an Auto Placement Cranial Implant that would allow the blood to escape and then reinject it further down in her system."

"I'm guessing you don't have one," Edens said.

"No, I don't."

Sternbach went through the items floating at eye level. He snatched an IV kit out of the air followed by an intraosseous needle. He closely considered the needle and shook his head.

"This is too long. I'd just be stabbing her in the brain. I need a drill," he said, looking up at Chavez. "You got one?"

Chavez shook his head.

"I can get one!" JD said. Before anyone could say anything, she disappeared into a small hole in the wall.

"She's pretty good at scavenging. She's the one who told me about this outcropping. This is an abandoned part of the mining operation. It was too unstable so they started drilling on the other side of their base."

Sternbach nodded and went back to what he was doing. He plucked a replacement respirator pump out of the air and daisy-chained it to the silver box already in place. He couldn't be sure what the battery life was but he figured that having two pumps condensing oxygen was better than one.

"Her pulse ox is rising, Chief," Bert said.

"Roger," Sternbach replied. He pulled a long, flat, gray object out of a deep pocket in his suit. He grabbed the handles on both sides and a screen flashed to life. He slowly panned it over Janet's body and the screen displayed a 3D image of her bones and organs. *Multiple fractured ribs, liver is swollen but intact, intestines look fine, her left lung is completely dropped.* He gave a quick glance at her neck. *No jugular distention so that's a bit of good news. Heart looks good. Left kidney is swollen but not bleeding.* He brought it back over her head. *That's not good.* The screen showed that an artery in her brain was bleeding.

"She's definitely got a brain bleed. It's the pericallosal artery. She needs a decompressive craniectomy but the best I'm going to be able to do with the drill is a subdural screw," he said.

The two men turned to him. "English, Doc."

"The appropriate treatment is nanocytes administered through an IV. They'd repair the bleed and help move the fluid away from the brain. I don't have any. Second best treatment is to remove part of her skull so the brain has room to swell. That is way the hell over my scope of practice. I haven't even assisted on one, let alone done it myself. The subdural screw is the only option," he held up the screw, still in its clear plastic case. "I drill a hole in her skull and feed this through it. It's got a one-way valve so fluid can escape but nothing can get in."

"Looks more like a bolt to me," Edens said.

"That's another name for it."

"Wait," Chavez said. "You mean you brought the bolt but not the drill?"

Sternbach nodded. "What can I say? Space was limited. I'll put the person responsible on report when I get back to the station."

"You mean Raditz?" Edens said.

"No, me."

"Well, don't go too hard on yourself, Doc," Chavez replied. "Common mistake. Could happen to anyone."

"Any chance you have good news?" Edens asked

"These kinds of bleeds often happen a couple hours or so after a traumatic brain injury. It's possible this is a new issue. On the other hand, both of her orbits have been broken and they are putting pressure on the brain," Sternbach said, pointing at her eyes. "In either case, she could have substantial brain damage."

"So, whatever she knows that's making her so important may be lost?" Chavez said.

"Possibly, yes."

They stood in silence for a few moments. Finally, Edens said, "Do the best you can, Doc."

"I'll send a burst transmission to see if the rescue ship can be here sooner," Chavez said. "The array is a few minutes' walk outside the airlock."

"I'll go with you," Edens said.

The two men disappeared. Sternbach set up the equipment he needed to place the bolt. He had done one during a rotation at a trauma hospital on Earth. He had the support of a mentor and a team of technicians, not to mention gravity; he had none of those luxuries here.

"Here you go, Doc," the girl said, startling Sternbach. She handed over a laser drill.

"I didn't hear you enter," he said.

"I have to be quiet or else the bad men will get me."

"I'm sorry you have to live this way."

She gave him a reassuring smile. "Not *everyone* is bad, Doc."

He returned her smile. "This is exactly what I was looking for."

She nodded. "Can I help?"

"Yes, you can. See that pen-shaped object with the red tip?" JD nodded. "Hold that over her head right here." He pointed at a place near the crown of the skull. "Press the little button on the side."

She nodded and carefully followed his instructions. Janet's hair began to separate from her scalp.

"I'm sorry!" JD said, quickly shutting off the machine.

"For what? You're doing a great job!" Sternbach said as he used a similar tool to sterilize the drill.

"Her hair is falling off!"

"That's what that thing does," he said with a smile. "I need the area to be shaved clean so I can place the bolt there."

She gave him a suspicious glance, "Are you sure it's not going to hurt Ms. Janet?"

He nodded. "She is well-medicated. She won't feel a thing."

JD turned her attention back to her task. After she cleared an inch of space, Sternbach told her she could stop. She let the tool float upward and collected the detached hair with her hand. She moved to a corner and released the hair so that it floated out of the way.

Sternbach looked at the scalp and gave her a thumbs' up. He changed the power of the sterilizer he had used on the drill and swept the tool over the exposed scalp. Finally, he used the device to cleanse his suit's gloves.

"Ok, I need you to hold this bolt but don't take it out of its bag until I tell you to, okay?"

She nodded. He unsealed the top of the bag and carefully handed it over to JD. He turned the laser drill's settings to the lowest possible strength, pointed it at the cavern floor, and activated it. The rock began to char after several seconds. Satisfied, he turned back to Janet's scalp.

"Here we go," he said. *I can do this...*

He activated the laser and cut through her scalp with ease. He moved the beam in a careful circle and then turned it off. From out of a sterile cloth holder, Sternbach selected a pickup, a tool similar to pliers but with the ability to lock in place. He used the tool to grab a piece of the skin and fat he had cut through and locked the pickup's handle. Slowly, he peeled the circular plug off Janet's scalp. He held the tool over her face and gently let it go so it wouldn't float away.

"You okay?" Sternbach asked his helper.

"Yup."

"Here comes the tricky part. When I tell you, be ready to squeeze the bottom of the bag until the bolt comes out the other end."

JD nodded.

"Okay, after I've made this incision, there's going to be a spray of blood before I can plug it with the bolt. Think you can handle that?"

She nodded again.

"Alright. Here we go," he said. *Don't fry the brain. Don't fry the brain.*

He aimed the drill and activated it. The skull was already charred from the first part of the procedure. He used the char as a guide and carefully followed it with the laser. Smoke began to fill the area between him and Janet making it hard to see. He turned the laser off.

"Bert, can you do a quick burst from the shoulder stabilizer?"

"Yes, Chief." Bert released a small blast of air that dissipated the smoke.

Sternbach continued to cut through the skull. There was one benefit of using a laser drill rather than a mechanical one. It automatically cauterized the tissue and bone keeping his surgical area clear of blood. At least, until the blood trapped between the skull and the brain pushed out the small cap of bone he had cut. True to his word, a spray of blood shot out from the hole.

"JD, now," he said.

The girl squeezed the bottom of the bag sending the bolt toward Sternbach who caught it. Making sure he was placing it in the right direction, he slid the bolt into place. At the head of the bolt was a wide rubber overlap that covered the exposed skull. Sternbach fired the laser at the rubber seal in short bursts. The rubber melted onto the skull anchoring it in place. Finally, he connected a cannula into the center of the bolt and connected it to a suction canister. He loosely strapped the canister around Janet's neck.

A small, but steady, amount of blood began to siphon into the cylinder. Sternbach powered down the drill and took a step back. He stared at the numbers on his HUD. The one associated with the pressure slowly went down.

"I think we got it," he said to JD. "Good job!" She smiled and gave him a high-five. "She's not out of the woods yet; but, this will help a lot."

Sternbach collected his instruments and put them back into the bag. He placed the skull and scalp plug into a sterile bag and clipped it onto Janet's shirt. "If her blood volume drops, we can recycle the blood that's in the canister."

JD nodded.

Sternbach checked the medication level in the IV bag as well as the respirators. Satisfied, he let himself float while he stretched his limbs.

"How did you come to be on Phobos?" he asked.

JD looked down at her feet. "My mommy was a hand on a supply shuttle. She got sick and died while our ship was docked here. One of the mean men took the shuttle and left me here."

"What about your dad?"

After a moment, she said, "I don't know who my daddy is."

"Nobody tried to take you to Mars or Earth where you'd be safe?" he asked.

JD shook her head. "No. I don't think the nice people can help me like that and the bad people only try to hurt me."

Before he could ask another question, Sternbach heard the zipper on the makeshift airlock open then close. He peered through the clear panel to see Edens trying to hold his ankle while opening the atmosphere knob. With some difficulty, the lieutenant opened the airlock and entered the cabin, cursing like a sailor.

"Fuckers shot me!" he said.

"*Chavez?*"

"No, the dickheads who run this shithole!"

He helped Edens sit on the other cot. The injury didn't look too serious. Sternbach grabbed his scanner and confirmed.

"It's a graze; not a big deal," Sternbach said. He pulled a large syringe filled with a pink material from the supply bag. He placed the tip on Edens' ankle and pressed the plunger. The pink gel covered the wound and part of the suit. After a few seconds, the goop turned black and became stiff. Sternbach ran his scanner over the leg. "You're going to be fine."

Chavez exited the airlock. "How is he?"

"It's a graze," Edens said.

"Good to hear. We got a bit of a problem, Doc."

"When don't we?" Sternbach muttered.

"The security team on this rock knows we're here and where to find us. They ambushed us on our return trip. Space Force has diverted a frigate to rendezvous with the station in fifteen minutes. Pack up your gear, we got to get out of here," Chavez said.

"We can't move her yet," Sternbach replied. "She's pretty damn far from stabilized."

"I don't think a bullet in her head is going to do wonders for her condition," Chavez shot back. "Fleet needs to know what she knows."

"Are you kidding? She'll be lucky if she remembers her own name!"

"We have to take the risk. She's lying on a pressure bag. While you're getting your shit together, Edens and I will get her in the bag."

"Fine," Sternbach said. "Having four people to help maneuver her will speed things up."

"Four?" Chavez replied.

"You, me, Edens, and JD."

Chavez looked at Edens, neither saying anything.

"What?" Sternbach said.

"We can't take her, Doc," Edens said.

Sternbach looked at JD whose face went pale. *She's scared shitless,* he thought.

"The fuck we can't! We got to get her out of here!"

"No, you've got get *her* out of here," Chavez retorted pointing at Janet. "As much as I hate to say it, JD is not the mission."

Sternbach looked back at JD who said, "It's okay, Doc. I'll be fine." She gave him a smile that broke his heart. She waved and disappeared into the tunnel.

"No, wait!" Sternbach shouted.

"She's gone, Doc. We need to go, too," Edens said, putting a hand on his chest. "Now."

Sternbach shook off Edens' hand and began throwing everything into his pack. He clipped it onto his web gear next to his spare oxygen bottle. By the time he was done, the other two had Janet sealed in her bag with two small oxygen tanks providing life support.

Edens walked to the emergency airlock and unzipped the flap. "Let's move!"

Leaving the interior open, Edens unzipped the external flap. Air rushed past them pushing the three men and their patient onto the moon's surface.

"We need to go left. They are going to do a hot extraction in this groove," Chavez said.

"I have acquired a communication lock with the frigate, Chief," Bert said.

"Call sign?" Sternbach asked.

"They're going by 'Mother'," Edens replied.

On cue, Sternbach's radio crackled and then a female voice spoke, "Mother to rescue party, status."

"Rescue 1, Mother, 800 meters to LZ," Edens replied.

"Copy. You have several bad actors closing on you. You're going to have to fight a bit before we get on the deck."

"Roger that," Edens said.

"The pressure in Janet's pod is rapidly dropping, Chief," Bert said.

"Shit!" Edens said.

Sternbach turned around and saw four people in black suits only a hundred meters behind them. They had their weapons shouldered and were firing.

"Doc, seal her bag!" Edens ordered.

Sternbach found the entry and exit holes with ease. He dug out two patches and slapped them on. He looked into the bag to see if Janet was further injured.

"She hit?" Chavez asked.

"Negative," Sternbach replied as he pulled out his sidearm.

"Keep moving," Edens said.

Sternbach gripped Janet's bag and continued to make his way toward the landing zone. He looked over his shoulder, leveled his weapon, and put four rounds down-range. One of the attackers went limp with a spray of blood and atmosphere emanating from his chest.

"Great shot, Doc!" Edens said.

"Thank—" mid-reply, Sternbach tripped over a rock.

Chavez didn't stop and kept moving toward the landing zone with Janet in tow. Edens skidded to a stop and dropped to one knee laying down covering fire.

"You good?" he asked.

Sternbach pushed himself up. "Yeah, I think—" A bullet ripped through his left leg. He let out a shout before pulling himself together. He grabbed the syringe he'd used on Edens from his suit pocket and slammed it into the entry hole. He felt like his entire leg was on fire. He pulled the syringe back and pushed it into the exit wound. The pink goo anesthetized his leg making the second part less painful.

With one hand on his leg and the other wielding his sidearm, he fired back at the attackers. More men had joined the original group of four. Now they were facing ten. Sternbach got to his feet with bullets bouncing all around him. Edens stuck by his side.

"Reloading!" Edens said.

"Mother, Rescue 1, 60 seconds to LZ. This is going to be a shoot-and-scoot so pick it up!" the woman said.

"Copy," Edens replied.

Those assholes are only 25 meters away, Sternbach thought. *We're not going to make it.*

"Down!" Edens shouted pushing, Sternbach to the ground.

Sternbach watched a white cylinder fly toward the attackers from the rim of the groove. It exploded, throwing shrapnel down onto the group. Some of them scattered, others just came to a dead stop.

Sternbach looked for the source of the explosive and saw JD scramble down the side of the groove making a beeline for him and Edens. She closed the distance with no difficulty.

"What are you doing?" Sternbach shouted at her as he gave her a hug. "It's dangerous out here!"

She nodded. "It's dangerous in there, too." She pointed back toward the station.

"Let's get out of here," he said, holding her hand.

Overhead, a small ship made of spheres and tubes dropped down toward the landing zone, a ramp already extending out of the bottom.

Sternbach and JD made it a few steps before he heard her grunt and go limp. He pulled her even with him and immediately saw an entry wound in her makeshift suit near her stomach.

"Shit!" he replied as bullets threw stone fragments into the space around them.

"We got to go, Doc!" Edens shouted as he grabbed for Sternbach's suit. "We have to leave her."

Sternbach threw Edens off him and slung the extra oxygen tank in front of him. He unraveled the tubing and placed it in the hole in her suit. He used the last of the syringe to fill the gaps. An oxygen meter on her wrist blinked green.

Sternbach dug his feet into the ground and pushed off toward the ship. He saw Chavez pass Janet to a crewman and then return fire. Sternbach made it a few more steps before he was hit again. It felt like someone had kicked him in the back sending him sprawling to the ground. He rolled over and pulled JD up to him.

"Mother, Rescue 1, we're putting down some heat. Get small."

Edens dropped to the deck next to Sternbach, who rolled on top of JD using his body as a shield between himself and the bad guys. He felt two more rounds hit him in the arm and back. He looked over at Edens and tried to speak but nothing came out. Using his good arm, he signaled for Edens to take JD to the ship. Edens nodded and then Sternbach's world exploded as the frigate fired shells past them. Their explosion caused a quake as parts of the crust were blasted off.

Sternbach felt lethargy creep over him. He looked back down at JD and saw her oxygen was still green. His vision slowly narrowed as if he were looking down a tunnel. This is it, he thought and then lost consciousness.

Sternbach blinked and tilted his head to get away from the blinding light. He coughed and pain shot down his back and legs like lightning bolts. He felt the thrum of engines through the bed he was laying on.

I'm aboard a ship, he thought.

Edens' face filled his vision. "Welcome back among the living, Doc," he said. "How are you feeling?"

Sternbach fought the desert his mouth had become. "Been better."

"I bet."

"What happened?"

"After the ship dropped the hammer, Chavez and I wrestled you aboard," Edens replied. "The ship's surgeon says you did an awesome job with that bolt. They don't know if she'll wake up but they *do* know that if you hadn't done the procedure, she definitely would have died."

"Where's JD?"

"Can you feel your right arm?" Edens asked.

"Where is she?" Sternbach demanded.

"Your right arm," Edens repeated. "Can you feel it?"

What a stupid fucking question to ask, Sternbach thought. He attempted to move his arm but something heavy anchored his hand. He looked down his right arm but couldn't see past a large amount of bandaging on his biceps. He strained to raise his head higher. He drew in a deep breath and tried to fight his tears. JD was asleep in a bed pulled close beside his. She had a death grip on his hand.

"Chavez and I brought her along, too," Edens said. "I know you crazy assholes have that old saying 'So that others may live.' You told me you didn't have any family. I think you do now. You might be all shot up but just remember... you can't die now. Not with her to live for!"

James Chambers
A BEACH ON NELLUS

James Chambers is the Bram Stoker Award-winning author of the original graphic novel *Kolchak the Night Stalker: The Forgotten Lore of Edgar Allan Poe* as well as the Lovecraftian novella collection, *The Engines of Sacrifice*, described in a *Publisher's Weekly* starred-review as "...chillingly evocative...." He has also written the story collections *On the Night Border* and *Resurrection House* and the dark, urban fantasy novella, *Three Chords of Chaos*. His story "A Song Left Behind in the Aztakea Hills," published in *Shadows Over Main Street 2*, was nominated for a Bram Stoker Award. His tales of crime, fantasy, horror, pulp, science fiction, steampunk, and more have appeared in numerous anthologies and magazines. He has also edited anthologies—most recently *A New York State of Fright*, nominated for a Bram Stoker Award—and written and edited comic books, including *Isaac Asimov's I*Bots*, *Leonard Nimoy's Primortals*, *Gene Roddenberry's Lost Universe*, and *Shadow House*. His website is www.jameschambersonline.com.

Brenda Cooper
CHILDREN OF THE LAST BATTLE

Brenda Cooper writes science fiction and fantasy novels and short stories, and sometimes, poetry. Her most recent novel is *Spear of Darkness*, from Pyr and her most recent story collection is *Cracking the Sky* from Fairwood Press. Brenda is a technology professional and a futurist, and publishes non-fiction on the environment and the future. Her non-fiction has appeared on Slate and Crosscut and her short fiction has appeared in Nature Magazine, among other venues.

See her website at www.brenda-cooper.com.

Brenda lives in the Pacific Northwest in a household with three people, three dogs, far more than three computers, and only one TV in it.

David Sherman
CONTAINED VACUUM

David Sherman is the author or co-author of some three dozen books, most of which are about Marines in combat. His books have been translated into Czech, Polish, German, and Japanese.

He has written about US Marines in Vietnam (the *Night Fighters* series and three other novels), and the *DemonTech* series about Marines in a fantasy world. *The 18th Race* trilogy is military science fiction.

Other than military, he wrote a non-conventional vampire novel, *The Hunt*, and a mystery, *Dead Man's Chest*. He has also released a collection of short fiction and non-fiction from early in his writing career, *Sherman's Shorts; the Beginnings*.

With Dan Cragg he wrote the popular *Starfist* series and its spin off series, *Starfist: Force Recon*—all about Marines in the Twenty-fifth Century; and a *Star Wars* novel, *Jedi Trial*. "Contained Vacuum" is set in the aftermath of *Starfist: Double Jeopardy*.

He lives in sunny South Florida, where he doesn't have to worry about hypothermia or snow-shoveling-induced heart attacks. He invites readers to visit his website, novelier.com.

Robert Greenberger
THE OATH

Robert Greenberger is a writer and editor. A lifelong fan of comic books, comic strips, science fiction, and *Star Trek*, he drifted toward writing and editing, encouraged by his father and inspired by Superman's alter ego, Clark Kent.

He is a member of the Science Fiction Writers of America and the International Association of Media Tie-In Writers. His novelization of *Hellboy II: The Golden Army* won the IAMTW's Scribe Award in 2009.

With others, he cofounded Crazy 8 Press, a digital press hub where he continues to write. His dozens of books, short stories, and essays cover the gamut from young adult nonfiction to original fiction. He's also one of the dozen author using the penname Rowan Casey to write the Veil Knights urban fantasy series. His most recent works include the *100 Greatest Moments* series and editing *Thrilling Adventure Yarns*.

Bob teaches High School English at St. Vincent Pallotti High School in Laurel, MD. He and his wife Deborah reside in Howard County, Maryland. Find him at www.bobgreenberger.com or @bobgreenberger.

Lisanne Norman
HOPE'S CHILDREN

Lisanne Norman was born in Glasgow, Scotland, and has lived in the USA since 2004.

"Strong-willed, independent, a whirlwind, a dreamer, she lives in another world." These phrases followed her around from her earliest days. They were partly right: she had grander plans than a world, though, she was already creating the universe of the Sholan Alliance, where Magic, Warriors, and Science all co-exist.

She began writing when she was eight because she couldn't find enough of the books she liked to read. How difficult can it be to write them myself, she thought with all the confidence of a child. After all, the libraries were full of books. It must be easy.

Real life took over as she entered college and began to work for the first time, but thanks to the constant nagging of two very good friends, one of whom is the sister of her editor, she finished a novel she'd started back in 1979. It was called Turning Point, and her friend's sister at DAW bought it. The Sholan Alliance Series is now nine novels long. She also has several short stories out in DAW anthologies, and one in Defending the Future series number IV, "No Man's Land" called "Valkyries".

Bud Sparhawk
COMRADES IN ARMS

Bud Sparhawk is the author of the novels *Distant Seas, Vixen*, and *Shattered Dreams*, as well as two print collections: *Sam Boone: Front To Back*, and *Dancing with Dragons*. He has three e-Novels available through Amazon and other channels.

Bud has been a three-time novella finalist for the Nebula award: *Primrose and Thorn* (Analog, May 1996), *Magic's Price* (Analog, March 2001), and *Clay's Pride* (Analog, July/August 2004). His work has appeared in two Year's Best anthologies: *Year's Best SF #11* (EOS), David Harwell, Editor) and *The Years Best Science Fiction, Fourteenth Annual Collection,* (St Martins Press, Garner Dozois – Editor.)

His short stories have appeared frequently in Analog Fact/Fiction, less so in Asimov's, as well as in five *Defending the Future* and other anthologies, publications and audio books. He has put out several collections of some of his published works in ebook format. A complete bibliography can be found at: http://budsparhawk.com.

He also writes an occasional blog on the pain of writing at http://budsparhawk.blogspot.com.

Robert E. Waters
MEDICINE MAN

Robert E Waters is a technical writer by trade, but has been a science fiction/fantasy fan all his life. He's worked in the board and computer gaming industry since 1994 as designer, producer, and writer. In the late 90's, he tried his hand at writing fiction and since 2003, has sold over 60 stories to various on-line and print magazines and anthologies, including the *Grantville Gazette*, Eric Flint's online magazine dedicated to publishing stories set in the *1632/Ring of Fire* series. Robert is currently working in collaboration with author Charles E Gannon on a Ring of Fire novel titled, *1636: Calabar's War*. Robert has also co-written several stories, as well as the *Persistence of Dreams*, with Meriah L Crawford, and *The Monster Society*, with Eric S Brown.

Robert currently lives in Baltimore, Maryland with his wife Beth, their son Jason, and their precocious little cat Buzz.

For more information, visit his website at www.roberternestwaters.com.

Eric V. Hardenbrook
SYMPATHETIC

Eric V. Hardenbrook is a fan, an author and an artist, usually in that order. Eric lives in central Pennsylvania with his gorgeous wife and daughter. He writes to try to get the stories out of his head. His stories can be found in *TV Gods, Best Laid Plans,* and *Dogs of War.* When he's being a fan he helps run Watch The Skies and assists in the publication of their monthly fanzine. He can be found (at least some of the time) at The Pretend Blog. When not working on those things, Eric enjoys the occasional video or board game and is an old school role player.

Danielle Ackley-McPhail
NO MAN LEFT BEHIND

Award-winning author and editor Danielle Ackley-McPhail has worked both sides of the publishing industry for longer than she cares to admit. In 2014 she joined forces with husband Mike McPhail and friend Greg Schauer to form her own publishing house, eSpec Books (www.especbooks.com).

Her published works include six novels, *Yesterday's Dreams, Tomorrow's Memories, Today's Promise, The Halfling's Court, The Redcaps' Queen,* and *Baba Ali and the Clockwork Djinn,* written with Day Al-Mohamed. She is also the author of the solo collections *Eternal Wanderings, A Legacy of Stars, Consigned to the Sea, Flash in the Can, Transcendence, Between Darkness and Light,* and the non-fiction writers' guide, *The Literary Handyman,* and is the senior editor of the *Bad-Ass Faeries* anthology series, *Gaslight & Grimm, Side of Good/Side of Evil, After Punk,* and *In an Iron Cage.* Her short stories are included in numerous other anthologies and collections.

Her newest book, *Eternal Wanderings*, released at the beginning of 2019. An elven mage joins a Romani caravan to help a friend fight his inner demons, only to be confronted with ancient demons of a more literal sort.

To learn more visit www.sidhenadaire.com or www.especbooks.com.

Jeff Young
BUCKET BRIGADE

Jeff Young is a bookseller first and a writer second – although he wouldn't mind a reversal of fortune.

He is an award winning author who has contributed to the anthologies: *Writers of the Future V.26, Afterpunk, In an Iron Cage: The Magic of Steampunk, Clockwork Chaos, Gaslight and Grimm, By Any Means, Best Laid Plans, Dogs of War, Man and Machine, If We Had Known, Fantastic Futures 13, The Society for the Preservation of C.J. Henderson, TV Gods & TV Gods: Summer Programming.* Jeff's own fiction is collected in *Spirit Seeker* and TOI *Special Edition 2 – Diversiforms.* He has also edited the *Drunken Comic Book Monkey* line, *TV Gods* and *TV Gods –Summer Programming.* He has led the Watch the Skies SF&F Discussion Group of Camp Hill and Harrisburg for nineteen years. Jeff is also the proprietor of Helm Haven, the online Etsy and Ebay shops, costuming resources for Renaissance and Steampunk.

Aaron Rosenberg
SLINGSHOT

Aaron Rosenberg is the author of the best-selling *DuckBob* SF comedy series, the *Dread Remora* space-opera series, the *Relicant Chronicles* epic fantasy series, and—with David Niall Wilson—the *O.C.L.T.* occult thriller series. Aaron's tie-in work contains novels for *Star Trek, Warhammer, World of WarCraft, Stargate: Atlantis, Shadowrun, Eureka, Mutants & Masterminds,* and more. He has written children's books (including the original series *STEM Squad* and *Pete and Penny's Pizza Puzzles,* the award-winning *Bandslam: The Junior Novel,* and the #1 best-selling *42: The Jackie Robinson*

Story), educational books on a variety of topics, and over seventy roleplaying games (such as the original games *Asylum, Spookshow,* and *Chosen,* work for White Wolf, Wizards of the Coast, Fantasy Flight, Pinnacle, and many others, and both the Origins Award-winning *Gamemastering Secrets* and the Gold ENnie-winning *Lure of the Lich Lord*). He is the co-creator of the *ReDeus* series, and a founding member of Crazy 8 Press. Aaron lives in New York with his family. Follow him online at gryphonrose.com, on Facebook at facebook.com/gryphonrose, and on Twitter @gryphonrose.

Christopher M. Hiles
SOMETHING TO LIVE FOR

Christopher M. Hiles is an emergency manager and nurse who currently serves as the Exercise and Training Section Chief for the Baltimore City Mayor's Office of Emergency Management. He, also, is a volunteer with Civil Air Patrol where he serves as the Maryland Wing Health Services Officer and Assistant Director of Safety. He has previously been published in *Dogs of War* and *If We Had Known*. He lives in Baltimore with his wife and his pup.

Mike McPhail
SERIES EDITOR

Author and editor Mike McPhail is the co-owner of eSpec Books LLC. He is best known as the creator and series editor of the award-winning *Defending The Future* series of military science fiction anthologies

His love of the science fiction genre sparked a life-long interest in science, technology, and developing an understanding of the human condition—all of which play an important role in his writing, art, and game design—these in turn are built upon his training as an aeronautical engineer, and dreams of becoming a NASA mission specialist.

As a former Airman, he is member of the Military Writers Society of America, and is dedicated to helping his fellow service members in their efforts to become authors, editors, or artist, as well as supporting related organization in their efforts to help those "who have given their all for us."

SUPPORT CREW

Alicia Blackburn

Allen

Anaxphone

Andy Remic

Andy Wortman

Angel Bomb

Anonymous Reader

Anthony R. Cardno

Aysha Rehm

Barbara and Carl Kesner

Carol Chapin Porter

Caroline Westra

Christopher Weuve

Curtis & Maryrita Steienhour

Dale A Russell

Daniel Lin

Dave Auerbach

David Perkins

Derek L Thompson

Douglas Vaughan

Evan Ladouceur

Gavin Sheedy

Gemini Wordsmiths

George

GMarkC

Ian Harvey

Isaac 'Will It Work' Dansicker

J.R. Murdock

Jakub Narębski

Jennifer L. Pierce

Jeremy Bottroff

Joanne Burrows

Joe Monson

John F. Bouchard

John Glindeman

John Green

Josh Mcginnis

Judith Waidlich

Kelly S. Pierce

Ken "Merlyn" Mencher

Kerry aka Trouble

Kierin Fox

Lark Cunningham

Lee Jamilkowski

Linda Pierce

Lisa Kruse

Louise Lowenspets

Marc "mad" W.

Maria T

Mark Carter

Mark Featherston

Mark Hirschman

mdtommyd

Michael A. Burstein

Michael Higgins — NobleFusion

Mike Crate

Mike Maurer

Mike Skolnik

Morgan Hazelwood

Neil Ottenstein

Niki Curtis

Pat Hayes

Paul van Oven

Pekka

Peter Young

Philippe van Nedervelde

PJ Kimbell

R. Garber

R.J.H.

Ralph M. Seibel

Ratesjul

Richard P Clark

Richard Stone

RKBookman

Robby Thrasher

Robert Claney

Robert E Waters

Robert Flipse

Rose Pribula

Samuel Lubell

Scott Elson

Scott Mantooth

Scott Schaper

Sheryl R. Hayes

Stephen Ballentine

Tim DuBois

Tony Finan

V Hartman DiSanto

Wes Rist

Finally, There's Something We Can All Agree On.

It's something we've all said many times. And it does seem to be one of the few things that Americans unanimously agree on. But it takes more than agreeing with each other. It takes the USO. For more than 60 years, the USO has been the bridge back home for the men and women of our armed forces around the world. The USO receives no government funding and relies entirely on the generosity of the American people. We all want to support our troops. This is how it's done.

Until Every One Comes Home.

Help support our troops.
888-USO-5566/www.uso.org

CPSIA information can be obtained
at www.ICGtesting.com
Printed in the USA
LVHW030457191121
703740LV00003B/419